FEROCIOUS
LOVE

Published by

AFRICA INDEPENDENT MAGAZINE CC
Reg: 2009/084401/23

Changing the mind-set

PUBLISHING DIVISION
+27(0)81 038 9797

Note for Librarians: A cataloguing record for this book is available from Library and Archives Canada at www.collectionscanada.ca/amicus/index-e.html

ISBN 978-0-620-60554-0 SA

Printed in Pretoria South Africa. Printed on paper with minimum 30% recycled fibre. Africa independent Magazine CC, Printing Division. The revised version has been printed by Africa Independent Magazine CC.

Offices in Pretoria South Africa.

This book was first published on-demand in cooperation with Trafford Publishing. On-demand publishing is a unique process and service of making a book available for retail sale to the public taking advantage of on-demand manufacturing and Internet marketing. On-demand publishing includes promotions, retail sales, manufacturing, order fulfilment, accounting and collecting royalties on behalf of the author.

The revised version is available in bookstores and on the market in south Africa and is shipped to countries worldwide.

AFRICA INDEPENDENT MAGAZINE CC

Reg: 2009/084401/23

Changing the mind-set

PUBLISHING DIVISION

ABOUT THE AUTHOR

Constance Mutale was born in the republic of Zambia. She graduated with a bachelor's degree in Accountancy in 1997, at the Copperbelt University and has worked with two of the big five international auditing firms in Zambia and as a lecturer of a private college in South Africa, where she permanently resides. She has since worked in the private sector as an accountant but now also works on her own in publishing and accounting field, focusing on a market niche. She recently completed her second bachelor's degree in laws in South Africa, through the University of South Africa and has made meaningful contribution in her employment in the legal industry.

She is a mother of two lovely boys and a daughter, and writing has been a strong point in her life. She believes that if exams were verbal, she would still be struggling to pass junior high school. (Just a thought)

Constance Mutale is now a very confident writer and believes that writing is a tool through which history can be preserved. She takes this introduction to welcome you to this life-long intriguing novel.

AUTHORS NOTES

This book is dedicated to my mother Felistus and my late father, Donald as a token of my love and appreciation for every single day; before now and forever.

ACKNOWLEDGEMENTS

Special thanks to my family and most especially my children, to Trafford my first publisher and I look forward to a long and spawned relationship with my current publisher, and to all the readers out there, thank you.

"Ask and you shall be given…
Seek and you shall find
Knock and the door shall be opened unto you." Mt 7:7

PREFACE

The modern era has brought about demand for wanting to be recognised in a world that is fast changing with time. Priorities are often made towards accomplishing things in life, thereby drifting away from the traditional set up, in which women predominately provided a supportive role to their husbands and families.

The need and desire for women to fit in the industrial world, normally leaves a gap that usually time does not fill. A big gap has arisen causing women to no longer be in the kitchen, but rather rubbing shoulder with men in the business world. This normally postpones the time for the happily ever after to be fulfilled, or does it ever happen? We come across a young naïve woman who meets with love for the first time and is swept off her feet, but she is soon drawn back to reality and back onto her feet, into the harsh business world when her love disappears.

She then gets obsessed with power, but will she ever want to trust love again? Is the power enough to substitute what could have been or do we still go back to the drawing line, which is the traditional setup where love is a basic human factor? We see the life story of love revolve through three generations. Does love remain a basic human need, which cannot be substituted with anything else? It is intriguing to imagine what holds a relationship when deceit, trust, careers and money are all put face up on one table. It shows women still trying to have their fantasy fulfilled to walk down the aisle, but how soon or ever is that dream fulfilled?

Enjoy every bit of the novel…that evolves from the Victorian era to our present-day setup, with women rubbing shoulders, with men in the business world.

BOOK ONE

CHAPTER ONE

$\mathcal{S}$he sat on a stool, leaning forward with her arms folded, resting on the windowpane. Her gaze was fixed on the treetops that were visible from her bedroom window, watching as the birds flew from tree to tree. Below the trees was a narrow, clear river to which she had become accustomed to over the years. It was a river to which she had so often run as a little girl, sitting by its banks and padding her bare feet into the waters. It was a river she'd hurried to whenever she needed time to herself, feeling the fresh aroma of the sweet-smelling flowers that lined up the riverbanks. She would watch as the butterflies flew from one plant to the next, a peace and serenity surrounding them that seemed to engulf her too.

She pulled herself from the windowpane and got up from the stool, the scent from the flowers beneath her bedroom window filling her nostrils. She leaned forward to close the window and with it shutting the noise from the insects and the birds in the nearby flower garden. She turned to face the rest of the room, shaking the gloomy feeling off her. She then took steady strides towards the door.

She opened the door leading her into the passage and was immediately greeted by the sweet savour of the dishes, which were being prepared in the kitchen downstairs and she stood for a moment, allowing her mouth to water. She heard her dear mother's voice above the clattering noise from the kitchen. It was her usual authoritative voice, and she imagined their maid, Alijah, working at the command of her elegant mistress's voice, although she was not by herself this time, but was with the rest of the cooks who had been hired to assist with the catering of the evening ball.

She walked down the corridor and the flight of stairs and was met by her mother's scornful gaze.

"And to where are you going? Surely, you should be dressed by now …" Begun her mother, who wore an expensive, yellow dress with golden slippers on her feet. Her radiant face was normally covered with a smile of honour and achievement, which she had developed over the years; her fingers were dressed in the finest jewellery.

"To have some fresh air." Came Kodelly's reply.

"Now, you and I both know very well that the guests will start arriving soon. I do not want them to find you looking like that." She spoke back firmly, gesturing at her daughter, who despite being in her early twenties, still carried the teenage appearance.

"I'm just out for a couple of minutes." She persisted.

"Alijah!" Called out Lidy, with her gaze still fixed on Kodelly.

Alijah appeared from the kitchen, fiddling with her apron as she approached her mistress and her daughter.

"Yes madam." She answered politely, only too delighted to have finally come out from the kitchen.

"Ensure to take Kodelly's outfit to her room upstairs, will you?" Spoke Lidy again.

"Yes madam." She replied.

"Do excuse me." Interrupted Kodelly.

"Do excuse you." Interjected her mother. "No fresh air." She continued harshly, having lost her patience with her. "It is your party, and a lady ought always to look presentable." She paused for a moment, "Now, no more talk about fresh air …"

"Do excuse me." Spoke Kodelly again, hurrying towards the door ignoring Lidy's interjection.

She opened the door and was soon out of the house, running softly in her sandals, dressed in a pair of shorts and a white shirt.

Lidy shook her head resignedly.

"And what will people think? What! A lady running her weight across the plain." Complained Lidy, to Alijah who still stood in the hallway with her.

"Go now and do what I told you." She continued. "But first wipe the flowers, they do lack the glow." She paused momentarily, looking at the potted plant at the foot of the stairway before walking away.

Alijah sighed, watching her mistress disappear into the lounge. She stared at the plant, which she had earlier cleaned before giving it the attention her mistress had requested again. She had served her mistress for several years and had come to terms with her fastidiousness with time.

She had watched Kodelly grow and over the years, seen her mistress struggle relentlessly at grooming her into a fine lady, but, the poor child had paid little attention to mastering all the skills she was so fortunate to learn from her mother; thought Alijah with another sigh, even though, she had at least portrayed good manners in the company of their guests on all occasions. She was not a natural born lady but had been fortunate to be raised in a well-cultured family. She grew up with family values, even though being exactly feminine was not much of her interest. Alijah was not a lady, except that she had served her boss for a considerable number of years to adapt to their quality of life.

*   *   *

The room was dimly lit, with music playing softly. On one end of the ballroom was the high table, from which lady Lidy would host the evening with her well-selected patrons. The middle of the room was reserved for dancing, while the space on the sides of the room were covered with tables and chairs for the rest of the guests. The walls were well decorated with an assortment of colours and at the far end of the room refreshments were being served. The guests had already started arriving and were standing in small social groups, sipping at their drinks, which they had been served in elegant glasses.

Standing in a pale blue, long evening dress with pale blue pumps, was Laura, Kodelly's cousin. She stood sipping at her wine glass, studying the crowd before Lidy walked in. She had changed into an expensive velvet evening dress. She paused in the doorway for a moment, as the crowd turned to admire her much expensive taste and then as though she had only remembered who she was, she picked up her steps firmly and with confidence, smiling and greeting her guests courteously as she covered the distance towards Laura.

"And where is Kodelly?" She asked Laura as soon as she'd reached her.

"I don't know." Came Laura's fairly uninterested reply.

"And what time shall she get ready for the ball?" She muted, but then, with an immediate glow in her eyes she exclaimed, "Oh, there she is." Seeing her daughter walk through the door.

"Do excuse me and do enjoy yourselves. Oh, I will miss you." She added, hugging Laura lightly.

"So will I." Came Laura's formal reply, looking over her shoulder as her uncle Bill and Kodelly walked towards them, with her beauty enchanting the crowd. She walked through the crowd not mindful of who was watching her; her confidence was as radiant as her looks.

The evening progressed as scheduled, with the crowd becoming merry, with Lidy and her husband Bill being the proud hosts of their daughter and Laura's send-off party.

"Oh, I will miss them." She said time and again within her conversations to her charming husband, who stood by his wife in all her expensive endeavours.

"Come love, this suit will definitely look nice on you." She'd advised him earlier in their bedroom.

"Why don't I put on this one?" He'd tried to argue.

"No husband of mine…" She begun then softened. "Oh, come on love, do wear this one for me."

"Alright." He'd eventually ceded.

"Oh my gosh! My feet are hurting." Spoke Kodelly to Laura, who was now standing on the balcony adjacent to the ballroom.

"I can imagine." She replied flatly, aware of the sensation her cousin was making among most of the bachelors', with her fine looks and aware of the so many people who still wanted to dance with her.

"Please Laura; do dance with Dinkley, for me?" She continued.

Dinkley Mills, Laura thought in disbelief, the gentleman who lived a few roads away from their two-story house. He was a good-looking man that she had admired from a distance for a long time. The man she had watched her cousin dance with for part of the evening.

"Are you that tired?" Laura heard him ask.

"Yes." Replied Kodelly, sitting down heavily.

"Don't you want to dance?" She asked Laura again.

"I'd love to. If that is okay with him?"

He nodded, offering her his arm before they walked to the dance floor.

As soon as the song ended, Dinkley excused himself from her company and joined a group of his peers and then helped himself to a few drinks. Laura too walked away from the dance floor and re-joined Kodelly.

"So, did you enjoy the dance with Dinkley?" She asked carelessly.

"Yeah." She replied. "But I just can't wait to leave for Cambel City tomorrow."

"I will miss Summerset. I will miss this place so much. But we are big girls now." She paused for a moment. "Aren't we?" Laura nodded, impressed with herself for having managed to change the theme.

Dinkley Mills re-joined the two ladies after the crowd had thinned out and Mr. and Mrs. Mollar were busy bidding the guests a good night's sleep before they departed.

"Do excuse me." He begun. "But I just came to beg your farewells." He continued with a grin on his face, having had too much Rum. "I will see you ladies off tomorrow. That is…"

Kodelly smiled back at him while Laura watched on. He extended his hand and held her hand, kissing the back of her hand as he spoke.

"To the woman who is more beautiful than the morning star!" He chuckled; she smiled and moved her hand away.

"Laura, do have a goodnight's sleep." He added casually, before leaving their company.

_____

CHAPTER TWO

The journey to Cambel city was long, but they both did not engage in much of a conversation with each other. They had both woken up at the dawn of day, despite having retired to bed late and only after ensuring that they had bid farewell to all their guests before doing so.

They had woken up early to a scrumptious breakfast, with Lidy looking very tired after an extremely exhausting but successful evening, with her guests marvelling at what a brilliant hostess she is.

The car, Mr. Mollar had hired to drive the two ladies to Cambel city had arrived as scheduled. Kodelly and Laura both walked to the car, with Alijah standing by. She watched her mistress' tearful face as they hugged to say goodbye.

"Oh, I will miss you, so." She finally managed to say in a sobbing voice.

"I will miss you too, ma'." Replied Kodelly.

"Do, God bless you," She paused for a moment. "both of you." She continued, extending her arms to embrace them both again.

Mr. Mollar stood watching his wife too, and then he hugged his daughter and then Laura, muttering a few words to both of them as he did so.

"Look at that!" Exclaimed Laura and drawing Kodelly's attention to the scenery they were just driving past.

"Wow, it's beautiful." Echoed back Kodelly, who for a moment had been trapped at the memory of the previous night's events.

She stared at her hands as the car drove on, wondering why Dinkley Mills had not come to see them off as he had promised. She wondered if he had probably overslept, or if he just did not consider it necessary to keep his word.

She sighed, as the car finally pulled to a halt in the driveway, opposite the tall apartment building, in which they would now be living.

"This is it madams." Announced the elderly man, who had been driving the car for a stretch of hours.

"It is most beautiful." Spoke Kodelly, as she stepped onto the driveway overlooking the fountains, with the porter hurrying to the car in order to carry their bags.

"Thank you." Spoke Laura to the elderly driver.

"My pleasure." He replied, entering the car again before driving off.

They walked into the foyer and into the elevator, led by the porter who was carrying their luggage.

"And this must be your new apartment?" He questioned knowingly.

"Yes." They both replied.

"Thanks for assisting with our language…" Kodelly added.

"Not without a tip, perhaps?" He interjected rudely.

"Oh, pardon us." Spoke Kodelly almost embarrassed. "But we were going…"

"Not a problem." He cut in again, quickly accepting the money that was offered to him before leaving their company.

*   *   *

The weeks that followed were hectic for both Laura and Kodelly, as they tried to adjust to their new busy schedules. Weekdays required of them to wake up early and prepare for work. They would leave their apartment on a cup of coffee or a ball of cereal to join the other city residents, in a race to get to their respective workplaces in time.

Their apartment was cosy, with two identical bedrooms that had been neatly furnished to meet both Mr. and Mrs. Mollar's high standards.

On the day of their arrival, they had found both doors with nametags on them. This, Kodelly had guessed to be her father's idea, since he was well aware of how the two would tag and pull if the felt that they deserved what they were fighting for.

Either room overlooked the city, which was well lit for most of the night.

"Nice room you've got there." Laura had said with a grin on her face, pleased to realise that their rooms were exactly the same and had been fitted with the same accessories.

"Thank you." Came Kodelly's ignorant reply. "May I have a peep in yours?"
"Sure." She'd replied.

"Oh, how could I have not guessed? Please give me a hug." She spoke playfully, after entering her cousin's new room.

"It's beautiful." She added, holding onto her dear cousin for comfort and assurance.

Days soon turned into weeks since the two had left Summerset and yet their weekends had mostly been spent indoors with a bowl of popcorn in front of them, either watching movies or listening to music.

Lidy had telephoned them occasionally to check on how they were coping, with their sudden change in lifestyle and environment.

Their meals were either hot take-away from a nearby restaurant or instant, ready-made food just to warm up. They had missed Alijah's meals and wished that they could ask Lidy to ask her to move to the city and live with them.

Laura had opposed the idea. It would be irresponsible of them, she'd often argued. She had, as such tried to learn how to cook faster than her cousin, since she was not yet ready to concede to her cousin's suggestion and have Alijah travel all the way to take care of two grown-ups.

"Oh, my goodness!" Exclaimed Kodelly. "Laura, look... a letter." She added, picking up an envelope from the floor as she spoke upon entering their apartment, carrying boxes of takeaway food from the restaurant across the street.
"Who is it from?" Laura enquired with enthusiasm.

"I don't know...but it is from Summerset," She continued, tearing the envelope open. "and it's addressed to me."

"Wow." Joined in Laura, sitting next to her on the couch, having put their parcels on the table in the hallway, but unable to read the letter's contents.

'My darling, angel.' It read in part.
'Do pardon my rudeness by not keeping

to my word at seeing you off.
I do however, miss your wonderful face
and graceful walk. My lady... my angel.
Please tell me about your stay in Cambel city.
I look forward to hearing from you...
From the bottom of my heart, I love you.
Dinkley Mills'

"Oh." She gasped, holding the letter to her bosom.

"What does it say?" Laura asked.

"I never thought that he would write."

"Who?" Laura asked exasperatedly.

"Dinkley." Kodelly informed her.

"Dinkley?" Laura echoed back, rising from the couch instantly.

"Dinkley is it?" She continued. "So, what does he say? How is Summerset?   How is the ranch?" She asked impatiently.

"Nothing much."

"Then can I read?"

"No, I will reply to his letter now." She answered back and getting up from the couch, before walking away to her room.

She sighed, after closing the door behind her, and then she sat on the chair by her study table to reply.

'Dinkley, things here are so different.
I work for a big company.
My boss used to tend the plants in the plantation,
now, he sits behind a big Mahogany table
making decisions.
I miss Summerset though.
Kodelly.
P/S
Laura sends her regards.'

———————————————

CHAPTER THREE

*M*ichael Yellern stormed into Kodelly's office, as he normally did and to which she had become accustomed. He was a plump figure, in his mid-forties. He carried about him some air of authority, although it was obvious that he did not have natural charisma. He was formal in his business dealings and appreciated attention. He had worked with the company for over twenty years, which was about her age. He had often preferred to address her as Miss Mollar. He had worked his way up the ladder, buying shares at a time that was most crucial to the business. He had committed his skills, time and resources at a time when the business was almost sinking, seeing it rise to its current position.

His business had almost become his passion, worrying about its future, especially since he had seen it almost hit rock bottom once.

"Ayah." He would say. "We had to go borrow from the bank and the rates in a recession, you wouldn't want to speak out…but slowly, things did look better and look at us now…" He would pause for a moment. "We are expanding into new markets…Ayah, be prepared, especially for a recession. It is not a good thing for a business. It is like sailing against the tide." Pulling at his cigar as he spoke.

"We have had to build this company brick by brick. Sometimes you go ask, 'and Dear Lord when do I get some genuine results, I'm doing some genuine work' and there, the recession is over…Ayah those were the hard times." He would stop his tale abruptly.

"Miss Mollar." He begun, wiping the smile from his face. "Meet Mr. Bobby Mitch." He introduced, gesturing to the man that was standing next to him.

"Sir, this is Miss Mollar…Kodelly." He watched as they shook hands before continuing. "He will be doing some research work on our new product and market."

The gentleman he'd introduced nodded politely to acknowledge her, as Michael elaborated his involvement with the company.

"You will excuse us now." He said after a while. "We do have a lot of work to catch up on, don't we, Mr. Mitch?" He continued, gesturing to him to leave her office.

Kodelly gave them a thin smile, watching them turn and leave, before she got back to her work schedule.

* * *

"Excuse me, excuse me!" She heard someone call out to her, as she walked down the pavement causing her to draw to a halt.

"Miss Mollar?" He spoke questioningly, as soon as he caught up with her.

She nodded, standing face to face with him again.

"It's amazing," He continued. "I haven't run into you since the last time we met. You must be one hell of a hard worker." He paused for a moment. "You do remember me, don't you?"

She nodded.

"Yes, I do."

"Am Bobby." He continued. "Just in case you've forgotten my name. Are you going for lunch?"

"Yes." She replied again.

"May I join you?"

"Well…I'm just going out for a quick snack." She tried to explain him away.

"I take it that you don't mind." He replied, crossing the road with her to a nearby restaurant.

In a moment they were both inside the restaurant and he led the way to the tables and gestured to her to sit near the window.

"Would you like anything to drink?" Enquired the waiter, who had followed them to their table, handing them the menu as soon as they were seated.

"I will have a beer." Replied Bobby confidently.

"A beer! Sir?" Enquired Kodelly.

"The lady objects." He continued without answering her directly. "So, I will have a soda instead."

"And the madam?" Enquired the waiter, turning his attention to Kodelly.

"A soda will be fine for me, too." She replied.

"I will come back for your orders." He said, before walking away from their table.

"You don't drink…?" He enquired, as soon as the waiter was out of hearing range.

"No." She replied firmly.

"How long have you been working for Michael?" He asked again.

"Close to ten months now." She replied.

"I see." He acknowledged, as the waiter returned with their drinks.

"May I take your order now?" He asked politely.

"Yes." They both replied.

The waiter took their orders and left again.

"You like working for Michael?" He asked again.

"Well…I, well I … his okay." She stammered.

His gaze was fixed on her as she spoke, studying her skin, looking deep into her eyes as though to discover the mystery of life, with her voice echoing softly in his ears. He watched her beautiful skin against her blouse with her shoulder length hair, hanging loosely above her shoulders. Her perfume seemed to hang loosely in the air about them.

The meal was served, and Bobby watched her intently, while they ate their meal. She stayed in control despite being aware of his scrutinising gaze. She pretended not to mind that he was sitting opposite to her, when all the while she wished that she had come to the restaurant unaccompanied. She stole a few glances at his serious but poised face, down to his broad shoulders and clear completion.

"Bobby." Called out a woman excitedly, breaking the awkward intensity that had built between them.

Her eyes popped out in delightful recognition, as she looked at him, not minding Kodelly. She had a dark shawl wrapped across her shoulders and her lean figure was supported in a red dress.

"Bobby." She repeated.

He shifted his gaze from Kodelly and turned to face her with concealed disgust.

"What?" He managed to say in almost clenched teeth.

"May I sit?" She said, pulling a chair next to Bobby Mitch.

"No. I'm unfortunately very busy. This…" He spoke.

"Oh, Bobby…I just wanted to…." She tried to continue.

"Do excuse us." He cut in again. "I'm in the middle of a... a..." He tried to explain.

She then turned to face Kodelly, whose presence she had not recognised all the while.

"I will speak with you some other time." He concluded; his gaze still fixed on her.

She nodded before turning away, hugging her handbag to her bosom, the shawl still hanging loosely about her shoulders, before she walked briskly onto the crowded pavement.

"I'm sorry about that." He stated firmly, looking back to Kodelly.

"How could you?" She asked in bewilderment.

"Never mind her." He replied, and then paused for a moment, "Oh, please.... she is not my girlfriend." He added.

"I did not say that." She replied before looking at her wristwatch and thereafter beckoned to the waiter.

"Our bill please." She said, as soon as he arrived at their table.

"Is everything okay?" He enquired. "You don't need anything else?"

"That will be all, thanks." She replied again.

"I normally pay my bills." She explained through a thin smile, after the waiter had left their table.

"That I can see." He replied carelessly. "Thank you for your company though." He continued. "I hope to be seeing you around more frequently."

She smiled politely again, getting up from her chair.

"I must get back to my office, seeing that we are running out of time."

"May I see you after hours, perhaps?"

"Not today." She replied. "Do excuse me." She added, wanting to leave his company.

"I will walk you back to the office." He insisted, causing her to cede.

They walked the short distance to their office building without talking much, calling an occasional greeting to the familiar faces that they ran into. She excused herself from his company as soon as they were in the foyer and hurrying the rest of the distance to her office. She opened the door and allowed herself in, closing it behind her with a sigh of relief.

She thought for a moment what her mother would say about him. He certainly was not a gentleman, judging by the way he had sent off the woman in the restaurant. Poor woman, she thought again, hating to be in her shoes. She sat in her office chair, remembering how embarrassed she had appeared to be, after she had been sent off rudely.

She thought about Bobby Mitch for a moment, remembering his gorgeous face from the few glances she had managed to steal off him and that he was a confident speaker, even though they had not spoken much.

Then slowly her lunch hour with him became a memory in the past, as she got engrossed in her work.

* _____ *

CHAPTER FOUR

"May I walk you home?" She heard Bobby's now familiar voice from the doorway to her office.

She stood thoughtful for a moment whilst packing her bag before answering.

"I'm fine, thank you."

"Come on Kodelly." He persuaded. "I kind of finished my work early today and I thought it's a fine evening, why can't I be honoured to walk your beautiful self, home?"

She stared at him for a moment.

"Please?" He spoke again, still leaning against the doorframe, with his hands in the pockets.

"Alright." She ceded.

She had not spent much time with him, since the last time that they'd had lunch at the restaurant, even though, she had run into him on several occasions. She had deliberately decided to avoid him, especially since she was not used to a man that was not exactly, etiquette. His reaction to the woman with the shawl at the restaurant remained vivid in her memory. He had asked her to accompany him to several places, though, but she just had not found it in her to spend much time with him.

She recalled mentioning about Bobby to Laura on one occasion, who immediately got interested in him. She had been keen to know, if perhaps, her poor cousin had been attracted to him and would then be torn between two men. She had in mind, Dinkley Mills, who had continued to write letters to her cousin, much to Laura's annoyance.

She had insisted that Kodelly was in love with Dinkley Mills, even though she had firmly refuted, stating that her interest in him was purely friendship. His letters to her had however, continued to atone her of his undying love for her.

> **"Kodelly, my most beloved, I cannot wait**
> **to see your beautiful face again. I shall visit**
> **you in Cambel city, but only as long as my**
> **work pressure at the ranch reduces.**
> **I love you endlessly,**

Dinkley Mills."

His letter read in part.

"See, he is in love with you." Laura argued firmly.

"But I only delight in his friendship." Argued back Kodelly innocently.

"Then why not speak out and tell him the truth as it stands?" She persisted.

"And what truth shall that be?"

"Oh! Come on, that you are not in love with him." She insisted.

"Why break a poor gentleman's heart, when I only wish to know information about Summerset. Laura, if I was in love, I'd let you know."

"Selfish. So flippen' selfish. You can't decide your love?" She'd retorted.

"Decide my love. Oh, Laura, can't you see that I'm not in love?"

"And what about Bobby." She paused "That good-looking city man?"

"He is my colleague and nothing more." She stated, blushing for a moment, before storming out of their apartment.

"Want some candy floss?" She heard him ask, pulling her from the memory as they walked down the street.

"Yes, thank you." She replied.

"My apartment is in the next block." She continued, after they had bought the candyfloss.

"I know that." He replied.

She gave him a quizzical look, causing him to raise his hand in the air in defence.

"Okay, Okay." He tried to explain; "I followed you the other day from work…" He paused for a moment. "I wanted to walk you home, but I guess I just didn't feel that you would want to walk with me."

"Why?" She questioned curiously.

He shrugged. "I don't know."

They got into her apartment building and into the elevator, walking onto the landing without either of them talking, before Bobby broke the silence.

"And I know which one exactly is your apartment." He announced cunningly.

"You followed me all the way?" She asked again in disbelief.

"Yes." He replied.

"Thank you…" She began, as they stood in front of her apartment door moments later, before the door opened and Laura stood in the doorway. "Good evening to you, sir." She greeted Bobby.

"Good evening, ma'am." He replied.

"I am Laura." She introduced herself. "And you must be Mr. Bobby…"

"Bobby Mitch." He filled in for her, amused that Kodelly had actually spoken about him to the fair lady standing opposite to them in the doorway, whom he supposed to be her flatmate.

"Do come in." She invited.

"Well…umm." He begun to answer before Kodelly interjected.

"He was only walking me home…. surely he has other places to go?"

"Not quite." He replied.

"Come in." Beckoned Laura.

He smiled thinly, before accepting her invitation.

"And this is our home." Continued Laura, as the trio entered the lounge.

"I have heard quite a lot about you," She said again, as soon as they were all seated, with Kodelly feeling a little bit uncomfortable.

"Really?" He asked curiously. "Is there much of a tale on me?" Looking at Kodelly.

"Not quite. I suppose it was more in passing than anything else." She replied feeling a bit embarrassed.

"Kodelly, do serve Bobby with a drink or something." She ordered on his behalf.

"In a moment." Came her reply, before she excused herself from their company and went to her bedroom to change into a more casual outfit.

"Why don't you join us for dinner?" Asked Laura, as soon as Kodelly re-joined them. "I'm sure Kodelly will be more than thrilled to serve us with dinner. Won't you darling?" She teased.

"Laura, I think his got other commitments."

"No. I have no other commitments …unless…" He tried to explain.

"Oh, that is lovely," Interjected Laura softly, patting him on the arm. "I stocked the fridge this morning, so there is no need for us to go to the restaurant." She continued, enjoying the look of bewilderment on her cousin's face.

"Okay." Replied Kodelly, unsure of what to say or do next. She walked into the Kitchen, stood for a moment before hurrying back to the lounge.

"Is dinner ready, already?" Teased Laura again.

"Nope, I just thought that I might need the telephone." She replied, taking the handset back to the kitchen with her.

Laura grinned.

"She is quite a cook." She reassured Bobby, who sat sipping from the glass of juice he had been offered earlier.

Quite a cook, thought Laura to herself almost chuckling. She recalled how hopeless they both had been at cooking when they first begun to live on their own. She remembered how they had missed Alijah's cooking and wished that she could be there to cook for them.

Laura's objection to have Alijah move in with them had made her learn the kitchen tricks faster than her poor cousin Kodelly. She recalled how the previous time that she had insisted that Kodelly prepare a meal for the two, Kodelly had objected and insisted that she would rather pay for them at a take-away restaurant than to dare fix a meal. She had however, relinquished, after Laura refused to leave the house for some lousy, take-away food as she had put it. Kodelly had then tried her hand in the Kitchen, but an hour later, they had both been disturbed by a loud knock on the door.

Kodelly hurried to answer the door and in the doorway, stood an old lady with a fire extinguisher in her hand.

"Come now, where is the fire?" She asked, while trying to push her way into their apartment, as soon as Kodelly answered the door.

"What fire?" Kodelly yelled back, with Laura laughing in the background.

"What fire?" She retorted. "I might be old, but I knows the smell of smoke when I do smell it." She paused for a moment, testing her nose.

"It is certainly coming from here." She persisted through her old teeth.

"There is no fire." Repeated Kodelly, embarrassed, as the smoke continued to come through the kitchen door, which was now shut.

"No fire and the smoke?" Gestured the old lady pushing her way in.

"Thanks for your concern." Kodelly tried to reassure her more calmly and to block her from entering the kitchen, to the smell of burnt food, which was still in the pot.

"But..."

"Oh, please do pardon her." Spoke a middle-aged woman, now standing in the doorway. "I'm sorry, she intruded." She continued, walking the short distance to the older woman and holding her on her arm.

"Intruded." She yelled again, shaking off her middle-aged daughter's grasp. "When will anyone ever appreciate an elderly woman trying to help?"

"Mom, let's go." She said softly to the old woman and getting the fire extinguisher from her hand, while Kodelly watched on.

"Oh, come on." She replied resignedly.

"I'm sorry." Spoke the woman again.

"It's okay." Kodelly tried to reason.

"I'm Mrs. Loika, we live next door to you, and this is my mother." She introduced after a short pause.

"I'm Kodelly;" Replied Kodelly, extending her hand to shake hands with her. "and that is my cousin Laura."

"Oh, I'm so sorry." She said again, turning to Laura as if to beg her forgiveness.

Laura gave her a thin smile.

"It's fine."

"Would you care for a drink?" Kodelly enquired.

"No, thank you."

"Yes." Came their simultaneous replies.

"Yes" Repeated the older woman.

She shook herself free of the memory, as she walked to set the dining table. She had been on the telephone for most of the previous hour, speaking to Alijah who had been instructing her with the recipe she had requested for. They had spoken for most of the hour, even though Alijah kept cutting the line, insisting that her mistress would find her talking on the telephone. Kodelly would then phone her again, despite her fear of Lidy, whom Kodelly did not mind at all, until she had gotten the final instructions for their traditional Sunday dish.

"Come on, I deserve something or even a pinch of salt, am hungry." She recalled Laura teasing her after Mrs. Loika and her mother had left. She brushed aside the memory, as she walked to announce that dinner was served to the two, with pride in her voice.

"The food is very tasty." Bobby complimented later on. "I had no idea that you would make such a perfect cook."

"Thank you." She replied, with Laura watching on in disbelief.

She wondered how Kodelly had managed to prepare their traditional Sunday meal. She knew Kodelly to be a pathetic cook and had been looking forward to seeing a disgruntled Kodelly, but instead she sat confident opposite to her. Her confidence was as evident as in one who had just won the title of being the best chef.

"This really is a break away from the usual microwave meals." He complimented again, "I had no idea that you had it all." He paused for a moment; his gaze fixed on her. "Beauty, charm and control in the kitchen."

She blushed, unsure of what to say, except to thank Alijah who had saved her face from embarrassment. She looked across to Laura, who could almost excuse herself from sheer disappointment, while eating a spoonful of the very tasty cuisine, indeed.

"Desert perhaps?" She enquired, before clearing the table.

"Yes, thank you. But I won't be staying long." He replied, looking at his watch, "I never meant to, but I guess it has been worthwhile." Looking back into her eyes, before she went to get the strawberry ice-cream and pudding.

*   *   *

"This is where I live." He said, unlocking the entrance door to his apartment.

It was a beautiful block of apartments, in a fairly expensive suburb. Kodelly stood looking at the surroundings, while he unlocked the door. She had finally accepted to visit his apartment, after having turned down his invitations on countless occasions. Curiosity had for a long time made her want to accept his offer. But she was uncertain as to whether it would befit her status as a lady, or so she thought her mother thought her to be. She often recalled her mother's tireless lessons on how a lady ought always to behave and Alijah was no exception at giving the lessons too, even though she was just a looked down upon simple maid.

She had resorted to avoiding Bobby Mitch, having been unsure of what her response to his constant invitations should be. This had however, proved futile, especially since they worked in the same office block, with her being just an extension away. She had no intention of giving away neither her character nor personality as yet. He knew her as an uptown, working woman and had no knowledge of her reserved background and cultured upbringing.

"After you." He said, gesturing to her to enter the apartment.

It was a beautiful maisonette apartment, with a view overlooking the tennis court and pool. She stepped onto the thick carpet and walked through the recently painted walls with various artistic paintings hanging on them. He then led her into the lounge, and it too was neatly arranged. She stood, to admire the painting against the wall, opposite the hallway.

"It is beautiful," She said, extending her hand to feel its texture. "I had no idea you are a collector of such fine art."

He shrugged wanting to be modest, an air of pride surrounding him while he listened to her soft voice.

"Whose signature is this?" She asked, her eyes still fixed on the painting.

"It's an original by Pedree Laskador." He informed her.

"Wow!" She marvelled at the abstract painting. "What does it exemplify?"

"His feeling. Pedree Laskador's feelings, I suppose." He replied with a grin.

"May I pour you some juice?" He continued after a pause.

"Yes, thank you."

"I have quite a collection." He informed her, while handing her a glass of juice. "Some are in the room upstairs. Come I will show you around."

She followed him up the flight of stairs onto the landing. "This is my bedroom," He continued, pushing the door open. "and that is another bedroom over there, a bathroom over there… and this is what I wanted you to see." He said, opening the door to the room opposite his bedroom.

It was a dimly lit room with antique bookshelves on two sides of the wall, and on one side of the wall was the window and, on either sides, and the rest of the wall hung other paintings and art works. Opposite the window was a table with a feathered fill-tip pen and a bottle of ink, with a chair on either side of the table.

"This is lovely. It is totally out of this world." She managed to say in admiration, moving from painting to painting.

"I hardly bring anyone up here, you must be very special." He remarked.

"Oh, aren't they so beautiful?" She continued, ignoring his remarks.

"And so are you." He said again, his gaze fixed on her.

She stopped in her tracks for a moment and looked back at him. "Shouldn't we go back to the lounge?" She said, almost on impulse.

"If you are more comfortable there."

"Would you like to dance?" He asked her, after they had walked back to the lounge.

"No." She replied with a chuckle. "No."

He held her hand gently, getting the empty glass of juice from her and placing it on the table, and then he turned to look into her eyes again before speaking.

"Must I pour you a glass of Brandy?"

"No. No. No alcohol, besides, I'd better be leaving. I'm sure Laura must be getting concerned."

"Why don't we sit on the balcony and enjoy the evening breeze." He spoke   softly.

"No." She replied again, before he held her hand again, lifting it to his lips and kissing the back of her hand almost on impulse, whilst gazing into her eyes.

They stood motionless for a while, before she pulled her hand from his and stepped backwards; she picked up her handbag and insisted on leaving.

He walked her back home, returning to his apartment where the smell of her perfume still hovered in the air. He took a deep breath, feeling her presence as he did so. His mind preoccupied with her beauty, her allure and the light moments he had so far shared and enjoyed with her. He went about his daily evening routine, his mind distracted by the loneliness he felt. He took the bottle of Brandy, drinking the remaining contents before falling asleep.

*_____ *

CHAPTER FIVE

It was a clear, warm evening, with the moon lighting up the sky. It was an evening Kodelly had been looking forward to, ever since Bobby had mentioned the big city summer dance party. It would be her first biggest jaunt since their arrival in Cambel city. She stood in front of her dressing mirror, with Laura watching her excited face. She was still in dilemma over what to wear to the function.

"Come on…make up your mind, he is sure to be here any moment from now." Encouraged Laura, who had just finished brushing Kodelly's hair.

"The long dress or the short one?" She asked for the umpteenth time.

"The short one," Replied Laura again, "It will go well with your sandals and hairstyle, since it exposes part of your shoulders. Besides it makes you look more mature." She advised.

"Do you think I will…?" She tried to rephrase her question, when the doorbell rang.

"Dress up." Ordered Laura hurriedly. "I will answer the door, I'm sure it must be him."

"Okay." She answered back, watching Laura hurry out of her bedroom.

"Good evening, Mr. Mitch." Greeted Laura, as soon as she had opened the door.

"Good evening." He replied back with a smile. "Where is the queen of my life?"

"Will be with you in a moment." Laura replied before allowing him into the apartment.

He was dressed in a dark suit with black shoes, an air of appeal surrounding him. His hair had been cut neatly earlier in the day. His confidence seemed radiant as he stood waiting for his date.

Kodelly joined them in the hallway, a few moments later. She appeared calm; despite the dilemma she had been facing earlier on. She had finally settled for Laura's advice and wore the short dress with a fur low neck and high-heeled sandals.

"You look adorable." He muted, extending his hand to her.

"Thank you." She replied.

"So, are you ready now?"

"Yes, I am."

"Do have fun." Laura bid, opening the door for them. Watching them leave the house for the party. She closed the door and then hurried to Kodelly's bedroom with one thing in mind. She wanted to go through the letters she had so far received from Dinkley Mills, which she had not been allowed to read. She sat on Kodelly's bed and retrieved the letters from the drawer, before enjoying their contents to her heart's satisfaction.

*   *   *

They arrived at the venue in a hired vehicle, Bobby stepped out of the car and opened the door for Kodelly, who had been sitting in the backseat with him. He held out his arm to her and then, they walked towards the building. They entered the building and were greeted by very loud, fast music. The atmosphere was very excited; their eyes met with young men and women, dancing to the rhythm of the music, as the psychedelic lights camouflaging their faces. They walked across the dance floor until they found another door, which led to the open platform, here also music was playing but not as loud as from the dance floor from which they had just come. The door that separated the platform from the dance floor also managed to separate the noise from the loud music.

Tables had been arranged on the sides of the pool and on one side beverages were being served. Tables had also been arranged for the buffet, which would be served later in the evening. The atmosphere was fairly different from that in the function they had just walked through. The music was playing softly, and the people were dressed differently. The ladies wore the latest fashion, in mostly mini dresses and high-heeled shoes. Little attention had been paid to coats, since the evening was fairly warm. The men were clad in expensive suits, carrying themselves about with style and charm.

A few waiters and waitresses were moving through the not so thick crowd, trays on their arms, serving refreshment as the music played on.

"What would you like to drink?" Enquired one waiter politely.

"I will have a brandy," Replied Bobby. "and she will have a…a…" He continued, turning to face Kodelly. "Punch perhaps?" He added. She nodded.

"Okay." He replied, before going to collect their order.

They sat at the table next to the swimming pool, watching the merry crowd. In a moment they too were enjoying the beverages that they had been served, with some snacks. The dance floor was covered with people dancing to the rhythm of the beat. They talked about the weather and discussed a few business issues, before he asked her to accompany him to the dance floor.

In the middle of the track, a man appeared behind Bobby, whispering into his ear and disrupting their rhythm.

"We need da' talk." He said above the noise.

"Not now." He replied above the noise.

"Now." He insisted. "It can't wait."

"Where is your jacket?" Bobby asked in an exasperated tone.

"Hey man." He replied. "Didn't know I had to dress formal. But we need da' talk." He insisted again.

"Okay." Bobby ceded, turning to face Kodelly. "Excuse me. I'm sorry, but I will find you at the table."

"Okay." She replied, having stopped in her tracks the moment the man had appeared behind them. She wondered who the rude stranger was that had just intruded on them.

She loved to dance, and that was the sole reason why she had accepted Bobby's invitation. She recalled how Lidy too had spoken proudly of the dances that she had attended as a young woman.

"Dancing is good for the soul. It makes you feel youthful." She would say, going through most of her memorable outings with the love of her life, Bill Mollar.

"It helps you to stay in shape." She would add with a smile, rising up and standing on her tiptoes, her arms in the air, demonstrating as she manoeuvred, dancing to a silent rhythm; the music still recorded in her memory.

Kodelly recalled whilst she sat by herself at the table that they had earlier occupied, of the few memorable Summerset, summer dances that she had been privileged to attend. She cheered up, as she watched Bobby approach her moments later.

"I'm sorry about that." He said, as soon as he was seated, sipping at a drink he had just got from one of the waiters.

She shrugged with a thin smile, expecting to hear more from him, but instead he spoke about other things and appeared a bit more alert, scrutinising the crowd as the evening progressed. Kodelly did not see the rude intruder again, whom she believed had most likely left the premises. She forgot about the ordeal after dancing to several tracks with Bobby, laughing softly with the merry crowd, and feeling a part of relief that Lidy had probably referred to, while she danced to the rhythm of the music.

The buffet was being served and most of the people had already gotten their portions, when Kodelly and Bobby joined the queue.

The man who had rudely interrupted their dance, reappeared and joined the short queue behind Bobby, this time he too wore a jacket, even though it was creased. He spoke to Bobby softly, almost without moving his lips, as they moved from dish to dish. Bobby had not turned to face him nor spoken back to him but was able to hear, even though Kodelly was not able to pick a thing of what was being said by the person she had definitely no liking for, although she had not been introduced or spoken to him. He lacked manners and seemed to have no regard for her presence, of which, she was so sure she had taken enough time to prepare for the evening and was as such confident of her appearance. They reached the end of the buffet and the stranger separated from them. They walked back to their table, putting the plates on the table before a loud scream was heard above the music.

"Loooook out." Came a scream, with Bobby being pushed onto the floor, while another man kicked the other person's arm, and a gun flew into the air before landing on the floor. Bobby quickly got up from the floor, pushing Kodelly against the wall, who had been watching all the events in a terrified state, as the noise of female screams accompanied what was happening.

The man who had pushed Bobby, tried to get up and pick the gun, and was immediately punched by the other man who had kicked him on the arm. Kodelly stood still, terrified, unable to move, wanting to hide but having nowhere to hide as another man approached them, he quickly began to exchange punches with Bobby, before another man pulled him from behind. Women screams were heard above the noise and soon it was six, seven and more people exchanging punches. Men were being pushed and falling into the pool and tables were being upset while, some people tried to escape. Then Bobby managed to free himself from the fight and he quickly turned to where Kodelly was standing, as she tried to cover her face from the flying objects. He got hold of her arm and began to drag her through the fighting crowd. She ran behind him towards the entrance door, feeling the discomfort from her high-heeled sandals, hearing the screams from the women and the cursing from the men as the fight was still at its peak.

They manoeuvred around the tables and chairs, which now seemed to be so chaotic, finally managing to reach the exit door into the dance hall from which they had initially walked through majestically. The music was still playing loud, but people were exiting because of the confusion and noise from the function adjacent. She was still determined to run, despite the discomfort. She ran out of breath, her mouth felt dry, holding onto her purse firmly, with her other hand still holding onto Bobby. They ran the distance of the dance floor from which they had initially come. They finally managed to reach the exit door and ran out onto the driveway. Tyres could be heard squeaking, as the cars pulled out of the driveway. Kodelly could hear herself panting, as they hurried through the parking. Panic engulfed her on realising that they would have to wait for a vehicle to take them back home. They began to run away from the cars, when one stopped by their side; Bobby quickly opened the door, simultaneously another loud scream was heard above the noise.

"Noooooooooo, not that one ..." Yelled the man who had interrupted their dance.

The driver of the car fired a gunshot; simultaneously Bobby slammed the car door, before he fell backwards. Kodelly hide behind a car that was parked, when she heard another shot. The car from which the first shot had come, squeaked its tyres and began to drive away.

Bobby had fallen between the parked cars in front of Kodelly. She gave out a loud scream, watching another man run in their direction.

"Go...that car." Yelled the man again, running towards them, when another car pulled to a halt in front of them.

Bobby slowly pulled himself together and rushed to the car that had stopped in front of them, Kodelly stood reluctant for a moment before she too dragged her exhausted body into the vehicle. She sat in the backseat, while Bobby sat in front with the driver. They drove past the man who had shouted to them to get into the car. He waved at them before he too jumped into another vehicle and drove off.

The driver of the vehicle Kodelly and Bobby had gotten into was muscular, wearing a sweaty, sleeveless t-shirt. He had perspiration on his forehead and was chewing vigorously on a bubble gum.

"Where to boss?" He asked calmly, as soon as Bobby had closed the passenger's door.

"My apartment." Replied Bobby, trying to keep calm and wiping perspiration from his forehead with a handkerchief.

"She? Your girlfriend?" He asked again, looking at Kodelly through the centre mirror.

"Just fucken' drive." He replied, with a bit of displeasure in his voice.

The man grinned, lighting a cigarette for himself and pulling at it to conceal himself from the rest of the occupants in the car. The car drove for what seemed to be an endless distance to Kodelly, before it finally came to a halt.

"That's it my man." Spoke the driver knowingly, parking in front of Bobby's apartment building.

"Thanks." Replied Bobby, pulling his wallet and drawing money from it. He then extended his hand to the man.

"No. No, man." He protested. "You can do that for me too, okay."

"Take it." He insisted.

"It has already been taken care of, my man."

"If you insist." He replied resignedly, withdrawing his hand from him. He put the money back into the wallet and thanked him again. He then opened the door and stood on the driveway, and then he turned to open the door for Kodelly, who had sat silently in the backseat.

"Let's go." He stated.

She got out of the car and followed him into the foyer, then up with the elevator to his apartment with her arms wrapped in front of her bosom. He opened the apartment door and allowed her in. She walked into the lounge and sat on the edge of the couch then looked up to Bobby, awaiting an explanation.

He walked to the table and poured himself a glass of brandy, taking a quick swig at it, before turning to face her.

"Want a drink?"

She narrowed her eyes, allowing anger to take control of her emotions and then she got up from the seat before speaking. "What was that all about?" She spoke angrily.

"That?" He repeated calmly. "Come now Kodelly, don't let that spoil our evening."

"Our evening?" She retorted. "That was barbaric. You hear. You understand." She stressed emotionally. "Barbaric!" She yelled.

He stared at her angry face for a moment, taking off his jacket and throwing it onto the chair, and then he unbuttoned his shirt and her eyes dilated in shock.

"Oh my…you mean that you were anticipating that to happen?" She said, after realizing that he wore a bullet-proof vest underneath his shirt.

"No. No. Not exactly…" He tried to protest.

"What about me? Who are you?" She asked again. "What if you had been hurt?" She continued with tears running down her cheeks. "What if?" She said, sobbing, too shaken to utter a word. "What about me?"

"I'm sorry," He said throwing his arms about her. "I'm sorry."

"Take me home." She said pulling away from him. "I don't believe that you actually anticipated that, and you just took me along."

"I didn't just take you along." He defended. "I wanted to spend some time with you."

"I bet you did." She said walking towards the door. "I want to go home now." She demanded having wiped the tears from her eyes.

"Okay." He said resignedly, upon gauging her mood and disappointment in him.

Barbaric indeed he thought to himself as he walked her home, without either of them saying a word to each other. What had seemed like a well-planned outing and was much anticipated seemed like a wasted evening after all, thought Kodelly. She had spent so much time and energy in trying to fit into the evening's function. She felt her feet hurt in her heeled sandals. She was afraid to admit that she had become fond of him. She had looked her best for him, but all that was futile. She had probably fallen in love with his allure. He filled her fantasies at times, but that was not all. She probably had fallen in love with him, which was quite an open secret that had been argued mostly by Laura and was noticed by Michael

Yellern, who had realised that the two had in the previous times, spent quite a lot of hours together. Or maybe she had just grown fond of him. Michael Yellern was an elderly man, with a wife and children. He had been initially attracted to Kodelly and had invited her to several functions, all of which she had turned down. He had then decided to have nothing, but a professional relationship with her, after several attempts. She had grown to trust him and discussed several things with him, but had so far not divulged her feelings for Bobby Mitch to him, not that it would be any of his business, but perhaps out of conversational interest. Kodelly felt ensnared in her emotions, being unable to share her feelings for Bobby with anyone. Could she possibly be harbouring feelings for him, she wondered? She sneaked quietly into their apartment, not wanting to wake Laura up. She took a long, warm bath to relax her sore muscles, and then she sat on her bed for a while and tried to block the night's events from haunting her, before finally falling asleep.

*   *   *

Kodelly had been absent minded for most of the morning. The weekend had gone by with Bobby Mitch not calling or checking on her. He had left her at her apartment door, after their disrupted evening. She had expected him to visit her the following day, with a bouquet of flowers and a big apology in his heart, but alas that had not transpired. She had looked forward to seeing him at work on the following Monday morning and had made a deliberate effort not to phone his extension. She sat waiting anxiously for her office phone to ring or to see him stand in the doorway, but again, none of that had materialised so far. She would startle when the phone rang, hoping that it would be him, but all she had received were business calls thus far. She blamed herself for his behaviour, thinking that she had probably overacted, after they had returned to his apartment. Maybe, she should have been a little bit understanding. She wondered why an evening so well planned could end up in the way it did. She longed to hear his voice, to see his face and laugh to his rare humour, she realized with a smile. The door swung open, jilting her from her thoughts and causing her to raise her eyes in anticipation.

"Kodelly how was your weekend?" He began, "I haven't seen or heard from you today." He continued before she could respond. "I can almost have bet that you did not report for work at all. You have been so quiet, almost invisible. Had a long weekend, too much to drink perhaps?" He said, putting his hands on the table for support, as he stood in front of her office table. "Yeah, Bobby any ideas where he might be at? I have tried his number at home and his not bloody picking up my calls. I hate people that stand me up, especially on a Monday. I need to draw up my plans and know what and where I will be at?"

She shook her head.

"Anything the matter. I need to know the flippen' plans for the week?" He stressed again.

"You are asking the wrong person." She replied flatly. "Besides, I need to work." She lied, only realising that he had not actually reported for work. Could something be wrong with him, she wondered, yet trying to conceal her concern for him.

"Come on, we all know that the two of you are close." He stated, getting out of his sour mood.

"Close?" She retorted in defence. "We are just friends. I only know him."

"Woo, woo don't get me the wrong way, but I'm sure you know where he is at or why he is not here?"

She shook her head again.

"Wrong question to the wrong person." She stated again. "I am busy, so if you will excuse me."

"Busy?" He asked in amusement. "I found you flippen staring in space. Is that being busy?"

"Okay." She said resignedly, giving out probably her first genuine smile of the day. "I will check on him after hours, if that is fine with you?"

"That will be great, coz I honestly have quite a lot of meetings this week. Tell him I'm … well never mind." Michael stood for a moment, before turning to leave her office.

*   *   *

A cold evening breeze hit against her face, as she walked briskly, down the busy pavement. She held her coat about her to keep the cold away. She finally got to Bobby's apartment. She stood for a moment in front of the door, looking about her, before ringing the doorbell to announce her presence. She looked on either side again, wanting to see if anyone was watching her and what thoughts could be going through their minds, seeing her stand in front of a bachelor's home. She rang the doorbell again, before she heard shuffled movements and the door opened before her. He appeared in the doorway, a bathrobe around his waist, his face looked clear and soft from the bath he had taken a few minutes ago. His eyes lit up momentarily, even though there was not much of a smile on his face.

"Come in." He invited, moving out of the way to allow her passage.

"Well…am not staying long. Michael asked me to check on you, so…" She began to explain embarrassed, a surge of anger coming over her. She had been worried about him, especially after what she saw at the dance venue and that he had not reported for work. She thought that perhaps something had happened to him, and yet there he stood. He had probably spent the whole day at home or had been up to some other endeavours that were more interesting than being jammed at the office.

He had not phoned her or checked on her since the Friday evening. Why had he been so quiet, she wondered to herself?

"Are you coming in?" He spoke again.

"Well…" She said, walking into the hall, wanting to know the reason why he had ignored her since that evening. She had a reason to be annoyed, she justified leading her way to the lounge.

"Why don't you wait for me upstairs in the other room, whilst I go and dress up?" He suggested.

She followed him up the stairs, he opened the door for her into his small gallery and excused himself to go and dress up. She sighed, after he had left her, marvelling at the paintings all over again. She allowed them to soothe her, and momentarily forgot about her disappointment with Bobby, for having not considered apologising to her necessary, for taking her out on such a worthless date. She deserved better than to be left to complete a puzzle for the so many things that seemed to have been left hanging. She walked to the table and on it was an ashtray with cigarette butts in it. There were also two empty wine glasses and an almost empty bottle of wine. She inspected the table further, a surge of jealous emotions overcoming her. She recalled Bobby telling her that he hardly took anyone to the room and yet, in front of her was evidence that someone else had been there earlier. Whoever it was must be special, she thought to herself. His girlfriend perhaps, she sighed again, wanting to leave his apartment immediately. She walked to the shelf, wanting to distract her thoughts again, and begun to read through the titles casually, before one book caught her attention. She pulled the book from the shelf. It was a book of poems; she read through the title and publication and then randomly began to flip through the pages. She recalled, how as a little girl she had recited poems for her mother and her friends. She would be dressed up adorably and then stand in front of her mother and her guests, who would be enjoying some homemade scones, with a fine cup of tea or coffee. Compliments would then be poured at her, as her pretty innocent face would lighten, her young voice echoing the rhyme of the poem.

"What a lovely voice that your little angel has."

"Isn't she adorable?" Other compliments would state.

"Thank you." Her mother would respond proudly.

She began to read one of the poems, her finger on the line of the page.

> *'Their hearts beat in unison*
> *as they stood face to face*
> *entwined in a passion they had*
> *never imaged,'*

She heard Bobby's voice from behind her, recite the poem after seeing her reading silently.

> *'It was emotions that could otherwise be*
> *trapped inside them, but had been allowed to*
> *flow. Like the river flows slowly to the ocean.*
> *Flowing the natural course*
> *So, their hearts' beat, rhymed in unison.'*

"It is beautiful." She said softly, closing the book and turning to face Bobby, whose voice she had heard over her shoulder.

"You recite Poetry?"

"Yeah." He replied. "A man ought to do what he gotta do."

"You?" He asked.

"Yes." She nodded.

"Maybe I should take you to the opera sometime, soon?"

"No. No, thank you." She replied. "You had company?" Gesturing to the glasses on the table.

"Oh, just some old friend." He replied again, with his arms folded in front of him.

She stood expecting to hear more from him, but he was quiet for a while.

"Why did you not report for work or even care to call?" She found herself asking.

"I thought you needed more time to yourself." He answered with a shrug.

"I have to go now." She said abruptly.

"So soon?"

"Yes." She replied, looking into his teasing eyes.

He obliged, walking with her down the stairs, they had hardly reached the foot of the stairs before they heard the doorbell ring.

"I will get the door." He stated. "Wait for me in the lounge, please." He spoke hurriedly.

She looked at him for a moment, uncertain of what to say, before walking to the lounge. She sat on the edge of the sofa, before Bobby opened the entrance door and spoke softly. Kodelly could not help but to eavesdrop.

"Oh, Bobby, where is he?" She heard a female's voice speak.

"We would like to see him." Continued another one.

"He is not here." He stated firmly. "Now, I have other things to do, if you will excuse me."

"Where can we find him?" Asked the second female voice.

"I already told you that I don't know." He responded irritably, slamming the door in their faces.

Kodelly sat puzzled at their conversation. She could not make out much of it though and was curious to see whom it was he was talking with. She thought one of the women's voices sounded familiar. It was almost as if, she had spoken to one of the two before.

"Wrong number." He said as soon as he had entered the lounge. "I'm sorry about that. Would you care for a drink?" He continued, pouring himself a glass of brandy.

The doorbell rang again, before she could even answer. She watched him leave the room again. She stood up and poured herself a glass of juice.

"Where is he?" She heard the voice she thought to be familiar speak to him again, prompting her to want to peep through the door that had been left slightly ajar, into the hallway to the main entrance. She looked through the ajar door, not wanting to be seen and there was the woman she thought to be familiar. It was the woman from the restaurant. She still remembered her vividly.

"Go away." He charged.

"Sorry to bother you, but..." Tried to explain the other one.

"Bother me? You heard me, leave. Go away, okay..."

"No, Bobby..." Said, the other woman Kodelly thought to be familiar. "We need to see him." She filled in, like little children rehashing for a play.

"Listen," He tried to explain calmly. "I can't help you because I don't know anything, okay."

They stood for a moment and looked at each other, before deciding to leave, after being satisfied that he had at least spoken to them calmly.

He closed the door softly, sighed and then turned to walk back to the lounge. Kodelly jumped and hurried back to sit.

"Wrong number again?" She asked, as soon as he walked in.

"Long day perhaps." He replied. "May I take you home now?"

"Yes." She replied, looking at his distracted face.

She was disappointed at the fact that she could not get through to him. There seemed to be a lot she had to learn about him. There seemed to be a gap that was growing wider between them. She wanted to know so much about him, but so far, he wouldn't let her. He seemed to be throwing caution to the wind. He certainly wasn't like any of the gentlemen from Summerset, who normally gave a month's prior notice, if they wanted to take a lady out to any function. Then they would be so mindful when speaking to the woman in their presence, in order to ensure that she remained feeling respected and the woman that they really were.

The lady too, would have to remember particularly who was in her company and carry herself about with esteem. She would speak with caution, not wanting to be anything less than what was anticipated of her, talking back with etiquette, and letting the man's ego grow as much as he wanted to, without talking back rudely or arguing back unnecessarily. But things were different with Bobby, she thought, sitting at her dinner table quietly with Laura, with whom she had spent less time with lately, because of their hectic work schedules. They had grown out of complaining of how much they missed Summerset, but had instead come to love working and living in the busy city.

Letters from Dinkley Mills had continued to pour in, speaking of how much in love he was with her and how much he missed her, except for the distance that had deprived him from seeing her beautiful face daily. He longed to see her again, he confessed time and again and yet, her replies to his letters remained neutral, ignoring his love confession, but responding in a rather general way. Love was the furthest thing on her mind. She wondered if she had directed her attention too much to Bobby, to ever mind about Dinkley Mills. Laura had continued to sneak into Kodelly's room, reading the letters from Dinkley Mills. Reading every word for the love that it stood for. Then sometimes, in one sentence, there would be a mention of her, enquiring of her well-being, but all the love and attention was directed to Kodelly, the queen of his heart.

* _____ *

CHAPTER SIX

*I*t was several weeks following the incident at the function and Kodelly had gradually renewed her trust in Bobby again, after spending countless hours with him. She had accompanied him to the opera and several other places but had deliberately avoided going to his apartment. He enthralled her days and seemed to set a direction in her life for which she had not anticipated. He did not fill her in on any of the things that she wanted to know. Indeed, there was a part of him that she never got through to.

"When is Michael sending you to check on me again?" He'd teased her on countless occasions.

"Why must I come checking on you?"

"You don't care anymore?"

She'd shrugged with a smile.

She stood by the window, looking through the rain as it hit against the closed window, while the music played softly in the background. There was a bottle of wine and two empty wine glasses on the table. Bobby lay on his bed, watching her. Her gaze was fixed momentarily on the city. She had finally accepted to visit him again. She had come with him and accepted to enter his bedroom. It was not an unusual room, although it was well arranged and comfortable. He got up from the bed and walked the short distance to the window. He stood behind Kodelly and put his strong arms over her shoulders, she turned and faced him. His fingers touched her face gently, and then he stroked her hair, kissing her gently on her forehead, then down onto her lips. She kissed him back entangled in a moment of passion, his arms sliding around her waist, then, abruptly she pulled away from him.

"Why?" He asked quietly. "Do you doubt my love for you?"

"No. No." She replied wiping her mouth.

"I tease you with words, but you certainly tease my emotions." He continued. "I love you; please don't deny my love for you."

She smiled and moved away. She walked to the table and poured herself a glass of wine.

"Want some?" She asked casually.

"I want you." He replied with his eyes focused on her tender, youthful body. He walked to her and held her hand, taking the glass away from her and looking deep into her eyes, before kissing her fondly again. His breath became heavy, as they continued to kiss; he sat her on the bed, his body next to hers.

"Bobby wait…" She said urgently, pushing away his hands from her body.

"What?" He asked in a deep voice.

"I need some time to think about this."

"Are you going home through the rains?" He teased.

"No." She replied, trying to pull herself together, "No." She repeated, softly, watching him take a swig from the glass of wine that, she had earlier poured for him.

*　　*　　*

The doorbell rung, causing Laura to jump from her seat, it was raining heavily, and she had just been wondering about Kodelly's whereabouts. She was wondering if she had been ensnared in the rain. She hurried to the door, wondering who could be calling on them, especially since the weather was bad for any outdoor activities. She was not expecting any of her workmates to call on her, despite it being a Friday. She had been engrossed in the local newspaper and was jilted from the stories, which were her only source of entertainment for the evening. She had become accustomed to spending most of the time alone in the apartment, especially since her cousin normally went to the opera, movies or for dinner depending on her mood. She opened the door and her jaws dropped in aghast.

"Oh, my goodness." She exclaimed, her hand covering her mouth, unable to conceal her delight. "Please do come in!" She added after a pause.

"How are you?" He asked upon entering the apartment, standing in the hallway, and taking off his wet coat.

"I'm fine, thank you." She replied, taking his wet coat from him after closing the door.

"I am sorry for intruding on you, but I had been trying your telephone earlier on, but no one answered." He explained.

"Oh don't. You would be the last person we would call an intruder." She replied, pausing for a moment again, before inviting him through to the lounge, after putting the coat away.

He followed her behind, a bunch of red roses still in his hands and then, he occupied the seat she'd offered him upon reaching the lounge.

"Do pardon my calling on you so late." He tried to apologise again.

"It's not a problem. It's good to see you." She interjected reassuringly.

"Where is Kodelly?" He asked abruptly.

She shrugged. "At the movies perhaps. I don't know for sure."

"I'm here on business. I am booked at the hotel, but I thought I can't sleep knowing Kodelly is just in the vicinity."

"I see." She replied, concealing her exasperation on realising that he was not at all thrilled to see her, but that his heart only longed for Kodelly.

"May I make you some tea?"

"Yes, thank you. What time do you think she is coming back?" He asked again.

"Soon, perhaps."

"Does she normally come late?" He continued.

"No." She replied, before walking to the kitchen to make some tea. She returned minutes later and found him standing by the hearth, looking at their childhood photos on the mantle, with the flowers still in his hands.

"I made some tea." She spoke to distract him.

"Oh, thank you. Isn't this beautiful?" He said pointing at the photo with Kodelly in it.

"Indeed, it is. May I put the flowers in the water for you?"

"Yes, do please." He said, sitting down before taking a sip from the cup of tea.

"What time did you say she would be returning?"

She sighed, putting the flowers in the water vessel.

"I can phone one or two places she might be?"

"No. No. Not a bother, I was just wondering where she could be?"

She sat in a chair across to him and was annoyed for a moment, especially to the fact that even in her absence, Kodelly still was the centre of attention. She wished she could have a meaningful conversation with him. She wished he could tell her about the endeavours in Summerset.

The phone rang and Laura got up to answer, Kodelly was on the other side of the line and was deliberately fiddling with the line, making reception poor.

"Laura. Laura, it's Kodelly." She spoke. "I will be quite late…"

"Hello? Kodelly, is that Kodelly? I can barely hear you…" Replied Laura, trying to strain her ears.

"I said…" She began before dropping the line.

"Now, where were we?" Spoke Bobby, pulling her to him, with her smiling back into his eyes.

"What did she say?"

"That everything is fine." She replied, as they continued to kiss and strip each other of their clothing, in merry unison, before making love to the rhythm of the rain.

"What did she say…Do pardon me, was that Kodelly? Is she on her way?" Dinkley questioned as soon as Laura had put the receiver back on the hook.

"Yes… Yes, it was." She replied, trying to make out what her cousin had been trying to say and yet also avoiding appearing puzzled.

"Anything wrong?" He asked again, urgently.

"No. I don't think so, except that the reception was quite poor. It might be due to the rain. I didn't get quite what she was saying."

"Maybe she is coming a little bit late. She could be delayed due to the rains." He suggested.

"Maybe." She replied back, wondering if her cousin was truly held up in the rain and if she was with Bobby. She always came home, and Laura did not doubt it in her mind that she would be home soon, maybe later, but certainly she would be home.

"I will be leaving soon. Let me not keep you up late. I will probably come tomorrow. I actually should have called before coming."

"The rains are very heavy. Are you going to brave them?"

"Okay…, I will wait for a while."

"Would you like anything to eat? I can fix us some sandwiches."

"I'm fine thanks."

"Do eat something, please." She said before disappearing into the kitchen. She returned moments later with a bowl of green salads, sandwiches, and juice. They ate quietly before Laura announced that she would be retiring to bed, after sitting for another hour watching TV with him.

"You can sleep on the couch if you don't mind. The rains are still too heavy."

"Well, I guess I have little of an option." He replied, watching her disappear again. She returned moments later to give him some warm covers.

"Good night." She said, before walking back to her room.

She stood in front of her dressing table, after changing into her nightdress and began to brush her hair when she heard a faint knock on the bedroom door.

"Hold on a second." She called from inside.

She opened the door and stood face to face with Dinkley. He looked into her eyes, watching her lean body, which was clad in her short night dress.

"I have never slept on the couch before." He said after a moment as a matter of fact, taking hold of her hand and raising it to his mouth.

He kissed the inside of her hand, his strong arms then surrounded her, lean figure. She felt the heat from his body as they begun to kiss. They fell onto the thick carpet and caressed. Laura ran out of breath as they continued to kiss, unable to live through the moment. She had never for a moment thought that she could end the day in a romantic rapture with the man she had for so long admired, the man who had written countless, love letters to her cousin Kodelly, the man who had entered their apartment earlier, looking forward to seeing the apple of his eyes. He kissed her urgently, down her neck to her bare shoulders, and then slowly he pulled away from her, without either of them saying a word for a while.

"I'm sorry." He began to say. "I shouldn't have..."

"Shh..." She spoke back, lying on her side and then raising her finger to his lips.

"I will take the couch." He reaffirmed, as he moved away from her and got onto his feet.

"Do you really want to sleep on the couch?" She asked while getting up from the carpet and walking to her bed, her mind still spinning on what could have probably transpired between them, if he was not just too careful and polite. It would have been a delightful moment for her.

It would have been a moment she had never anticipated, but that she could have cherished forever. She got into her bed and between the covers wanting to invite him, but wondering how he would take it.

"Yes." She heard him say after a pause, before he walked back to the lounge, and finally fail asleep on the couch, in the warm bedcovers she had provided him with earlier.

*   *   *

She woke up the next day, as the sun rays entered the room. She pulled the bedcovers over her. She had no clothes on and for a moment wondered where she was? She turned and saw Bobby still in his sleep, and then she recalled the previous night's events and where she was. She slipped out of the bed, not wanting to wake him up. She felt a sense of guilt about her, and yet a part of her told her that he must be in love with her. She felt a sense of belonging with him, even though the only thing she wanted was to be back at her apartment. She wondered if Laura had realised that she had not returned home the previous evening and wondered what could be going through her mind. She quickly put her clothes on and hurried to the bathroom, still not wanting to wake Bobby up. She washed her face and sneaked her way down the stairs, getting her bag from the couch before leaving his apartment. She walked onto the pavement and quickly stopped a taxi with one fantasy; to get home and take a warm bath and relieve herself from all the aching that she was experiencing. The taxi stopped in front of her apartment building, she paid her fare and got out onto the sunny pavement, with no evidence of the previous day's heavy rains. She walked into the foyer and into the elevator and walked the distance to her apartment door, moments later.

She hoped, as she turned the key that she would not meet with Laura. She felt guilty all over again. She hoped that Laura would still be fast asleep, it being a Saturday morning. She opened the door and was greeted by a radiant Laura, a warm smile on her face, dressed in an expensive outfit, with an equally expensive ring on her left, middle finger.

"Good morning." She greeted her cheerfully. "Care to join me for breakfast?"

"No, thank you. I need to... well."

"Sorry, I couldn't hear what you were saying yester night…"

"No need to bother. If you will excuse me…"

"By the way, I have some news for you."

"Me?" She asked quizzically, stopping in her tracks and turning to face her.

"Yes… Well, yes."

"What is it? Can't it wait?"

"No." She said firmly, "No." She paused for a moment, looking at her cousin's face, watching her every expression, wanting to convince her to join her for breakfast. Surely it would be the best way to break the news and not with her standing in the doorway, on the verge of a rare mood. It was almost as if she wanted to run away. But then, Laura couldn't wait to share the news with someone, anyone, especially family.

"Dinkley and I are engaged." She said with a sparkle in her eyes, blushing a little.

"What!" She exclaimed. "Are you crazy? What…?"

"I am engaged to Dinkley Mills. He is picking me up for dinner this evening. He was here last night." She reaffirmed, as if reciting a story.

"What the hell are you talking about? I know you like Dinkley, but get off it, Dinkley in Cambel city without calling?"

"I was going to tell you last night, but your line was poor…so poor in fact…"

"Listen, Laura, I need to take a bath… rest perhaps." She replied, starting to walk away.

"You don't believe me?"

"No." She, said flatly.

"Look at the ring he gave me." She continued, showing off her engagement ring and entering her bedroom after her.

"It is nice." She complimented with little interest.

"But what…?"

"But nothing."

"Are you jealous?"

"No. Listen; give me some time to myself, maybe I believe you, maybe I don't."

"He said that he loves me." She continued.

"Read my lips, 'congratulations Laura'. Satisfied? Will you excuse me." She said, gesturing to her to leave and closing the door in her face.

She then just realised that all she wanted was to be with Bobby again, and that she couldn't get him out of her mind, not for a second. She took off her clothes and stepped into a warm bath, a part of her wanting to wash him off, yet a part of her still wanting to hold onto him. She thought about Laura for a while, wondering why her poor cousin was lying about Dinkley's visit. He definitely would not come without calling her first, neither would he engage Laura. She got out of the bath, before falling asleep on top of her bed covers.

Laura sat in the kitchen, unable to eat, with a cup of tea in front of her and staring at the gold ring on her finger, still in disbelief. Dinkley Mills had slipped it on her finger earlier in the morning, almost in a hurry, saying that he had some business meeting to go to. He had spent the night on the couch. Then, suddenly, she became unsure of his feelings for her. What if Dinkley had changed his mind about seeing her again? What if he had walked back to the hotel room and realised that it was Kodelly he loved and not her? What if, he was just jealous or hurt because Kodelly had not come back, or perhaps he was just hurt? No. She told herself, she was just being paranoid, and he meant every word he said. No. She tried to convince herself, he meant the ring he had slipped on her finger in the morning.

*   *   *

The doorbell rung, waking her up, she had slept for almost the entire day and woke up only to eat. It was almost dusk, when she heard Laura's footsteps rush to the door and then she heard her talking. She could not make out whom she was talking with, though. She then realised that the last person she wanted to face was Bobby. She got her relaxed body from the bed and slipped into a warm outfit. She washed her face, and then she went to the lounge and before her sat Dinkley Mills with Laura. She stood for a moment trying to recall her earlier conversation with Laura.

"Kodelly." He exclaimed, jolting her from her thoughts. "It is good to see you."

"It is good to see you too." She replied back dumbfounded, looking at Laura who suddenly seemed insecure.

"Congratulations." She continued, looking back to Dinkley. "I heard about your engagement."

"Oh, thank you." He replied, blushing.

"If you will excuse me." She continued, not wanting to talk at length with him. "I have to fix myself something to eat." Before, leaving the two in the lounge, with no regrets on her previous night's decision.

————————————

CHAPTER SEVEN

*S*he stood in the flower garden, dressed in her long satin dress, with white heeled-pumps and a white sunhat over her head. It was not the same white dress she wore during her wedding ceremony, exchanging vows with Dinkley Mills and assuming the title of Mrs. Laura Dinkley Mills, she thought, standing face to face with her husband, this time without a veil to shield her from him. They held hands, the sun seeming to smile on them, as they kissed, not minding who was watching them, with the smell of the familiar flowers surrounding them. They were officially married, and nothing mattered anymore to them, except for the love that they felt between them. Nothing could transcend the joy that had encompassed Laura since Dinkley had visited Cambel city. Nothing would ever exceed the joy and excitement that she still felt. Dinkley Mills had made her a woman. He was all that she ever dreamt of. He was all that she ever wanted and thought she could never have and yet, like a scene from a dream, she now wore his ring and was committed to him for life.

Kodelly sat, looking through the window, thinking about Bobby Mitch, who was so far away from her. He had declined to accompany her to Summerset for Laura's wedding, and yet all she wanted was to go back to Cambel city and be with the man that she loved. She had been counting the hours delightfully after the ceremony, having watched Dinkley Mills and Laura Mollar exchange vows to be tied in marriage. She recalled how frantic Lidy had been when she first saw her in the restroom of the hotel in which the wedding reception was held, even though, she had put in all the effort in preparing one of the most memorable weddings in Summerset, with her husband Bill and Dinkley Mills' parents. She had appeared excited all the while, until she ran into Kodelly, who had arrived on the actual day of the wedding ceremony.

"How could you let her do this to you?"

"Do what mom?"

"Steal him from you?" She stated.

"But, she didn't." She protested.

"Oh! Don't pretend. It was you that Dinkley Mills was in love with. It was you that he came to the house for and asked about." She paused for a moment, narrowing her eyes. "Oh, how could she do this to you?"

"She didn't. I was not in love with him …" She tried to explain, pulling her petticoat up her waist.

"Oh, don't pretend." She repeated, "Now, I have to go back in there and pretend to be very happy when I know that it was you, he was in love with?" She paused for a moment, trying to get hold of herself, before Kodelly interjected.

"Mom, let it go."

She sighed, seizing her daughter and looking her in the eyes.

"It was you that he was in love with." She repeated. "So, when is your wedding?"

She blushed, feeling uncomfortable for a moment as she looked back into her mother's eyes, wanting to explode and tell her all about the city man, Bobby Mitch. But then, how could she? Where could she start from, she wondered, as she smiled, embarrassed with herself.

"Let us go and celebrate Laura's wedding and stop saying that she got him from me." She said cheerfully, embracing her mother, wanting to get reassurance from her, feeling the tender familiar warmth from her, trying to block Bobby from her mind and just be a part of the wedding celebrations. They joined the merry crowd smiling happily, with Lidy forgetting her misgivings about Dinkley's feelings for her daughter, Kodelly.

They had no courtship, from the night that they had spent in the same apartment, they had announced their engagement, a week later to make it official, and now barely a month after, they had exchanged their vows and were now husband and wife with just one or two dinner dates before their wedding.

Kodelly sighed, still hearing some of the guests' voices in the rooms downstairs. She had already packed her bag, too eager to go back to Cambel city, to an apartment she would now occupy by herself, as Laura was to remain in Summerset and start a new life with her husband on the ranch. Pulling away from the window, she sat on the bed, in the room that she had occupied for most of her childhood, a feeling of loneliness engulfing her, and yet a poem kept coming to her mind.

"To harvest a love that is not yet ripe

**To follow a course that does not lead the river to the ocean
To harvest a love that is not yet ripe….
Sweet like candy at the beginning…
To harvest a love that is not yet ripe
Like bubble gum, bitter at the end, with only one desire
To depose of it
To harvest a love that is not yet ripe…"**

She sighed, as she thought about Bobby. She had spent several nights at his apartment, since the first time when Dinkley had called on them, and yet she could not tell if he truly loved her as much as she loved him or as much as he said he did. Despite all that, all she wanted was to be back in Cambel city, to be back in the arms of the man she felt would love her forever.

*　　*　　*

"I have got two executive tickets for the art exhibition." Announced Bobby whilst flashing two tickets in front of Kodelly's face, who sat behind her office desk looking back into his excited face.

"Oh!" She replied, having little knowledge of it.

"Pedree Laskador, is exhibiting and you, my love are gonna' go to the exhibition with me." He continued.

"Thank you." She replied casually.

She had heard talk of Pedree Laskador's exhibition for the previous week, with everyone who was an art enthusiast ticking his exhibition days at the gallery in their dairies. The gallery was to open to the public during the day, and then, in the evening only the executive ticket holders would visit the gallery to see his works.

"The bastard." Michael Yellern had complained earlier to Kodelly. "His out to get money only. Ayah, there are hundreds of people who want to see his work and then, his got them rich folks who will go on executive tickets. Pity, I never managed to get hold of one. Got sold out faster than I can talk. His got the talent."

"So, you enjoyed yourself?" She recalled asking him, wanting to know more about the exhibition that had gotten everyone so keen.

"Ayah, too many people." He paused, pulling at his cigar, and seeming distant for a moment. "Lots of people, like I said and maybe seeing imitations of his work. Who knows, the rest they put away for the executive guests, perhaps. I suppose he shall auction some of his work. So, aren't you going?"

"I am not sure yet." She had replied and yet she now looked at the ticket Bobby had just presented to her in the comfort of her office.

* * *

They entered the well-lit art gallery, which was filled with guests, who were elegantly groomed. The sight was breath taking, with the crowd showing off their expensive jewellery, which formed part of their dressing. The evening tour was just about to commence, and the entourage was talking softly. Bobby walked abreast Kodelly, dressed in a dark tuxedo, an expensive perfume about him, with gloss shoes which showed off his height. Walking gently, yet majestically was Kodelly, thinking only of Lidy and how she carried herself about, picking one foot after the other with much poise, trying to master the allure that always encompassed her, adorned in a well fitted, long dress, with a slit on either side, a scintillating handbag in her hand and heeled shoes that seemed to add to her height, a few inches.

"Ladies and gentlemen," Spoke a clear, well cut voice. "Good evening and may I have your attention." Clapping his hands simultaneously to draw the crowd's attention.

The noise and shuffled movements slowly subdued and there was a relative calm, with their eyes focused on the person that had called for their attention.

"May I introduce Mr. Pedree Laskador?" He said, gesturing to the man that was standing next to him. "He will guide you through the gallery and hopefully you will all come back for the auction on the date indicated. Thank you. Mr. Laskador, please..."

"Good evening." Greeted Pedree Laskador.

He was an elderly man in his fifties, tall with a lean figure, small glasses on his eyes and wore a white dust coat over his neat outfit. He held a small pointing stick in his hand and within a moment he was taking the audience from painting to painting, talking in brief about what had prompted him to do each particular work. The crowd listened intently, showing varying enthusiasm as they followed along. Walking by Pedree Laskador's side, was a young, humble looking gentleman, with dark hair.

"That's his son." Whispered Bobby to Kodelly, as he held her hand in his.

"I see." She replied, paying attention to Pedree Laskador, whilst he guided them through.

There were about two or so people taking notes and a few others taking photographs, probably freelancers, trying to get the selling pictures and make a living. After about three quarters of an hour, they reached the last painting.

"Last but not the least..." He introduced the final painting, before concluding. "To our honoured guests, we do have some refreshments over there," He said, gesturing to a table on the other end of the gallery. "Which, we would like of you to part-take freely, as you go through the gallery, at your own leisure, with the knowledge we have just imparted. Please enjoy..." He ended, giving the pointing stick to the man that had earlier introduced him to the audience, and then gracefully walking to the table with refreshments on it and an assortment of finger snacks. He poured himself a drink, whilst the guests joined in.

"Let's have a drink." Suggested Bobby, leading her to the table.

"Good evening. Now, don't tell me the name." Spoke Pedree Laskador, holding a drink in one hand and rubbing his forehead with the other.

"Good evening." He replied.

"And how do you do, my Lady?" He said, taking Kodelly's hand in his hand and kissing the back of her hand politely.

"How do you do?" She replied, smiling thinly.

He let go of her hand and rubbed Bobby on his arm.

"Do remind me, please."

"Bobby..." He began to speak.

"Ah, Mr. Bobby Mitch." He quickly interjected; his memory having been triggered.

"Mr. Bobby Mitch." He said, shaking hands with him all over again, with renewed enthusiasm.

"And the lady?"

"My fiancée. Miss Kodelly Mollar." He replied.

"I'm honoured to meet with you." He bowed gently at Kodelly.

"I'm honoured to meet you too, sir." She replied.

"Anything for the Lady?"

"Some orange juice, pure if you have, otherwise natural water is her choice." He replied on her behalf.

"I see, she is a lover of nature. Pure orange juice it shall be." He replied, pouring her a glass of juice and handing it over to her. "The gentleman will help himself." He advised, seeing Bobby pick a glass and fill it as the other guests joined in too, to drink to their satisfaction.

"Do tell me before you leave." He spoke to Bobby again, before turning his attention to some other guests.

"And when did we get engaged?" Enquired Kodelly, teasingly as they moved away from the table.

He shrugged.

"Pedree Laskador doesn't see a beautiful woman. Besides aren't we in love?"

She nodded, a sense and feeling of pride filled her and she wished that she could stand on top of the roof and tell the whole world about the strong bond of love she shared with Bobby.

"How do you know him?" She asked impulsively.

"What?" He asked back dumbfounded.

"I mean you and Mr. Laskador?"

"Oh...I bought some paintings some time back...His paintings I mean. The one in the lounge." He struggled to explain. He paused, looked at the now empty glass still in her hands. "Want a refill or must we leave?"

"I'm fine...we could as well leave. We will come back for the auction, won't we?"

"I suppose so." He replied, taking the glass from her, before leading her back to Pedree Laskador.

"It's been a wonderful review of your work, Mr. Laskador, but we have to leave now. I have quite a handful of things to do after here." He explained, choosing his words carefully.

"Don't worry. I will see you off and thanks for coming." He said, excusing himself from the man that was standing next to him.

"I will walk you to your car. It is always good to see familiar faces." He added, as they exited the gallery.

Car, thought Kodelly in panic. Car? What car would he walk them to? They had not come in a luxurious vehicle like most of his elegant guests. They were just a moderate couple, which had what it takes to convince the masses that they were part of this entourage, even though they did not exactly meet the standards. They had come in a hired vehicle, unlike most of the guests. The driver had dropped them and driven off and that was it. They would have to call for another cab to pick them up. What an embarrassment the evening would end in, she thought in disgust, wanting to tug at Bobby's arm and ask him to stop the charade, she told herself. They walked through the parking lot with the two men talking softly between themselves. What would he think of them, she thought in panic? Just then Bobby stopped in his tracks.

"Here we are." He said, stopping in front of a parked limousine, and simultaneously the driver got out of the vehicle.

"Good evening, Mr. Mitch." He greeted knowingly to Kodelly's astonishment.

"Good evening, sir." He addressed Pedree Laskador, "And ma'am." He beckoned, turning to Kodelly.

"Good evening." They all replied, watching him as he opened the passenger's door for Bobby.

"Thank you so much for coming," Spoke Pedree, "Your support is my inspiration."

"I'm always honoured to be present at your exhibitions." Replied Bobby, shaking hands with him.

"And to your beautiful fiancée, I am honoured to have met you and do enjoy the rest of your evening."

"Same to you." She replied, still baffled at the limousine that she was standing next to. She wondered how Bobby had managed to call the driver without her knowledge, especially one that actually knew his name.

They got into the back seat of the limousine, while Pedree walked back to the Gallery. The car pulled off slowly from the parking lot, concealing them from the hustles and bustles of the city.

"I had no idea that you had a car waiting out here for you." She began.

"Shh." He said, smiling in her face. "It shows how much I love you." Kissing her gently on the lips with his hands moving down the length of her leg.

"I can't wait to get us home." He mumbled softly.

She kissed him back and then moved away.

"I deserve better than the back seat of a limousine." She said chidingly, watching him pull away in the shadow of the night and instead focusing their attention to the city they were driving through. A sense of security and love surrounding them, as the car drove on gently. She felt very secure, wondering why Bobby had told Pedree that they were engaged, other than just to flaunt his esteem. She curdled next to him, with no fear of the past or the future, whilst his strong arms encircled her. She felt loved, as the car gently rolled its wheels on the smooth road in the quietness of the night.

_____

CHAPTER EIGHT

*H*e was holding three brochures in his hands; he stood for a moment in the lounge before continuing to pace up and down again. Kodelly was in the bathroom, wetting her face, she watched the water roll down her cheeks through the mirror. She felt a quiver go down her spin, unsure of her own emotions. Not wanting to go back to the lounge to face him again, slowly she pat dry her face, wishing that this whole moment would never be. She wished that, it were perhaps, just a bad dream and she would wake up into the loving arms of the man that she was so much in love with. She put the towel on the side rail and walked back into the lounge.

"So, as I was saying," He began, stopping in his tracks as soon as she re-entered the lounge. "The procedure is very easy." He continued in a flat voice. "I have got the very best doctors in town. I will foot the bill." He explained.

"I heard you the first time," She said, shaking her head, feeling the tense atmosphere between them. "I need to go and get myself something to drink." She added, walking the short distance to the kitchen.

She returned, moments later with a glass of milk in her hands.

"Do you really have to drink that?" He spoke harshly.

"Well…" She stammered. "Yes."

"I am disgusted." He continued walking the distance to her and getting the glass from her hands, before putting it on the side table.

"Sit down." He said softly, beckoning her to sit. He knelt in front of her and held her hands in his as soon as she was seated.

"It is the best thing to do. Not now, not yet. You've got your whole career at stake. Not now Kodelly."

She pulled her hands from his.

"It is the logical thing to do." He reassured, as he looked back into her eyes.

"Logical?" She said in a whisper, getting up from the chair. "There is a baby shop around the corner. That is logic. What about all those lovely things? I can't just decide to do it now. I can't go through with the procedure." She added in a raised voice.

"You are being irrational." He retorted, looking her in the eyes again, as he too had stood up after her.

"Maybe, but I really can't."

"Can't what? You think you will cope on your own? Goodness!" He cut in sharply again, before taking a deep breath.

"I have to go now; I will leave you with this." He continued, putting the brochures on the table. "If you make up your mind on doing the right thing, you can always refer to this." He added, before walking quickly to the door, opening and slamming it behind him.

She sighed, placing her hand on her stomach, a quiver running down her spine at the memory of his angry face as he stormed out of her apartment. She had not seen him since that evening, even though she had hoped that he would walk through the door and tell her that everything would be back to the way the used to be. She had gone back to the office two days later, with one hope in mind, at least she would be able to see him at the office, by then, he would have calm himself down and come to terms with the situation. He would probably apologise for having been harsh to her on their last encounter. She had barely sat in her office chair, before she heard a voice in the doorway.

"Good to see you, beautiful lady...So how was your two days off?" Spoke a cheerful voice.

"Oh," She replied a bit startled, not wanting to go back to the previous days' events, feeling a big weight on her shoulders.

"Had a nice time, I suppose?" He persisted.

"Well …I would like to think so." She replied.

"You went on a rendezvous, perhaps; or would you like to extend your leave?" He continued, lighting a cigar and patting his stomach.

Extend her leave, she thought? The last thing she wanted was to be alone again. She had been so used to having Bobby around her, such that, her two days without seeing him had been like an endless time in space. She hoped that the feeling of desolation would end today. She would see the love of her life again and they would be able to talk things over, like two rational adults. As a matter of fact, Michael Yellern was wasting her time chatting her up. All she wanted was to talk to Bobby and be able to perhaps, put reason in his mind. He would certainly understand, she told herself.

"You seem distracted?" He spoke again. "Anything the matter?"

"No. No. I'm fine."

"Thinking of how you will cope without seeing your lover?"

"What?" She asked startled. Did everyone already know that she and Bobby had an argument? That he had stormed out of her apartment, and she had not seen him since then, she wondered?

"I mean cope without seeing Bobby anymore?"

"I. I…" She stammered, looking for words but unable to have anything logical to say.

He pulled at his cigar, enjoying the moment.

"Well…I bet he gave it enough thought." He continued.

Thought, what was Michael talking about? How could anyone possibly think that she deserved to suffer? How could anyone think it would be okay for him to just walk off her like that?

She raised her hand in resignation.

"I don't want to discuss this any further."

"Tell me about it. I am just as disappointed as you are, that is if you are?"

"What do you mean?" She yelled, losing control of her emotions.

"I mean, his flippen resignation… I didn't think he would just walk off me like that."

She felt a surge of heat come to her face. Resignation? She was not going to see Bobby again, at least not in a couple of minutes, as she had anticipated. Why did he resign? Was it because of her or what? Is that what she had meant to him, all along?

"His contract was coming to an end anyway, but I thought that he would have the decency to see it through. Flippen bastard." He added, pulling at his cigar again. "I bet you must have all the details of why he cut his contract short."

"No. I mean no." She replied a bit perplexed.

She had no idea that he would resign without even telling her. What else didn't she know about him? What other surprises was she in for? How much information did Michael Yellern have about her relationship with him? What if, she had agreed to what he had wanted, would things have been different then? Would things be the same as when they first started out, or could he still have left?

"He probably got a good pay-out at the gallery." She heard Michael speak again.

"What pay-out?" She found herself asking.

"He was part of the organising team at the exhibition. That is how come he managed to get those tickets." He filled in. "But at least he is still a part of your life, so you will see him outside working hours." He tried to console her.

Outside working hours, she assured herself, a feeling of relief came over her. That means he does not know about her sour relationship with Bobby. What a relief. Then, she would have to play happy, until such time that she figures out what to do. She told herself. She could pretend to be in control. She sighed, still feeling a big weight on her shoulders.

"Are you okay?" She heard him ask again. "I'm sure he has flaunted to you how much he got from the exhibition." He paused for a moment and then continued to speak without waiting for her response. "The bastard, he was not even supposed to be part of the organising team, but he and his friends played around with the committee that was supposed to select and they got the deal. I heard the ended up having a fight at some club or something with the losing team. Big money it was. Very big money…"

The fight at the dance party Kodelly recalled, feeling a quiver go down her spin at the memory of that barbaric incident.

"You are rather moody today?" He said again. "Are you okay?"

"No, am not. I just think I need to get down to work than to spend my entire day discussing… well, Mr. Mitch."

"Oh, don't make it sound too official, I know that the two of you have been seen several places together. I will miss the bastard; he is really good at his work. Really good." He said, turning around to walk out of her office.

She felt the exhaustion, disappointment and pain of not having really known Bobby for what he was all those nights that they had spent together. Yet no amount of time could ever have betrayed their love or his lack of love for her. She had been blinded by love and to her, he had been nothing but a loving and charming man. She would never for a moment, have imagined that he would walk out on her the way he did. She recalled him slamming the apartment door again and she instinctively covered her face with her palms to ease the pain. He could have at least told her that he was leaving the company. She was looking for answers, but she could not find them. Would it have really mattered if he had told her that he was leaving or not? She felt trapped in her decisions.

Decisions that she had made, and decisions she still had to make. Should she really turn to face the other option available for her, by going through the brochures that he had left behind and do the 'logical' thing as Bobby had suggested? She wished that she could talk to someone about how she felt, and she wondered if there was anything right anymore.

*   *   *

She lay in bed with a bar of chocolate in her hand, reading a magazine on parenting skills and thinking of how much her life had changed before the baby had even arrived. She had completely cut off her social life and hardly ever went out of her apartment, unless it was absolutely necessary. She still had not gotten over breaking up with Bobby and couldn't help but to blame herself. She couldn't believe that she had not seen it coming at all; as if that would make the pain any less.

He was bound to leave her anyway she consoled herself. She recalled how frantic her mother had sounded, when she told her over the phone about her condition, especially since she had never told her any details of her love life with Bobby Mitch. She could have probably assumed that her daughter was seeing someone, particularly since she did not seem perturbed at Dinkley's marriage with her cousin Laura. Kodelly, had so far created the impression that she was all too busy with her work and the hectic city life schedules and had definitely no time for a social life.

"Hello, my sweetheart." Lidy had fondly greeted her daughter as soon as she had recognized her voice.

"Hello, mum. How are you?" Came her reply.

"You haven't been calling me lately. Why? Anyway, I'm well thank you and yourself?" She spoke again in a familiar well-toned voice.

"Well, just a bit of this and that… I'm okay though."

"Okay though … darling you do not sound sure of yourself." She paused for a moment. "Do you have a cold or something? Oh, they can be such an irk."

"No, I do not have a cold, I'm okay mom."

"Then do sound cheerful. You overspent your money and you need some money? It is nothing to be ashamed of my daughter…"

Ashamed, thought Kodelly, why couldn't this woman keep quiet for a moment and not decide what she wanted to hear. She was not the one who had phoned, Kodelly thought, so she should learn to keep quiet and listen.

"Are you still there?" She heard her ask, sensing the pause. "It is money? How much must we send for you…I know ladies' expenditure can be quite high, especially if you want to dress up in the finest designer clothing and expensive jewellery and perfume to dignify your eminence? I don't blame you love. So how much do you want?" She enquired confidently.

"No. No, I'm not broke. I don't need money." She defended.

"Mom…" She continued hurriedly, not thinking she could go on another moment, without losing her composure and fail to tell her why she had actually called.

"Mom." She repeated.

"Yes dear, am listening. Oh, we had such a fabulous dinner party last weekend. Your dad and I were guests of honour at the City Charity ball."

"Oh, is that so and Laura. How is she?"

"She visits sometimes. I must say that she is such a nervous wreck in my presence. She stole Dinkley Mills from you." Accused Lidy again.

"I thought that we had discussed that already. Dinkley and I were not in love…"

"Oh… tell me now, are you seeing someone?"

She shifted her weight in the chair; that was more than she was ready to answer. It was too direct a question and she was just not ready for it. It was more than what she had anticipated; maybe it was not such a brilliant idea to phone her mother after all. Then, impulsively, she heard herself speak.

"I'm going to have a baby." She replied flatly.

"Sweetheart, no. I don't get it, are you planning on having a baby or what do you mean?" She asked frantically.

"I mean …" She tried to explain.

"No." She cut in. "If you are planning on having a baby, my advice is for you to wait. Get married and then…"

"Mom you do not understand…. I'm going to have a baby."

"My goodness… a baby." Came the uncontrolled voice.

They were both quiet momentarily, with Kodelly wondering the kind of shock that she had inferred on Lidy.

"Oh, sweetheart how could you, and the father of the baby?"

"Mom, we will talk about that later." She answered flatly. "I have to go now." Cutting the line hurriedly.

A moment later, she heard the phone ring.

"Kodelly," Spoke her mother in a shaky voice. "I'm so sorry sweetheart… do you need anything? Must I come visit you…?" She asked beginning to sob.

"No, mom… I still have a long way to go. I'm sorry, mom. I well…I …" She tried to talk, hearing her mother sob.

"Call me later if you want to. Bye for now." She said cutting her mother off again.

The next time they had spoken, Lidy was more composed and asking as many questions as possible, but of course not getting the answers that she wanted to hear. She had rephrased her questions, but alas, her daughter did not tell her if she was getting married or not.

She sighed again, putting the magazine aside and getting the local newspaper. She browsed through and there in black and white, she saw an advert on Pedree Laskador's exhibition in the city. She sat up and began to read it word for word. It was at the same gallery and the times were the same as the last time that he had visited the city. She looked at the date on the newspaper, wondering if she was reading an old newspaper, only to reaffirm that it was the current paper. She felt the adrenaline begin to race up her spin, as she recalled Michael Yellern linking Bobby Mitch to the organising group. Maybe, she thought, she would be able to see him there. Maybe, he would be there for the evening exhibition like the previous time. Then, she would see him again, and maybe they could talk. Probably, things would be back to what they used to be. She picked up the phone and quickly dialled the number at the bottom of the advertisement to book herself an executive ticket. Then her mind immediately began to think of what boutique she would go to. She wanted to look stunning for the evening, despite all the weight that she had put on and having lost her waistline.

*   *   *

Satisfied with her reflection in the mirror, she walked out of the apartment and drove to the gallery. She kept asking herself the same questions over and over. She reminded herself of the need to stay calm once she sees Bobby again.

She parked her car securely, and stepped onto the pavement, her heartbeat beginning to race upon entering the gallery. The tour of the evening had already begun; she walked calmly to join the elegant audience that was being led through, like the previous time. She had obviously missed the introduction, she realised, as she briefly gazed through the crowd, wondering if Bobby had perhaps seen her already.

She begun to follow the tour, like everyone else and realised that there were new paintings, which seemed more intriguing than before, despite her continued effort to spot Bobby. She continued to walk through the exhibition, frantically wanting to see the one man that she had gone there for. She moved from one angle to another, in an effort to see him, yet being so discrete so as not to be noticed by anyone. She tried to keep herself calm by concentrating on the paintings from time to time. She had not seen Bobby yet and they were nearing the end of the exhibition. She felt her feet hurt from the weight she had gained over the months, despite the shoes that she had carefully selected.

Pedree Laskador invited the guests again, to have some refreshments at the end of the show. Kodelly watched on desperately, as the guests went on to have some refreshment. She remained standing at the last painting, watching in dilemma, wanting to leave, yet at the same time, unsure if she had scrutinised the audience thoroughly enough for Bobby.

"Good evening, Kodelly." Came a familiar voice over her shoulder, jilting her out of her chain of thoughts. She immediately turned to see who had greeted her and there she stood face to face with him.

"It is good to see you again." He continued, looking at her startled face.

"I suppose that you are now married." He continued, gesturing to her stomach, and kissing the back of her hand.

"Where is your husband?" He asked, with his eyebrows raised.

"His …well…his out on business." She quickly replied, surprised at herself.

"Good. So, you will be joining me for dinner perhaps…?"
She quickly remembered the remarks she had heard about him and found herself replying.
"No. No, I have other commitments."
"You can always cancel them." He advised. "Come; let me get you something to drink, while you make up your mind."
Make up her mind, she thought in dismay; her mind was already made up. She was not going anywhere she had not planned to go. This was her first social outing since Bobby left her, and the only reason that she had come, was because she had wanted to see Bobby Mitch. She had not managed to see him and yet Pedree Laskador thought that she knew where he was and that they were married. The bastard, how could he possibly think of even taking her out on a date in her condition? How pathetic of him.

"He loves women just as much as he has passion for his paintings."
She recalled Bobby Mitch explain to her the last time that they had been there.

"I am afraid I will not join you for dinner." She said firmly, after sipping at her glass of orange juice.
"It will be a grand dinner party." He explained, slipping his hand in the pocket, and handing her an invitation. "That's the venue, in case you decide to join us later."

She got the invitation as a matter of courtesy and finished her drink, before excusing herself from his company. She walked the distance to the door and then out onto the parking lot. She felt a surge of tears come to her eyes as she walked, with the cool evening breeze gently caressing her face. She had been looking forward to seeing Bobby Mitch tonight and she was more than sure that he would be there, and then she could lay her faithful eyes on him again. She wiped the tears from her eyes and then she sat in the car, resting her head on the wheel for a moment, then slowly she took a deep breath, calming herself down and accepting the fact that she could not lay her eyes on him again this evening, yet praying deep inside her that she would get over him somehow, soon.

*　　*　　*

She sat in a rocking chair, a baby in her arms. Her eyes were filled with joy and pride. She could hardly get her eyes off him. She had never imagined that she would feel so much love for anyone. It was worth everything, she'd repeatedly told herself. It was worth all the sacrifice. It was worth her dignity and all that she stood for, even if Bobby had not been there for her. She had redecorated her bedroom to announce the presence of her new-born baby. Lidy walked in, she had only managed to travel to Cambel city, a week after the baby was born.

"Sorry love, I couldn't be there to hold your hand through the pains." She apologized casually. "Your dad and I had decided to go on our honeymoon. We didn't celebrate our anniversary. He had been quite disgruntled with news about you, the baby and all..." She'd explained as soon as she had entered her apartment.

"I see...." Replied Kodelly, after they had hugged each other formally.

"So, where is my grandson?" She enquired.

"In the bedroom. He is sleeping." She replied leading her into the bedroom.

"Oh, he is so wonderful. He is so beautiful...may I get him up?"

"Sure."

"He is adorable." She continued, lifting him up in her arms. "May God bless you, my grandson." She paused for a moment.

"I'm so proud of you." She whispered to Kodelly, totally losing control of her emotions.

"Thank you...would you like anything to drink?"

"No. No. Nothing but a warm bath, but first let me take a good look at, what is his name again?"

"Olly." She replied.

"And the father...," She paused for a moment. "aren't you setting a date for the big day now?"

"No." She replied firmly. She hadn't seen him since and she didn't care at all, she thought to herself. She had actually gone through the difficult part on her own, having people comment on her as she walked through the streets because she wasn't married. Having the baby without the man she had believed loved her at her side. The rest, she would now handle day by day. She did not need Bobby now and she had totally gotten over him. Who cares what nasty comments people make, for all she cared, she had about the best gift anyone could ever give her...little Olly.

"No." Retorted Lidy.

"No...we are not getting married. I thought that I had made that clear already."

"Why?" She persisted.

She shrugged.

"Do you still love him?"

"We are not seeing each other anymore." She stated firmly surprised at herself and yet wanting to bring the interrogation to an end.

"Are you happy now?" She added to cut through the ice that her answer seemed to have created in the room.

"Honey..." She said soothingly. "It's not like it's my fault."

"It's not your fault...I just want to well...get things together. I really feel that I don't need him anymore?"

Need him? She thought to herself, even if she needed him, he would not be there for her, so what's the point? He probably was in love with somebody else by now and had totally forgotten all about her.

The door opened and Michael Yellern walked into the bedroom, conveniently disrupting the seemingly awkward conversation that the two ladies were having. He was startled for a moment, looking at Lidy, who was still a very attractive, well-maintained elegant lady. Lidy on the other hand thought him to be the possible father of the child she was still holding in her arms, especially since he had allowed himself past Kodelly's maid and right into her bedroom. He must be the baby's father she thought, her face lightened into a smile. She would finally get to meet the man that her daughter never wanted her to know.

He certainly had to be the one, for indeed he had just barged into Kodelly's bedroom without even knocking.

"I'm sorry for not knocking." He began to apologise.

Kodelly gave him a thin smile. He had been to see her almost every day since the baby was born. He had spoiled them with presents, even though Kodelly was not at all flattered. She had too much to live for to bother about who saw her or who didn't see her. He had tried to be supportive of her, upon learning that she was expecting Bobby Mitch's baby, whom they both didn't even know where he had vanished to. He had tried to apologise for having made insensitive remarks about him.

He felt as though, he could have read through him and would have possibly spared Kodelly from being disappointed by him. Maybe, just maybe, he could have prevented them from being intimately involved. But then, what woman could have resisted his charm. He seemed to have all that any woman would want in a man, most of all he had charisma.

"Indeed, your mother must have taught you to knock when you was a little boy." Replied Lidy.

"Mom, meet Michael Yallern, my boss."

"Oh … Oh, pleased to meet you, Michael." She replied with little enthusiasm.

"Well, I'm sorry again…I just brought this for Miss Mollar."

"Oh, not another present from you." Kodelly protested.

"Actually, it is not from me, but it came through our office…it is for you."

"For me?" She enquired quizzically, getting the tall, sealed parcel from him.

"Won't you open it?" He suggested, curious to know what the sealed parcel was.

"I will open it later." She replied, putting the parcel away.

"Can't the two of you discuss business in the lounge… the baby is trying to sleep." Spoke Lidy in a firm tone.

"I'm actually leaving, madam." He paused for a moment, turning to face her, "It is a pleasure, finally meeting you. I have heard so much about you. You are more beautiful than I could have imagined." He complimented and to that she cheered up.

"Oh, thank you, at least someone appreciates what a lady ought to be, just that a lady. Do enjoy your day, Mr. Michael…"

"Yellern…and thank you ma'am." He replied walking into the lounge with Kodelly.

"You won't open it?" He asked eagerly again, standing in the hallway with Kodelly.

"Not now." She replied flatly.

"I want to see what's inside."

She shook her head.

"Thanks again…. Thanks for everything." She said opening the door for him.

She walked back to the bedroom wondering what the parcel might be or whom it might be from. A part of her insisted it could be from Bobby and yet she still doubted it. She unwrapped the parcel, not wanting to keep herself in suspense and before her, was a beautiful painting of her. The painting was done on the evening of the exhibition at the gallery. Someone who had a photograph of her must have painted it. It was so accurate, she thought, reading Pedree Laskador's engraving on it.

"Oh, it is so beautiful." Gasped Lidy. "You must have paid a fortune to have it done." She remarked.

She shrugged, deciding to put it away as she did not want anything to remind her of Bobby Mitch. She watched her mother put the baby back in the cot. Then she went and sat on the couch whilst her mother went to take her long-anticipated bath.

_____

BOOK TWO

CHAPTER NINE

She sat on the chair whilst talking on the telephone with Lidy; her watchful eyes were on Olly, who was playing in the middle of the lounge with some building blocks. He was a very handsome, soft-spoken boy and Kodelly had over the past five years focused her life on building their future. Her life revolved around Olly, seeing him happy was all that mattered in her life. They still lived in the same apartment that she had first occupied with Laura, even though she had grown weary of it, especially since it had no playing ground for little Olly. Despite her busy schedule, she always made a point to have enough time to spend with Olly. She always travelled down to Summerset for the Christmas holidays in order to be with the rest of the family. She had a higher rank though; facing more challenges, although she sometimes felt that she'd had enough working for Michael Yellern. The thought of changing employers had often crossed her mind even though the fear that, that might upset her well-structured schedule had made her not consider it as an immediate option. She loved going for picnics with her peers and to be involved in her little boy's school activities. He was a brilliant little boy, who always seemed to make her happy. She enjoyed hosting her son's birthday parties, being in the company of Olly and his friends and sitting in the background with her friends and watching the children play alerted her.

Life was sometimes hectic; however, she had decided to put up a fight. She woke up early in the morning to prepare Olly for school before she could also get ready to go to work. Then she would instruct her maid on what food to give him once he got back from school, what time to play and what time to take a nap, until she would get back from work and take over from the maid, with her own job not being any less demanding. It required her every ounce of the working hours. She loathed working late, even though she sometimes found herself doing that. She needed the extra money to pay her bills, but most especially, to buy a bigger house. She envisaged a two-story house, something a bit like her parent's house in Summerset.

She knew that Olly was not just fond of his grandparents, but that he also enjoyed running around in their big house, playing in the garden with them and running back to the house with muddy feet. He enjoyed the clean, evening breeze unlike all the pollution that they were plagued with in Cambel city. He enjoyed watching the sunset in the evening, the family braai just added to some of the reasons why he enjoyed visiting Summerset.

Lidy had noticed how fond Olly was of both his grandparents and she had, therefore, decided to host his sixth's birthday party, although she had other ulterior motives. She had over the past years watched her daughter go into seclusion. She had completely cut off her social life and worked her life from the start of the year to the next. She had focused her life on Olly, which had caused much concern for Lidy, who had mentioned it several times to her husband. They had over the years tried to get her to let them live with Olly, but to that, she could not concede. They had been hoping that that would perhaps help her to pick up her life from somewhere, but alas, all that was in vain. Kodelly had developed a very responsible, mature but passive attitude, even though she attended their family braai's each time that she was in Summerset, she never allowed herself to get carried away with any man. Lidy had on several occasions tried to rouse her daughter's interest in dating but that had not been achieved thus far.

"Honey, I am concerned about Kodelly?" She'd told her husband once in the morning, while he was shaving his beard.

"What about?" He'd asked back curiously, looking back at his image in the bathroom mirror.

"Because of how she carries on about Olly. True, a mother ought to be protective of her offspring, but Kodelly has cut off contact with possible men that she could get married to. She is not getting any younger you know."

"So, what do you have in mind?" He'd replied calmly, wiping the shaving cream off his face.

"I think, I will go to Cambel city and convince her to allow Olly to come stay with us for a while."

"But you know that she has opposed that several times." He reminded her.

She sighed, watching him pat dry his face after washing the shaving cream off.

"Besides, she is a big girl, she must know what she is doing." He added, walking back to the bedroom with Lidy following behind.

"I feel I can convince her, look at Laura, we brought them up precisely the same way. Why can't Kodelly be like her? Get married and just ... be what we expect her to be. Happy."

"So, you think that you are going to Cambel to get Kodelly to get married?"

"No, but I need to convince her, maybe, she does not know what she is doing to herself." She insisted.

"Honey if you need a break from me just say so...go visit her, but don't expect a miracle."

"But honey, I thought that we would go together." She protested.

"I have a business preposition to attend to. The Charity club is holding elections this weekend. In short my dairy is full." He pointed out to his wife, holding her hands in his before kissing her on the forehead.

"I love you." He said softly.

"I love you too." She replied.

"I will arrange everything for your trip. So, when would you like to leave?"

"Tomorrow." She replied excitedly.

"Okay, then I will see you in the evening." He concluded, walking out of the bedroom.

Lidy left for Cambel city the next day. She arrived late in the evening after a long and exhausting journey. She was met with Kodelly, who had just arrived from work. They then spent the evening chatting casually, despite how exhausted Lidy felt. Olly was thrilled to see his grandmother and to show his excitement, he kept running around the lounge. Lidy did not explain her reason for visiting though, but she strongly believed that she would somehow get Kodelly to allow her to travel back to Summerset with Olly. But like Bill had warned, she still could not hear of it. The next day Lidy become infuriated and talked bluntly, explaining how much she wished to see her get married and lead a normal life as she deserved. But to her utter dismay, Kodelly had instead made a mockery of her mother's desire, asking her if perhaps that was the only reason why she had travelled all the way to Cambel city?

"I'm doing fine, mom. There is no need for you or dad to worry."

"Are you sure that you are okay?"

"Yes"

"And happy?" She insisted calmly.

"I'm very happy. I don't think that I can ask for anything else. I'm content."

"But when will you get married?"

"Married!" She exclaimed putting the hot cup of coffee back on the table, even before tasting of its contents.

"Yes married?" Her mother repeated.

"I don't know. You are free to stay with us as long as you want. I shall not have you travel back with Olly either, or am I getting married this weekend." She paused for a moment, "We are happy to have you visit with us and we would like you to stay as long as you please… that is if you are not missing dad already. By the way, I know that you have only my interests at heart." Taking a sip from her cup of coffee. "I love you greatly for that. Believe me I do."

"Oh, come give your mommy a hug." She said emotionally. "I will leave after the weekend; maybe, we can go shopping on Saturday." She said, after getting a soothing hug from her daughter which seemed to cheer her up.

Lidy returned to the loving arms of her husband, who did not appear surprised that his wife did not succeed in her mission to come back with Olly, especially since he knew that their daughter had a strong bond with her son.

"So how was your journey and visit?" He asked, after kissing her tenderly.

"As you had predicted…Oh, that stubborn girl. She couldn't even hear of it. Come on love, I thought that we was a good example to the children. But no, not Kodelly, she don't see things our way."

"Maybe she needs more time…"

"More time to get older?" She interjected. "Anyway, how did the voting go?"

"You are looking at the new chairman." He announced proudly.

"Sweetheart!" She exclaimed before hugging him again. "Congratulations. I wish that I was there."

"You will be. The inauguration is only two weeks from now."

"Oh, I am so proud of you." She said, forgetting about her fruitless journey to Cambel city ephemerally.

Kodelly then put the receiver down, after ending her conversation with Lidy.

"Mummy, Mummy, can I have chocolate please?" Came Olly's excited voice, as soon as he saw his mother put the receiver back on the hook.

"Only after you drink your soup. Your grandmother sends her love. She says, she can't wait to see you again. She is going to throw a big party for you."

"For me …a party?" He repeated excitedly.

"Yes, my love." She replied, walking into the kitchen with him following behind. She handed him a bowl of warm soup, continuing with her conversation with him, with a bar of chocolate on the table to which his eager eyes watched with content.

Lidy sighed as soon as she'd ended her conversation with her daughter. She had managed to convince her to come a few days before the actual day for the party; this she believed, would enable her to get acquainted with her idea.

*   *   *

They had arrived in Summerset the previous day in the evening and were greeted to a warm dinner which was a welcome gesture for their visit. Olly had retired to bed a little bit later than usual, after listening to some bedtime stories from his grandfather.

Kodelly woke up later than usual the next morning, with her mind set at not going to visit anyone. She had decided that she would meet them all at the party the next day. She had breakfast with her family and watched Lidy pack a picnic basket for Billy and Olly, who had decided to go fishing. That would definitely leave the ladies with enough time to go shopping for new clothes and other things that they might need for the party. She hoped that she would not meet anyone she knew, but unfortunately, she kept on running into delightful faces and they were just too glad to see her after a long time. She politely turned down the several invitations that she got from friends, explaining that she had other commitments, when in actual fact all she wanted was to spend some time alone.

She returned home after an exhausting shopping spree with Lidy, who was always fashion conscious. She had a quick, light meal before going to her bedroom to change her clothes. It was a bright summer afternoon, so she wore a long summer dress with sandals and a straw hat. She walked out of the house and into the woods. It was only until later in the evening that Kodelly walked back to the house. She entered into the hallway and was met by Lidy at the bottom of the staircase.

"Where have you been the whole afternoon?" She paused for a moment, yet not necessarily waiting for an answer, she continued.

"Come, I'd like you to join us for tea." Gesturing to Kodelly to follow her.

She had just taken off her straw hat and her hair looked dishevelled, yet even with that as a probable excuse, Lidy was not ready to let her off, least she disappears again as she had done before.

"Come." She beckoned, noticing her reluctance to follow her to the coffee room.

"Okay." She replied, following Lidy behind.

They entered the coffee room and sitting at the coffee table was a man she had known from their neighbourhood in her younger years. A fine gentleman he was known to be. He was very handsome and still was, she realised, despite the weight he had gained over the years. Yes, Andréa she recalled, remembering how much of a crush all the girls seemed to have had on him. She recalled how she and Laura with her other friends would giggle to get his attention. But then they were so immature and would decide to play Goose instead. Alijah who normally accompanied them to their dance classes and sat through them would scold them, as Lidy would have it.

"I won't have a lady of your calibre play goose…what in front of these fine gentlemen. You ought to be ashamed. You ought to be ladies; that is what your mothers' is bringing you all up to be. Fine ladies." Alijah would caution.

Then, they would look back at her innocently and beg that she does not tell their parents that they were behaving anything less than the well-mannered children they were indeed being raised up to be.

For the first time in a long time, she minded about her appearance with regards the gentleman that stood up from his chair the moment the door opened to allow the two ladies in.

"Good evening, Miss Mollar?" He greeted from across the table.

"Good evening." She replied, her straw hat in one hand, shaking hands with him from across the table.

Lidy watched on with content, before speaking.

"Kodelly, I am sure that you remember him don't you, my love." She introduced informally.

"I do." Came her reply.

"Could you please have tea with him, there is something else that I have to do." She talked hurriedly before walking out.

Kodelly stood awkwardly for a few moments, before Andréa spoke.

"Have a sit." He said, pulling the chair for her to sit.

She could almost not believe herself, first she was in the same room with a man that almost every girl had a crush on as they were growing up and besides that he had just pulled the chair for her. This was totally different and hardly expected in Cambel city, where women were hardly given the due attention that they deserved, to which she had almost gotten accustomed. Andréa reminded her of what a treasure of culture and manners Summerset actually had to oyster.

He sat on the opposite side of the table, looking across to her as they talked, first very formally, then laughter accompanied their conversation as they enjoyed a warm cup of tea with homemade, honey cookies.

It was a bit easier than she had imagined, she thought, after they had finished their tea. She walked him out onto the patio with the evening moon beginning to give light to the woods about.

"I'd like to see you again." He suggested.

"I do not think that will be possible." She replied firmly, surprised at herself. She certainly was not a sorry excuse of a person and was not just about to allow her mother to play matchmaker for her. She definitely was the one who had asked Andréa to have tea at their house.

"Why, are you seeing someone?"

"No. I mean…that is none of your business. But if that makes you any happy to know, I'm only here for a few days, during which I expect to be much occupied."

"I also only came to see my family. We can perhaps travel back to Cambel city together?" He suggested.

No. She felt like saying. No. She took that to be his first step to want to control her. She was not yet ready for that. She recalled how much she admired him when they were both young, but that was so long ago. A lot had happened in her life and she just didn't feel like letting anyone in her life.

"No." She heard herself say. "No, thanks."

"Why?"

"Because...because," She stammered. "I...I well..."

"Is it anything to do with me?"

"No. I'm just not sure I want to travel with anyone. I'm sorry, you will have to excuse me." She replied hurriedly, beginning to walk away from him.

"I will see you tomorrow afternoon." He called out to her, watching her as she walked the short distance back to the house before he turned to walk away.

Kodelly travelled back to Cambel city, without giving Andréa another opportunity to be alone with her, much to Lidy's disappointment. She had however, accepted his friendship and that was as far as her relationship with him developed to Lidy's dismay.

_____

CHAPTER TEN

Olly had just turned sixteen, when Kodelly decided upon moving to Goldring city. She had gotten tired of her routine lifestyle, working for Michael Yellern. She had long ceased to find her job challenging and had been looking for other openings. She had finally found the job that she felt was worth leaving her current position for, besides that, she had managed to buy her dream house in Goldring city. That was all so the reason that she was leaving. Michael Yellern was devastated when she handed in her resignation letter, asking her if perhaps there was anything, he could do to make her change her mind.

"Tell me, is it money? Do you need a raise?" He prompted.

"No. No. I guess I just need… new challenges."

"What new challenges. I can promote you if you want. You are indispensable. You know this company, in and out…"

"Don't flatter me. You know that I'm not indispensable. Besides, I already bought a house there, so changing my mind at this point is quite not possible."

"I will offer you double the amount." He challenged.

"I need to move on, Michael. Thanks, anyway for the offer."

He had eventually given up challenging her and had instead set his mind to throwing her a big party. He knew that he would not only miss working with her, but also her friendship. He had seen Kodelly build herself into a strong woman of character, who knew the direction she wanted to take in life. He was aware of how fond of Olly she was, and he knew that whatever decision she had made had been thoroughly considered. She was a brilliant woman he often admitted.

Mrs. Loika, her neighbour for so many years, was equally devastated. She wished that Kodelly would continue to live in Cambel city. They had finally become friendly with one another, not after her elderly mother stormed into her apartment with a fire extinguisher, a time that seemed so long ago, but after her son who was just about Olly's age had left a toy gun in her apartment. Mrs. Loika knew that Olly was a very spoilt child, who had grown up with undivided attention from both his mother as well as his grandparents.

Her son Troo, had gone to play with Olly, under his maid's supervision and returned home before Kodelly got back from work. When Kodelly got back from work, carrying shopping bags in both hands, she entered the apartment, but when she walked into the kitchen her seven years old son was standing at the opposite side of the kitchen table with a gun in his hands, which he immediately pointed at her.

"Don't move or I will shoot!" He shouted imitating a scene from a movie.

Her mouth opened in aghast as her eyes dilated.

"Who gave you that?" She asked freezing as instructed.

"No talking …Freeze."

"Okay. Okay, mom is freezing, now put that down." She tried to command.

"No talking." He said a little bit disappointed.

"I heard you, now mummy's hands are getting a little bit tired from the groceries, besides I got your favourite chocolate in my bag."

"I will shoot, if you move again…Okay put the bags on the table." She moved towards the table and put the bags on the table.

"Now, do you want the chocolate?" She asked hoping to distract him.

"Where is my gun?" Enquired the little boy, standing in the doorway to the kitchen with his mother behind him, who had been let into the house by the maid.

"I have come to get my gun." He said walking towards Kodelly.

She felt heat come to her face, watching as Olly shifted the gun from her and targeting it at the boy. She quickly pushed him down, as Olly pulled the trigger letting out a shout as she did so. Olly began to laugh, satisfied that his mother was playing along so well. Mrs. Loika watched in total dismay. When Kodelly realised that it was just a toy gun, she charged at her son grabbing it from him and then, turning, she walked to Mrs. Loika and handed her the toy gun while speaking furiously.

"I don't want my son playing with such things. You hear me? You must keep your damn toys to your son, don't bring them here."

"I think you are overacting." She'd replied in a steady tone.

"Overacting…Overacting?" She repeated, in a raised voice. "What if it was a real gun? I suppose that next time you will give them a real gun to play with?" She continued.

"I can't do that. I wouldn't do that."

"Oh, yes you would."

"I don't believe you." She replied, getting hold of her son. "Come Troo." She spoke, dragging him out through the lounge and out of the apartment.

Kodelly sighed, convinced that she had done the right thing. She then called her maid into the kitchen, threatening her that she would lose her job if she did not know how to take care of Olly, and taking care of him included not allowing him to play with hooligans in her absence. Having satisfied herself that she had gotten herself heard; she went back to her normal routine. Unfortunately, it was only two days after the incident before her son began to threaten to refuse to go to school, unless he could be allowed to play with his friend from next door again. She now found herself in a dilemma, one she could not untangle herself out from, without going back to Mrs. Loika. This, she would have to do in order to keep her spoilt son from carrying out his threat of not attending school. She took her son to school the next day, promising him that she would speak to Mrs. Loika later in the day and ask her to let Troo play with him again.

When she returned from work, she found Olly sitting on the couch waiting for her. He jumped up from the seat as soon as she entered, reminding her that they ought to go and visit his friend Troo from next door.

"Okay sweetheart, let mummy just have a cup of coffee." She said, hoping that he would probably forget about it. But alas, he had not been distracted at all, until they stood in front of Mrs. Loika's apartment door with Kodelly hearing herself apologise for having been so rude, blaming her outrage on possibly… fatigue.

Mrs. Loika seemed more understanding and allowed her son to go and play with Olly, especially since her son too had nagged her over the last two days. He kept asking, why he could not go and play with his friend from next door. Her relationship with Kodelly had grown from that day onwards.

"Oh, I will miss you." Mrs. Loika said time and again, after realising that nothing would make Kodelly change her mind about leaving.

"I will truly miss you, but I bet it must be for a better job and besides, Goldring city is a very rich city."

"Yeah, I intend to enjoy my work as well as the 'rich' city." She replied cheerfully as they hugged. "I will miss you too."

*   *   *

The first day at her new job in Goldring city was hectic. She had to learn the system and the other routines that pertained to her job description. But despite all the things that she had to get abreast with, she made a new friend, Rena, as she had introduced herself. She was of medium height and fairly built, with slightly big breasts that seemed to emphasise her feminine appeal. She had well maintained hair of medium length. She wore a very fine perfume with properly matched clothes. She was a very outspoken woman from their first meeting. She had barged into her lunch hour, asking her questions about Cambel city and then filling her in on the events of the big corporation. It was towards the end of the year and Rena spoke excitedly about the year-end party.

"It is awesome. Everybody just dresses up for the party. We normally have it on the last day of the year into the new year." She explained reminiscing. "Oh, it is awesome."

Kodelly listened to most of the conversation, not wanting to do much talking as she was just settling in. She was only too glad when her lunch hour was over. She returned to the office to carry on with her work. She had been in Goldring city for just over a week. Her son was just adjusting to his schoolwork and making new friends in his final grade in high school. He liked their big two-story house, even though it was sometimes too quiet for his comfort, but making new friends and visiting new places seemed to make him content. He had grown into a well-mannered teenager, whom Kodelly thought had learnt a lot from his grandparents, who were forever so eager to have him visit with them. He had been happy to move to Goldring city and seemed to like his new school. It was almost time to knock off, when Rena found her way back into Kodelly's office.

"I'm going to the club for a drink, would you care to join me?" She asked in a carefree tone.

"Mmmh…well I have to go home early. There are a few things that I need to buy, and I'd like to get my son registered at the Tennis club."

"Your son, how old is he?" She asked curiously, looking at her well-maintained figure.

"Oh, he is now a teenager; fortunately, he is not 'a hassle'. I'm sure that you will meet him someday soon."

"I look forward to that. So, do you know the good shopping malls? I can accompany you there, besides, we need to start window shopping for the year-end party."

"Oh that…" Replied Kodelly, wondering how she would get rid of her company. "We will do that some other day, cause I'm in a bit of a hurry today."

"Okay, then I will see you tomorrow." She said, giving up on her.

"Have a good night." Replied Kodelly as they walked out of the office together.

She was looking forward to the peace and quietness that greeted her when she entered her immaculate home. She had no plans for the evening and had decided on leaving all her other endeavours for the weekend.

_____

CHAPTER ELEVEN

The big, long, awaited day finally arrived. Kodelly stood for a moment in front of the mirror. It was going to be her first major jaunt since she arrived in Goldring city. She felt a quiver go down her spine, in anticipation of a probable wonderful evening. Her son was now a grown-up lad and she felt that it was time to loosen up a bit. Rena had talked endlessly about the event, making Kodelly feel as if she had already attended one. She picked up her bag and walked out of the bedroom, into the passage and down the stairs. She was dressed in a glittering long, red dress with slits on either side, with high-heeled pumps. Her hair was tied back, and a lovely perfume lingered about her.

"Mum you look sixteen." Complimented Olly, as soon as he saw her.

"Oh, come on love, you the one that is sixteen."

"You look lovely," He repeated. "And I hope you will enjoy yourself."

"Are you going to be fine, on your own?"

"Yes, don't worry about me, I'm a big boy."

"I know, but I can't help wondering or be concerned. I still feel that I should be tucking you in bed."

"I'm actually watching a late-night movie. Just have a good time."

"Alright love, if you insist that you will be fine and please do eat a decent meal."

"I will."

"I love you and take care." She called out, as she walked out of the house. She was surprised at the enthusiasm she felt for the year-end party. She had been looking forward to the function. She had not been avid for a jaunt, as she was feeling now in a long time. Maybe, Rena was the cause of her enthusiasm. She got into the car and drove to the venue. She and Rena had spent hours on end looking for the appropriate outfits, visiting one shop after another over several days; until Kodelly had finally decided to settle for the dress she now wore.

Rena had then insisted that they would each need a date, to which Kodelly had firmly objected. Rena had however, gone ahead with her plan. Kodelly looked forward to spending less time with Rena, since she would be with her date. She would not want to spoil their fun. It was a work function; hence she believed that she would have other colleagues to chat with.

The venue for the function was the eastern side of the office premises on the ground level. A platform had been erected and the tables and chairs were properly arranged. Executives from other companies had been invited adding flavour to the whole event. A catering company had also been hired for the evening. Kodelly was greeted with a glass of punch, which one of the waitresses served her with, upon arriving. She looked from side to side at the already filled venue, the music was playing loud and some of the guests were dancing to the rhythm of the beat. It was an outdoor function in order to allow for the fireworks at midnight. She stood undecided as to the direction she should go, before Rena approached her.

"Wow, you look lovelier than I imagined in that dress, dear." She complimented.

"Hi Rena. You look lovely too." She replied, sipping at her glass of punch.

"Come, I'd like for you to meet my date." She invited, allowing Kodelly to follow her through the crowd. "You can actually join us." She suggested after a short pause.

They arrived at the table that Rena and her date were occupying which was close to the platform.

"Kodelly I'd like you to meet Mr. Woulm. Woulm actually." She introduced with a giggle. "And this is Kodelly, my good friend."

"Pleased to meet you." She said with courtesy, as they shook hands from across the small table.

"Pleased to meet you too." He replied, "I need another beer, please." He called out to the waiter walking past their table.

"Take a seat." Invited Rena again.

Kodelly sat down and mused herself with Rena's date. He was queer, she thought to herself. He wore spectacles, a neat shirt, and a pair of trousers. He was small in built and seemed unsure of himself, except for the satisfaction with which he gulped his beer. He was more an introvert and seemed to be enjoying nothing more than his beer; he definitely was not the kind of man that one would expect the loud-mouthed Rena to date. Several colleagues however, invited Kodelly to the dance floor, but she had decided not to mingle just a little too much. It would spoil her reputation, she had told herself.

"You don't need a date." Commented Rena, after Woulm excused himself to go to the restroom. "It is almost as if everyone has been longing to talk with you, over the few weeks that you have been working here."

"What do you mean?" Enquired Kodelly innocently, yet sure of the heads she was making turn.

"Oh, everybody who is anyone wants to dance with you and look at me. My date is so boring. I'd do anything to get away from him." Rena complained.

"Come on. He is not that bad." She consoled her.

She waved her hand in the air excitedly to disregard her comment and cheering up in an instant.

"So, which one of the men do you have a thing for?"

"No one." She replied quickly.

"Oh, please. I would suggest…Tom." Rena encouraged her.

"Tom." Echoed back Kodelly laughing softly. "No, I wouldn't."

"Why not. He is good looking; he earns a good salary…Oh, but then his house is not even half the size of yours."

"Oh, come on, that is not the criteria." She protested.

"Then what is, my love?" She asked back. "Then what is?"

"I really don't know." She said, stopping abruptly as Tom reappeared to ask her for another dance.

"No thanks." She replied to Rena's disappointment.

"Okay, I will check you later, perhaps." He said before excusing himself.

"He has a crush on you, I suppose." Rena commented again, "Everyone likes Tom." She added with envy, before Woulm re-joined them.

Kodelly checked her watch, it was barely twenty minutes before midnight and the microphones on the platform were being checked.

"The Managing Director will be here any minute." Informed Rena. "He normally gives a speech before midnight, before the fireworks."

"Oh…I see." She replied.

She had heard Rena talk about the MD on several occasions, even though she so far had not met him. She was not amused by that since the corporation was big. She envisaged him to be a very busy person, but he certainly had the employees' interest at heart, judging by the effort and expenditure that had gone into making the year end party.

"Let's move forward, I'd like to see his every expression as he talks." Suggested Rena in an excited tone. "All that area will be filled up when he comes."

They moved forward, even though it was not as close as Rena would have liked. They'd had several snacks and were now just sipping at their beverages, as they continued to chat.

"Attention please." Addressed one of the managers, as soon as the music had been turned down.

"Good evening, ladies and gentlemen." He continued, "Please, let us give the floor to the MD, just for a few minutes, before we begin the count down to the New Year. Hip …Hip…"

Part of the crowd laughed while the others applauded at the speaker.

The MD walked onto the platform. He was a well-built figure, dressed in an expensive suit. The crowd applauded in unison as soon as he stepped onto the platform, walking the distance to the microphone. He raised his hand as soon as he was standing in front of the microphone, to signal that he appreciated their acknowledgement of him.

The chatting and all the noise in the crowd subdued. The dim light shone on his face, concealing his features.

"Good evening." He began to speak proudly.

"Oh, my goodness." Kodelly said in a whisper, "It's Bobby." loud enough to be heard by Rena.

"Of course, Mr. Mitch is the MD." Filled in Rena, not realising what could be so amazing about it. He had been the MD from as far back as she could remember, despite that she had only worked there for a few years.

She stood for a moment, unsure of what to do. She was able to see his lips move, but unable to hear a thing that he said.

"*Not now, Kodelly.*" She vividly remembered him speak to her those far years back and then he'd slammed the door and walked out of her life.

There was no evidence of their ever having been together, as he stood on the platform. She quickly turned and began to hurry through the crowd away from the platform. She felt perspiration come to her forehead as she pushed through the crowd, her head having immediately assuage, despite the alcohol that she had taken.

She heard his voice through the loudspeaker as she hurried towards the carport not wanting to see his face again. Not now, this could not possibly be happening. That could not possibly be Bobby Mitch. She finally got to the car, fiddling with the car keys before finally opening the door and quickly letting herself in. She felt her mouth dry, as her eyes became watery.

"Not now Kodelly, not now." She recalled those haunting words.

She sat for a moment trying to calm herself down, before starting the engine. She pulled into the driveway and then the sky lit up with a big noise from the crowd, cheering at the fireworks that signalled the end of one year and the beginning of another. She drove off, wanting to be as far away from the party as possible.

This cannot be happening she told herself, hating the realisation that Bobby Mitch was actually the MD. She wished she had instead gone to Summerset for her holidays, and then this could not be happening. She finally got to the house, after driving for what seemed to be an endless time. She hurried into the house with one thought only. She was relieved to find the lights off, since that would mean that her son had already retired to bed. Her thought was to leave Goldring city as soon as she possibly could.

*   *   *

She woke up late after an evening of exhaustion. She was glad that it was not a working day. She covered her face in her palms, as she recalled the previous night's events. Bobby Mitch, she thought, still unable to believe that it was actually he that stood on the podium to address the employees the previous night. He was the MD that she had so far not run into, since joining the corporation. There he stood, dressed in an elegant suit, without a trace of their ever having been together. She got up from her bed and went to take a bath, her mind still preoccupied, wishing that she could talk to someone and yet not knowing whom she could confide in. Eventually, she walked back to her bedroom; she heard a soft knock on her bedroom door. She stood for a moment wrapped in a towel.

"Yes." She finally called back, after a second knock.

"Madam, Madam Rena is here to see you." The maid announced.

"Tell her that I will be down in a moment."

She stood for a moment, wondering what she would say to Rena; maybe, she should not have run away. Maybe, she should have stayed and left in a more decent way to avoid being interrogated by Rena. She got dressed quickly with her hair loosely tied back before going downstairs.

Olly had left for Summerset earlier in the morning with the first flight. He would spend the rest of the festive holidays with his grandparents. Kodelly would have loved to join them too, but her holidays were too short. She would have to go back to work in a day or two. Maybe it would give her more space to come out of this predicament that she was now faced with. She had decided against leaving Goldring City, maybe, the best option would be to leave her current employer, she thought. That would give her more time to do other things and never to crossroads with Bobby again. She couldn't leave Goldring City; her son had already acclimatised to his new school and had made a couple of friends. She did not want to disturb him for her personal reasons and yet she could not even discuss the situation with him.

"Hi." Greeted Kodelly, as soon as she'd walked into the lounge.

"Hi there." She greeted back.

Rena was dressed in an elegant outfit as she normally did.

"Where did you run off to yesterday?" She said as a matter of fact.

"Me, run off? No, I didn't."

"Yes, you did."

"I'm starving, I haven't eaten since last night."

"I will gladly join you." She replied, following her into the Kitchen.

"Listen, about last night, I'm sorry. I should have told you that I was leaving but … I forgot."

"Forgot? I was right next to you…So did you enjoy yourself?"

"Sort of, it was not bad. I must admit, I just had to leave."

"Why…? Did the MD's speech bore you?"

MD, she thought again. There was no way she was going to call Bobby Mitch the MD and no way was she going to discuss him under her roof.

"Listen, it was just coincidental that I left during the speech."

"Make me believe, honey."

"I don't have to. You just have to take my word for it."

"Oh, isn't he handsome. He is gorgeous and has such expensive taste."

"Has he?" She replied back, not wanting to appear too keen and yet wanting to know more about him.

"Very expensive taste." She repeated, taking a biting on a burger that Kodelly had quickly made.

"How was your date?" Kodelly tried to distract her, whilst stirring her cup of coffee.

"Date? My word I was so bored. I will never hang around with him again. The jerk got so drank and well I just had to leave him and have fun with other mates."

"I see." She replied, before Rena begun to fill her in on all the things that had transpired after she had left, such as who ended up dancing with whom. Who she thought was improperly dressed and that made her forget about asking her about the MD, until she was just about to leave.

"So, you don't like the MD?"

"Whatever gave you that idea? I did not say that."

"Okay, that is all I wanted to know." She replied, walking across the lounge. "Coz everybody just loves the MD."

"I see… I will call you tomorrow, perhaps." She cut in, wanting to be left alone again; maybe by then, she would have tried to make sense of her predicament.

*   *   *

It was a few weeks into the New Year and Kodelly had just returned from lunch. Her office was big and spacious. It had a huge table and a swivel chair, with two other seats on the other side. The other side of her office had a lounge suite and a small table and on it were company brochures; adjacent to her office was her secretary's office. She handled all of Kodelly's calls in her absence and screened all the visitors to her office.

Kodelly sat in her chair, addressing her busy schedule, when she heard the buzzer on the intercom and simultaneously the door swung open. She looked up to see who had entered her office.

"Could you sign this for me?" His focus was on the documents in his hands before he lifted up his eyes to face her.

"The MD is here to see you." She heard her secretary announce, a few seconds after he had stormed into the office.

He stopped in his tracks and for a moment, wondered where he had seen her before. He could not remember who she was; he walked the short distance to her table and placed the papers in front of her. She got the papers and began to sign on them without either of them uttering a word. She felt the tense atmosphere as he stood there. She tried to maintain her calmness while handing him back the documents and yet trying not to look back, directly into his eyes.

He got the papers from her and turned to walk away from her; he opened the door and let himself into her secretary's office and into the corridor. He entered the elevator and got off on the floor on which his office was. He hurried past his secretary and into his office. He felt like someone who had been running for a long time, such a long time, yet not sure of what he had been running from or towards. That cannot be her, he told himself. That woman in the Sales and Marketing department couldn't possibly be Kodelly. Kodelly Mollar, he remembered with a sigh. He recalled his Human Resources manager talking about a vacancy in that department, but it would never have occurred to him that Kodelly would fill it. No. Not Kodelly, not now he thought in panic wiping the perspiration from his face. If it really was Kodelly what happened after he had left? Did she do as he had advised her or, did she go ahead and have the baby? If she'd had the baby, how old could the child be now?

He sat heavily in his chair after pouring himself a glass of water. He loosened his tie, still wondering if she'd had the baby, if she was perhaps married? He needed to find out all that immediately, he told himself, picking up the phone and asking for her personnel file from the Human Resources manager. He felt as if he had been running for a prize just to be caught up with and getting no prize in the end.

Kodelly sat through the rest of the afternoon, unable to concentrate. She could not believe that after all those years he could not even have the audacity to greet her properly but had treated her like a total stranger.

It was time to leave the corporation; there was no way she could put up with such malevolent treatment, especially not from Bobby Mitch. Not after what they had once shared or what she believed that they had shared.

* ———————————— *

CHAPTER TWELVE

Rena stood at the opposite side of Kodelly's office table, her eyebrows raised curiously. She wanted to know more about Kodelly's relationship with the MD. Her curiosity had been galvanised after she'd noticed that the MD was spending more time than usual in the Marketing and Sales department. He had kept a close eye on her, after the day that he had first set eyes on her again. Resorting to her personnel file did not do much to answer his questions. It had nothing on her personal life, making it impossible for him to know if or how her life had been since he last saw her in Cambel city.

He was basically monitoring her work, requesting for one report after another and analysing the department's performance over the months that she had been head of the department. He enquired from her, if she still felt that they were meeting the targets; asking her about her advertising methods and which one of them she thought to be most effective? He reviewed the master budget and enquired from her if the amount allocated to marketing was sufficient? He enquired from her how much of the budget had been spent to date and if the funds were sufficient to cover the rest of the year? What new strategies she had for the year and if at all she was targeting any new markets? She sometimes gave him answers intelligently and sometimes she was just off the picture. No questions had been raised about the past. She wondered if the close supervision was perhaps, a way to catch her off guard and ultimately relieve her of her duties. His constant supervision meant that she worked extra hours, leaving her less time to spend with Rena and her other new friends.

Rena, however, made every effort to spend time with her new friend, even during working hours. She had noticed the frequent interaction between Kodelly and the MD, but even that did not explain or put the pieces of the puzzle together.

"Why does he always call on you?" She asked trying to sound innocent.

"Who?" Kodelly asked back dumfounded, looking up from the paper she was reading.

"The MD of course." She replied in a raised tone. "Don't be all dumb with me."

"Mr. Mitch." She answered back with little enthusiasm. "Believe me, it is purely a working relationship and nothing more…"

"Working relationship my foot! He is always calling your office and asking questions and the like. I have seen other managers in this office and certainly Mr. Mitch never took interest in their work, and he never called them on the hour for sure." She explained, sitting comfortably opposite her.

"Well, I will not explain things I don't know. You are trying to insinuate…"

"I am not insinuating. It is a fact, so cut out the charade. The MD is interested in you."

"He is not." She refuted firmly. "It is all so man and woman for you…everything…'his attractive, his got money'…" She accused her, whilst imitating the sound of her voice, in her meaningless dialogue, causing Rena to laugh.

Just then her buzzer on the intercom sounded.

"Kodelly speaking." She said in a firm tone despite the irritation in her voice a few moments ago.

"Ah, Kodelly," He began. "There is a conference the day after tomorrow by the coast. Your air ticket has been booked as well as your accommodation. It will run for a week, so please prepare yourself for that after work."

"Conference on what?" She heard herself ask; half embarrassed that Rena was there, listening in to this conversation, which had caught her completely off guard.

"Marketing. It is good for the company of course. It is more likely to increase our sales, but we have to marry that with our level of production and bearing in mind our finances."

"I see. Is anyone from my department going with me?"

"Not that I know of, I'm sure that you now want to know who else is going?" He paused for a moment. "It might suffice to know that I am also travelling along for the seminar, and I don't think anyone else was included for the trip."

"Okay, then…" She stammered with a quizzical expression on her face, as she looked back at Rena who made her feel more uncomfortable.

"The driver will pick you up in the morning so as to take you to the airport. I guess that is all. Oh, and by the way, sorry for the short notice"

"Thank you." She said, cutting the line between them.

"And that?" Rena said excitedly, "And that." With a hint of envy in her voice.

"That is business." She replied again, trying to assimilate what he had just briefed her on.

Olly was old enough to remain in the house for just a couple of days, even though going to the coast seemed like a good idea, except for keeping company with Bobby Mitch, she reminded herself. The notice she thought, was more like no notice at all.

"Hello." Rena spoke again, snapping her fingers in the air to get her attention, after noticing that her mind had strayed.

"I have a lot of work to finish off; maybe we can meet when I knock off or perhaps when I come back from the Coast."

"Oooh, I wish it was I. So, any bikinis you would like to carry along?"

"Rena it is not a leisure trip. I wish it was, but alas it is WORK, WORK and just work. And I don't think it will be anything more than that." She snapped.

"Oops, I didn't realize it was that bad. I will see you later and please, don't forget to fill me on the juicy bit."

"Get out." She charged playfully rolling the ballpoint pen between her fingers, nervously.

She watched Rena leave her office, before she covered her face with her hands. What was she getting herself into? When would this nightmare end? Maybe she should not have left Cambel city, then she could not have run into him again. She recalled the pain and humiliation that he had put her through all those years back, the loneliness and now the constant patronising, made her wonder if he was set to destroy her enthusiasm for work and her natural being.

* * *

The driver arrived early the following morning to collect her, as she had previously been informed. She had packed her bags the previous evening, selecting only her finest clothes. She had almost been tempted to buy new bikinis in case she managed to have time to go to the seashore. She had instead just packed one of her favourites from her old collection. She could not imagine that the MD would give her time to go gallivanting, it would be a purely business trip she reminded herself.

They were booked in the first class with her occupying the seat next to him. They did not talk much. He greeted her upon seeing her, and then when it was time to board the plane, he got in after her and got engrossed in the newspaper, being interrupted from time to time by the air hostess, who kept enquiring if everything was okay or if they needed anything more. It had reminded Kodelly of the time she and Laura had left Summerset and were driven to Cambel city. They had both been filled with expectations and the package that life had to offer and she had gotten her share of it. She sighed, putting the book in her hands aside, wishing that they would land soon and then she could be away from Bobby.

They arrived later in the afternoon, exhausted from the flight before they were driven to the hotel. It was a lovely, expensive, Victorian hotel, overlooking the ocean and there, they would spend the next couple of days. The porter carried their luggage to their rooms.

They had been booked in separate rooms, which were adjacent to each other, with a door connecting the two rooms.

"I will see you in the dining room, at 7 pm. I will then brief you of what is expected of you." He said pausing for a while, "So did you enjoy the flight?"

She nodded, not knowing what else to say.

That will be all thank you, she recalled whilst taking a shower. What would be expected of her she mused? She wished that she could slip on her bikinis and run off to the coast, but she needed time to rest a bit before meeting with Bobby again.

At 7pm Kodelly walked into the dining room. It was a warm evening, so she wore a thin summer cotton dress, with heeled pumps and was carrying an expensive purse in her hands. Bobby Mitch was already seated at the table, with a glass of beer before him. He raised his eyes and watched her as she advanced towards him.

"Good evening." He said, standing up before pulling a seat for her.

"Good evening." She replied, beginning to feel awkward again.

"Do you want us to order now, or would you like to have a few drinks before?"

"I will order dinner and perhaps you can brief me on the seminar." She answered with little interest, getting the menu from the waiter who had just arrived.

"A drink for the lady." Bobby spoke again. "Give us one of your best wines, please."

"Yes sir." Replied the waiter, before walking away.

"I will have just a soda, if you don't mind." Replied Kodelly after the waiter had left.

"Relax, am not going to deduct that from your salary." He teased, sensing her uneasiness.

The waiter returned minutes later, with an expensive chilled bottle of wine and two glasses. He poured its contents into both glasses without saying a word, and then he stopped and took their order for the meal.

Bobby lifted up his glass to hers, smiling briefly from across the table and then he took a sip at his glass of wine, watching her as she drank from her glass. He looked at her with concealed content, a part of him wanting to tell her of how beautiful she still looked, but then, a part of him cautioned him against doing that. He cleared his throat, before breaking the silence. He briefed her about the whole seminar, emphasising her role to participate and put their corporation on the map.

"You must try to be aggressive, but not arrogant. Remember the market is not waiting for you to act. There are so many players out there, who will certainly act before you do and get the best slice of the cake. You must always aim to be the first in the market." He cautioned.

She acknowledged and they ate their meal quietly. She felt the wine go to her head and she refused his next offer for a refill. What if she got drunk, too drunk in fact and failed to be effective the next day or perhaps if she got too drunk and told him exactly what she felt about him; the bastard that he truly was? He had walked out on her and still had the audacity to sit opposite to her as though he had no memory of the past.

He kept wondering if it would be appropriate for him to refer to the past. He needed to know about what had transpired after he had left Cambel city. Did she have the baby? What if he apologised? Apologised, he thought with a grin.

"What's funny?" She asked, wiping the corners of her mouth with a paper handkerchief.

"Funny ...? No, nothing." He replied hurriedly, having been caught off guard.

She had desert without talking much and managed to excuse herself from his company as soon as she had finished. She walked back to her room and realised just how taxing her meal with him had been and indeed what a long day it had turned out to be. Yes, such a long day, she thought, wiping the makeup from her face delicately. She could not imagine that she would have to cope with several more days like this one. She deduced from his briefing that she would not even have time to go to the beach. She would be confined to the conference room during the day and would have dinner in the evening, with executives from various segments of their prospective market; especially for the product that they had just launched. They had already been notified of the dinner dates, so all that was required of her was to market the product in a conducive atmosphere, which she hoped, would at least keep them apart.

It was a day before the end of the seminar, and she had just returned to her room from having dinner with one of their would-be clients. She took a quick shower and slipped on her nightdress, with a light gown on top of it. She sat on top of her bed covers and began to read a novel. She had spent little time with him since the day on which they had arrived. She was glad since spending time with him would have been stressful for her. He had, nonetheless, spoken to her after the first day of the conference.

"I didn't see much of you." He'd complained, "You need to be aggressive." He had almost scolded. "You can do it. Don't be intimidated by the crowd. You understand?"

She had then unfolded with the conference and enjoyed the challenges which were posed her way. She marketed their products and almost saw the possible results with her efforts.

The door that connected the two rooms opened, she lifted her eyes from the book and turned to look at the door. Her eyes were momentarily locked with his. He walked towards her, without saying a word. He stopped by her bedside, looking intently at her transparent nightdress before speaking.

"Hello."

"What do you want?"

He sat on the edge of her bed, extending his hands, and taking her hand in his gently.

She pulled her hand away, wondering for a moment what she was doing, and if there was anything right or wrong in her world.

"I wanted to… well, have a chat with you."

"I'm sorry, am tired."

"Don't pretend that reading that book is all that you want to do right now. Don't pretend that you don't want me to kiss you and touch you."

"I think you ought to leave." She answered obstinately, pulling the gown about her.

"Why?"

Because I hate your guts. I hate you. She felt like saying, but then a part of her told her not to let him know exactly how she felt about the past. How much pain and rejection she'd had to live with after he'd left. She ruminated, especially the fact that, he had denied her when she had needed him the most, considering her situation. She felt the pain surge again.

"I need to be alone. If you don't mind." She said politely instead.

What is it with you? He felt like asking, why can't you scream or say what you feel about me? Why can't you tell me what transpired after I had left? He got up from the bed and just looked at her again before leaving.

The next day the seminar ran for part of the morning, she was then free to go about her personal business, including the day that followed, advised Bobby Mitch, who acted as if he had no recollection of having walked into her hotel room the previous night. What a bastard, she told herself in disgust.

She went to her room upstairs and wore her bikini, taking her towel with her and wrapping it around her waist. She could hardly wait to get to the beach and lie down on the sand, to feel the cold water and allowed it to touch her body. She heard the children's laughter and watched some couples that seemed to be having fun on the beach nearby.

She got into the water and swam for a while, before deciding to lie on the towel, on the beach, enjoying the heat from the sun. She soon drifted into a deep sleep from exhaustion, from all the work that she had done since the beginning of the week. The next time she opened her eyes, she was on a raft on the ocean, a boat sailing next to her.

She looked around in panic, wanting to understand where she was and how she'd gotten there?

"Hi." Spoke the crude looking man, a grin on his face in the boat next to her.

She looked at the coast that was not too far from where she was. She held onto her towel, which was still tied around her waist.

"Hello." He said again exposing his broken teeth.

She instinctively jumped into the water, beginning to swim back to the coast.

"Bitch." He said through a laugh, "Bad boys are everywhere…" He shouted, watching her splash the water in panic.

"Bitch you want a rich boyfriend, aah?" He continued, paddling his boat towards her.

She continued to swim away from him, without looking back, feeling the strength in her arms reduce from the strong tide that she had to swim against. She remembered a raft next to her before she fell asleep, but she had no idea that she could be put afloat on it. She finally got to the coast and out of the water. The man that had been giving chase, had stopped paddling his boat, but continued to watch her from a distance.

She picked up the other towel she had been lying on and continued to run the distance back to the hotel, not wanting to have anything more to do with such bizarre people. She finally got to the security of her hotel room, almost out of breath.

She met with Bobby at the cocktail bar, at 8 pm, as instructed on the note that she had found on her dressing table.

"You can go on a tour tomorrow; it is part of the whole treat." He informed her. "Some other executives and I went off today." He continued, pouring her a drink in a glass, "You should be very careful out here. Don't talk to people that you don't exactly know."

She looked at him and acknowledged. She had already realised that it was not a safe place, going by her experience on the beach. She still felt the pain in her arms from the quick strokes; what if she did not know how to swim, she thought feeling a quiver go down her spine. She had lost zeal for the rest of the tour; she could not afford to have her life in jeopardy all because she wanted to have a feel of the rest of the city.

*   *   *

They arrived back in Goldring city with souvenirs from the coast. Nothing about their relationship had changed, realised Bobby disappointedly, as they got into the car at the airport. He still had so many unanswered questions. He had asked the driver to drop Kodelly off and then he would go to the office, before heading home. She sat in the back seat with him. She opened her purse to get her lip gloss when he saw a picture of Olly.

"May I see that picture?" He asked without concealing his interest.

"Why? No." She heard herself say, closing her purse quickly.

"Is that your …your…?" He asked at loss with words.

"Yes. It is." Dreading the conversation, wondering how far it would go.

His face lightened, certain that he would now get the answers that he had over the weeks been battling to get. He could not bear to live in suspense anymore. He had to find out if that was his child, but then again what if it was not his? What if she'd had another child years later?

He was not prepared to make a fool of himself and yet his conscience wanted to come clean. But how could he ask her without uncovering the past? She must have long gotten over her relationship with him, so maybe it would not hurt to ask her? They probably would reach her house any minute from now, anyway. Maybe she would allow him to enter her house and see his child. His child he thought with discomfort. A child whose sex he did not even know. He cleared his throat, feeling uneasy while fiddling with his fingers.

"How old is your child?"

"Let's change the subject, shall we? Besides, I don't think that it's any of your business."

If it was not any of his business then she did not have his baby, he reassured himself, as the car came to a halt in front of her house.

"I have to go now." She spoke politely, "I will submit my report in a day or two." She opened the door and allowed herself out of the car. She then got her bag and stood comfortably on the pavement.

"Greet your child for me?" He addressed, watching her emotionless face.

"Okay." She replied, only too glad to be home again.

She watched the car drive off and then she walked to the house. She entered the warm friendly house and realised that there was nowhere else in the world she would rather be, but here in her house with her son. The maid took her bags after she had entered the hallway. She warmly hugged her son who had come down to meet her. For a moment she questioned what her intentions were? Maybe Olly deserved to know his father? Maybe Bobby Mitch, deserved to meet his son? Sighing, she walked upstairs to her bedroom, with only one desire to take a long, warm, bath before taking a nap.

———————

CHAPTER THIRTEEN

"So, how was your trip with the boss?" Enquired Rena excitedly.

"Official." Replied Kodelly whilst hugging her back.

"Official! If you ask me, you are glowing with excitement."

"It must be… the heat." She replied, pulling away from her.

"So, did he say he loves you?" She asked again, lowering her voice and rubbing her hands in anticipation.

"What does the word 'official' mean to you?"

"Actually, the two of you are quite suited for one another." She persisted.

"Does he have a wife?" Kodelly heard herself ask as she walked around the table to get the other side.

"A wife? I haven't heard of a Mrs. Mitch. But of course, he probably has a girlfriend." She replied, pausing for a moment. "Are the two of you, falling in love?"

"No. I was just curious." She replied sitting in the chair opposite Rena who had just pulled a seat for herself.

"You had sex with him?" She asked bluntly again.

Sex thought Kodelly for a moment.

"No. No …" She refuted firmly with a frown on her face.

She looked across the table to Rena, whom she had agreed to meet at the restaurant after work, watching her as she gulped her beer, lighting a cigarette and pulling at it and then puffing the smoke in the air. She had visited Rena's cosy apartment and had met with her two daughters, who were both in high school. She had been married at some point to the father of her two daughters but had later gotten a divorce.

From what she had tried to explain, Kodelly really could not make out who was right or wrong, or whose fault it had been that the marriage had ended up in shambles. Some misunderstandings perhaps, but whatever it was, it had cost them their marriage. She had not exactly vowed not to get married again, but would if she met a loving, reliable man; she had told Kodelly time and again. She enjoyed her beer and going out to parties whenever she was invited. She enjoyed having an active social life, even though, she was torn between being a reliable parent and having a good time. Kodelly, thought Rena had quite overwhelming responsibilities and could not for once understand why she was always so talkative.

"I'd say that you are lucky." She continued. "The MD is everything a woman dreams of in a man."

She sighed, recalling the time that Bobby had walked out on her in Cambel city. Indeed, he was such a mean and heartless bastard, no wonder she did not feel remorseful about denying him the opportunity to meet with Olly. She had concluded that, he did not deserve to meet with her precious Olly. O, she had once thought the world of him. She had held him in such high esteem once, she had given him her all, but that was all in the past now and nobody needed to know.

*   *   *

She had just left the office with a pile of files in her hands when she heard footsteps behind her; she turned and saw Bobby walking towards the carport, when he motioned to her to stop.

"Kodelly." He said, as soon as he had caught up with her.

"Yes." She said, after stopping in her tracks.

"I was wondering if you could come to my house, for a drink this Saturday afternoon. I'm hosting a small party, by the pool." He continued as they walked the short distance to her parked vehicle.

"Is it?" She replied with little interest.

"Yes...Here is my address." He said leaning on the bonnet of her parked vehicle, he wrote it on a piece of paper and then handed it to her.

"Please come…"

"I will think about it." She said, putting her files in the car.

"Did you mention that your car had a problem yesterday?"

"Yes. Why?"

"No, I saw it being driven in the afternoon by a man, and for a moment I thought that was your boyfriend or something. But when I looked closely, I realised that it was your son."

She stood motionless for a moment. Was that what the invitation was all about? It was a stance to get close to her because he wanted to meet Olly, now that he had seen him in person.

"I thought about Saturday, bad day, am afraid that I am totally engaged." She said on impulse handing him back the address.

"He is very handsome." He continued, ignoring her sudden change of temperament. "I will see you on Saturday." He said, walking away from her.

She looked at the piece of paper in her hand, before getting into her car. She sat in the car for a moment, unsure of what to feel or think. She managed to regain composure moments after, and then she started the engine and drove off feeling disgruntled.

_____

CHAPTER FOURTEEN

*H*er car pulled into the driveway; she'd had a tough time turning down his offer completely. She was curious to see his house and how much he had changed over the years. She had nothing to do for the afternoon; contrary to what she had told him and so popping in to see what sort of friends he now had, was not a bad idea. She was expecting to find several cars in the driveway but there were none. She wondered if, perhaps she had come to the wrong house or had got her time wrong before the butler approached her.

"Good afternoon, ma'am."

"Is this Mr. Mitch's home?"

"Yes, it is." He replied politely.

"Is he here?"

"Yes ma'am, you must be Ms. Kodelly, he is expecting you." He informed her.

"Yes." She replied, closing the window and getting out of the car.

"This way please." He invited her, after she had stepped out of the car.

She followed him into the elegantly furnished mansion, with possible antiques here and there. She followed him through a narrow passage, out onto the patio. She heard splashing water and recalled that the party would actually be by the pool side. She was the only guest, she realised as she approached Bobby who was inside the pool.

"Hello." He called out to her.

"Did everyone else turn your invitation down?"

He laughed, swimming the distance to the steps, and getting out of the water, clad in his swimsuit.

"Am I not worthy of your company?"

"No, you are not." She replied firmly.

"Why not?" He paused for a moment. "Shhh, would you like anything to drink?"

"No, what I want is to get away from here, okay."

"Come, let's not fight. I know that I hurt you in the past and it was not intentional."

"It was not intentional?" She heard herself charge. "You walked out on me deliberately. You didn't even have the guts to say that you were leaving, and you say…"

"I'm sorry. Very, very sorry." He cut in again.

"Oh, and what am I supposed to do? To forgive you and tell you that it was so much easy without you. You made me feel like a …a nothing…a nobody. You understand? I was worthless and I'd like things to remain that way and as for your cheap excuse of a party, I am not interested and never will be again." She continued in a raised voice.

"Kodelly, no you can't do that. I'm sorry. I had no idea what I was doing."

"Sorry indeed you are." She replied, pouring the juice in his face.

"Women! What the hell is wrong with you? I am practically down on my knees. Can't you see it?"

"Oh, I got something that you want now, again? Tell me what you want from me this time? Back then I was young and naive. I didn't know things would turn out the way they did. I believed everything that you said. I thought we had a chance…anyway never mind."

"No, it is good for both of us to talk." He said wiping the juice from his face with a towel.

"I have to leave." She charged further.

"Kodelly, listen, I'm sorry. I just want you to say that you have forgiven me."

She shook her head.

"You can't force me to forgive you." She said pointing her index finger at her chest. "You did what you thought was right, so face the consequences like I did."

He held her on her arm and swung her around as she was trying to walk away.

"I have a right to know my son." He said through clenched teeth.

"Oh, now he is your son? Now he is your son that he is old enough? Previously he was that foetus that you could just get rid of in a flash of a moment by visiting a doctor! Now it makes sense to call him, your son?"

"I had no idea what I was asking of you to do."

"I have to go."

"No. Not until you tell me that I can see my son and be a part of his life."

"No. I can't do that."

"You don't understand. I had to leave when I did."

"Oh please, don't tell me that soap story of you being 'afraid' of those people you were in a fight with at the party. That is not reason enough to leave without ever contacting me."

"I was afraid that they would hurt you, if they knew that I was close to you."

"Oh, let go of me you bastard. I want nothing to do with you ever again." She charged swinging her hand in the air and walking away from him.

He got her by the hand again.

"Listen..." He began, before she tried to pull away from him and before she knew it, she missed a step, tripped off her balance and then slipped and fell right into the swimming pool.

She fell right to the bottom of the pool, before she began to swim to the surface again, still wearing all her clothes and shoes.

"Oh, I am so sorry. I did not mean for that to happen." He began to apologise.

She swam to the edge of the pool and was clearly embarrassed but outraged, if only she had kept her cool and then this could not have happened. This would certainly give him an upper hand over her. Why did this happen, how could she make an utter fool of herself in front of him? He offered her his hand and helped her get out of the water, thereafter, he put his towel about her, while she stepped out of her wet shoes.

"Let me get you inside the house and let's try and dry them clothes for you."

She obliged, feeling her every nerve twitch with fury. She followed him into the house and up the stairs. He led her into his bedroom and handed her a dry towel.

"I think I will need some privacy now."

"Privacy?" He repeated, "Let me help you out of your wet clothes." He continued, walking to her and turning her around, and then he unzipped her skirt, allowing it to fall to the floor. Then he began to unbutton her shirt; he gently kissed her shoulders and loosened her bra, kissing the length of her stomach. He pulled himself up and kissed her on the lips, she kissed him back hungrily, while they stripped off the rest of their clothes. He lay her on the bed and made love with her passionately before they both fell asleep.

She woke up, wondering for a moment where she was. She looked on the other side of the bed, but it was empty. She tried to get up, pulling the covers about her, when she saw him enter the room.

"I managed to wash and dry your clothes in the machine. Now no more games. I'd like to work things between us."

"Between us…. 'Us' implying what?" She asked sarcastically.

"Come on, you know what I mean." He replied with his arms folded in front of him.

"What I think is what is important now. You understand. Pass me my clothes please, as I need to get out of here."

"I want to meet my son." He said stupidly, handing her the clothes.

"You think what happened between us means anything to me?" She paused for a moment. "No, it doesn't. It does not mean an iota to me. In fact, it would be best for us to forget it happened. I hate you Bobby Mitch."

"And you have every reason to."

She looked at him, stunned for a moment having put on her now dry clothes and then she quickly picked up her bag and stormed out of the bedroom. He hurried after her.

"Kodelly, wait."

"I can't. I'm sorry I just can't." Running her fingers through her dishevelled hair while she descended the stairs with her damp shoes in the other hand.

"I'm sorry…I truly am sorry." She heard him shout after her before she stepped onto the parking and hurried into her car. She closed the door to her car and closed her eyes momentarily as if to block him out of her mind, opening her eyes with a new focus, just to drive home and feel at ease.

*   *   *

She sat in front of her dressing mirror, still unable to believe that she had permitted herself to be persuaded into allowing Bobby Mitch, to meet with her son. A part of her, had told her that maybe that was best for him. But she still was not ready to let him meet him as his father, that they had discussed and there would be no compromise. He would meet Olly, only as his mom's friend and not as his father. But still, she felt uneasy about the whole situation. She heard the doorbell ring and she immediately jumped from the dressing stool, she wanted to go and meet Bobby downstairs before he ran into her son. She reached the hallway and was met with her maid.

"I think I will attend to that." She excused her maid.

"Yes ma'am." She replied before disappearing into one of the other rooms.

She wore a big smile on her face. It was the first time that Bobby Mitch would enter her house. She had been to his house on a number of occasions following their first date there, however, she was ashamed that she had actually let herself sleep with him again. She had made sure not to let Rena know about her relationship with him. She made it a point to ensure that nobody else knew that she had slept with him, except of course his butler, who had given her a very interesting look before she left his house, making her wonder if that was the look he gave every other woman that Bobby brought home? Of cause, she could not fool herself that she was the first woman to enter into his house and be treated like the best thing that ever happened to him.

"Hello." She said excitedly, upon opening the door before her smile went into a complete surprise. She was the last person she expected to see, especially on this particular day. This couldn't be happening. She could not remember the last time she had called on her.

"Laura." She exclaimed. "Wow, this is a surprise."

"I know. I should have called to tell you that I was in town."

"No. No. You don't need to. It is good to see you."

"You've got quite a nice house here. So, how is Olly?"

"Oh, he is fine. He should be upstairs. Do come in. Would you like a drink or something?"

"No. I'm fine, I won't stay long." She replied following behind her. "Dinkley is waiting for something in town, so I thought I should just pop in and say hello."

"You did well." She said pouring her a drink, ignoring her objection.

She wondered what she would do if Bobby walked in now. She was certain that the two would remember each other from Cambel city and probably either of them would say something that would refer to Olly, or his father and she was not about to let that happen. She could not bear to have Bobby introduced as Olly's father. But then, how could she ask her cousin whom she had not seen in a long time to leave?

"I will have a scotch." She informed, seeing that her cousin was determined to offer her a drink.

"Here you are."

"Thanks, I won't stay long though; I did not tell my husband that I would go far." She informed her again. "How is Olly? Is he here?" She asked again.

"He might be gone already. His going for a tournament this afternoon and I am supposed to be going for a meeting somewhere." She lied.

"Ooops, then I should not keep you long. Let me not delay you."

"Oh, it's fine. It's good to see you." She replied, relieved that she was leaving before Bobby got there.

She then walked her to the door a few moments later and watched her drive off, before retreating into the house.

Minutes later, another car drove into the driveway, this time it was Bobby Mitch, dressed in one of his finest designer casual outfits. He looked charismatic as usual. He got out of the car and walked towards the house, Kodelly hurried to open the door before he could even ring the doorbell.

"Kodelly." He said, as soon as she opened the door. "May I come in?"

"Sure." She replied, directing him to the lounge to which she had been just a few minutes earlier with Laura.

"A drink?"

"Anything."

"Brandy?"

"I would do with an orange drink, I had one too many last night." He confessed.

She asked the maid to bring him a glass of juice and a plate of snacks for the two of them.

"So, where is Olly?" He asked seeming impatient and nervous at the same time.

The door opened before he could get an answer and a teenage boy dressed in a tennis outfit, with a tennis bag in his hands stood in the doorway.

"Oh, sorry mum, I had no idea that you had company."

"No, not a problem, you can come through."

"Good afternoon, sir."

"Good afternoon." He replied, waiting for Kodelly to introduce them.

"Mom I wanted to borrow your car. You said that I could use it this weekend."

"Sure son. Here are the car keys." She replied. "Enjoy your game. By the way, this is Mr. Mitch, my boss, his the MD and that is Olly, my son."

"Nice to meet you, sir."

"Same here."

"Well, you'll have to excuse me. I have a big match ahead."

"Bye love." Called out his mom as he hurried out of the lounge.

Bobby watched the door close dumbfoundedly. Was that it? Was that the introduction that he had so looked forward to? He could not even touch his own flesh and blood? He could not even let him know who he really was to him? He tried to memorise his personality, what his son really looked like. It was the first time that he had ever stood in the same room with him. He was a strong, young lad. He thought about the brochures he had left in Kodelly's apartment and wondered if this triumphant moment would ever have been, if she had acted on them, if she had followed his advice?

"He is very handsome. Isn't there another way?" He paused. "Isn't there, something else?"

"No Bobby, you said you just wanted to meet him, and you did. There is nothing else that I can do for you, unfortunately." She stated.

He got up and began to pace up and down with his hands in his pockets. He watched the maid enter the room and put the drink on the table, and then she walked out of the lounge, again leaving them alone.

"You met with Olly, so what else do you want?"

"To be his father." He replied flatly, stopping in his tracks, and looking at her squarely. "I want to be his father."

"His father! No. No. You can't just be his father out of the blues…"

"Are you going to punish me forever for some mistake I made?"

"Well, you never stopped to think that I would have to be haunted for the rest of my life if I had actually gone ahead and seen 'the best doctor' as you had suggested? The cost would have been on you." She said mimicking him. "That was all that mattered. You did not love me enough or I was not good enough or whatever the damn reason was." She spoke back emotionally whilst he stood level-headed and looked back at her.

"Well bravo, bravo." He said clapping his hands mockingly, "You acted as the bigger person and I was the coward and I'm sorry but am trying to make amends, too."

"Well then, not in this lifetime. Not with me. Not with my son, so please get out, Mr. Bobby Mitch. I don't care if I don't see you again. I don't..." She charged.

He looked at her squarely, before he obliged and walked out of her house. She stood for a moment in the middle of the lounge with her hands holding onto her waist, wondering what she was doing. She needed some time alone. What was life worth? She wondered, walking out of the house. She hurried through the driveway and out onto the pavement, walking without looking back, wanting to run away from herself. She heard the laughter from the people in the streets and wondered if it was directed at her. She kept on walking feeling her legs wobble, whilst her eyes became moist. She kept blaming herself more than anyone else; if she had not decided to leave Cambel city then this would not be happening. She would not have had to stand there and tell her son that Bobby was just her boss and hide the fact that he was his father. Or maybe, if she had decided not to be friends with Bobby again, she would not have had to do what she just did, lying to her son right in his face.

She stopped only after bumping into someone.

"Gosh, I'm so sorry." She began, trying to clear her eyes. "Sorry." She said again, clearing her dry throat.

She looked at the person she had just bumped into and realised that he was a priest. This was blatant by the white collar in his long gown and the rosary in his hands. She turned to look to her side and realised that she had actually walked as far as the local church, no wonder her legs ached.

"It is okay. I had actually seen you coming but I thought that you had noticed me standing here. Anything the matter, my child?" He enquired politely.

"Yes...no...no." She answered.

"I'm father Timdel, the Parish Priest." He paused for a moment, expecting her to introduce herself, but instead she stared back at him. "Come." He continued. "Let us sit on the bench over there, if you are not in a hurry."

Hurry, she certainly was in no hurry. She thought, following him to the bench. All she needed was some time to herself. She never thought for a moment that she would walk this far.

"It is a beautiful afternoon, isn't it? Look at the wonders of creation. The trees to give us shed. The birds, entertain us with their wonderful melodies and to imagine that we too are a part of this creation. We are not just a part of creation, but also very special persons. Is there anything you would like to talk about?"

"No." She replied, fiddling with her fingers.

"What do you do on Sunday mornings; perhaps you can come and share mass with us? Or if you need to talk to someone, you can always call." He continued, looking at her troubled face. "What did you say your name is?"

She looked at the elderly man realising that his faith lay in his words. He seemed to have great faith in creation and all that stood around them. Maybe his world was different, or maybe he had overcome, decided to stay the hell away from trouble and not look it in the face like she did. He seemed noble, making her feel like a skimming bitch. She had to go. She had to get away from him. The wonders of creation, she thought looking at the sunset with a different view, which she had not done in a long time. Where were her happiness, her peace of mind, and her joy? She smiled, allowing the smile to reach her eyes.

"I'm, Miss Kodelly Mollar." She replied. "I was just taking a walk." He smiled back, not wanting her to realise that he found her pace rather amusing, for she had been practically running.

"I'm going back. Thanks a lot, father Timdel." She spoke politely.

"Any time my child, remember we are here on earth to help each other."

"Thank you." She said, pausing for a moment before beginning to walk away.

She walked back home thinking about Bobby Mitch again.

"I need to meet Olly. His my son too, you know."

"What must I introduce you as? His guardian angel?"

"Well…"

"You don't for a second think that I would introduce you as his father. After all…"

"Shhh…we are in love again. Aren't we?" Watching her brush her hair in front of his dressing mirror.

"Well, my relationship with you has nothing to do with…"

"It does not mean anything to you? Come on Kodelly, you would rather sneak into my house, have sex with me and then pretend to the rest of the world that you are some decent woman?"

"Decent? The only thing that is absurd is how I got involved with you again?"

"Cut the sarcasm." He said in a lower tone and taking her hands in his. "I love you and maybe we should be talking of getting married."

She paused for a moment.

"No Bobby Mitch. Not now, not ever do you understand?" She retorted.

"Then what are you doing here with me?"

"Well, you can come and meet Olly, tomorrow and that is as far as it can go." She said picking up her bag and kissing him lightly on the lips, before leaving his house.

She got back to the house after walking the distance from the local church. She went to take a bath, wondering why she was still so upset when everything was done just according to how she had said they would. Olly did not have to know that Bobby Mitch was his biological father, she insisted.

*　　*　　*

Rena walked into Kodelly's office; she stopped, watching her end a business call.

"Kodelly, you won't believe this." She said excitedly.

"What?" She asked back a little amused.

"Rumour has it that the MD's girlfriend is back in town." She informed her heartlessly.

How could she do this? How could she openly tell her that? Couldn't she have found another way of breaking the news to her? Surely, by now it was common knowledge that the MD was having an affair with Kodelly, everyone knew about it, including Rena. Kodelly had come to terms with her insensitive introduction and had been in touch with the old, father Timdel. He made her believe that she was not suffering at all, especially when he talked about people who had real needs in life. The underprivileged, the deprived people in society, surely none of those deserved to suffer, whereas for her, she went through the heartache because she had compromised her morals. Most of the other people that father Timdel normally mentioned, had done nothing to find themselves in those situations.

She on the contrary, had become almost accustomed to the expensive dinner parties she went to, being whisked as the lady behind the successful, Mr. Mitch.

"Yes honey" She continued, nodding her head, "I did hear that, now don't ask me where from?"

"Well I... I'd asked you before if he was involved?"

"And I said he don't have a wife, but I did say that he could have a girlfriend." She continued with a big smile on her face.

"Mmmh, how do you expect me to feel? You just walk in here and lash out on me that the man, I'm currently involved with has a new aficionado on the block. So, tell me, is she younger than me, pretty I suppose, with lots of money. Ayah?"

"Well, I had no idea you would react so badly."

"Badly, it is my reputation we are talking about here." Kodelly retorted.

"Are you upset?"

"Wouldn't you be? How did you know about it, anyway?"

"I ran into them, at the coffee shop."

"Oh', so they are actually dating?"

"Kind of. So, are you gonna' phone him?"

"No." She replied firmly. "I have to get back to work now, if you don't mind."

"Well, that's fine with me." She shrugged before walking out of her office.

Kodelly took a deep breath, before she sat down heavily in her chair, to contemplate her stance. How could he do this to her, first he gets into her pants again, then he demands to meet Olly and then he devotes his attention to another woman, he is just unbelievable? But what if he knew her before Kodelly came to Goldring City? Who cares? He should have been loyal to her. He knew Kodelly since a long time ago. He owed her some respect. Why was she upset when she acted as though the intimacy between them meant nothing much to her? But if it was not about the intimacy... then what? She wondered to herself remaining distracted for the rest of the day. She had so far done nothing to show him any ounce of respect or devoted any of her attention to his ego.

——————————————

CHAPTER FIFTEEN

Kodelly's relationship with Bobby had not changed, despite Rena's allegations as she had decided to call them. Maybe Rena was just jealous of her and wanted her to break up with him, because nothing so far had indicated that he was having an affair with another woman, nor had she run into his 'old girlfriend'. She could not ask Bobby about the allegations or else he would think that she was perhaps being possessive or jealous. Jealous indeed she would turn out to be. But she was not ready to be referred to in that regard, not at her age and with her repute.

She left her office to see Rena a little while after midmorning. She needed to ask her to meet her during their lunchtime. She walked to Rena's pool office and definitely made everyone look up to see the MD's girlfriend. It was the least place anyone would expect to find her and coming from the opposite direction of the corridor was Bobby with a lean woman of medium height. Bobby walked by her side confidently as he showed her around the corporation. Rena seemed to notice them first and tried to draw Kodelly's attention to the local paper that was lying on her table, but alas, Bobby walked into the big office, unknown to him that the woman he confessed to love was actually standing there. He continued his ego tour.

"…and this is part of the production department of which I also oversee, in short am the boss of the entire corporation."

"Wow." She said in a soft voice, enjoying the tour, holding her bag in front of her and scheming in her head of how lucky she was to get herself such a rich man.

"Boss indeed you are," Spoke Kodelly, who had only noticed them after they had reached the entrance to the pool office, leaving Rena's table and walking towards them.

"Oh, he is boss, yes indeed, maybe to the whores or something." She said between clenched teeth, almost in her face, with the rest of the staff watching in shock.

"Excuse her rudeness. I think I will take you around some other time." He said trying to remain calm.

"But I thought you said…"

"Go home or something."

"You won't take me home?"

"Take a taxi." He said, beginning to walk away from her, "Take a taxi." He said again, leaving her there and hurrying to the elevator.

Kodelly walked past the woman and began to walk back to her department before Rena caught up with her.

"Are you out of your mind or something?"

"Do you think I will stand and watch him insult my intelligence, my… well everything I am?"

"What if he fires you?"

"I don't care." She replied angrily.

"So, is that the girl you meant?"

"No, she is different. That is not Jill."

"Oh, so you even know his girlfriend's name?"

"Hello, I'm not gonna' close my ears if people are gossiping about your man."

"Well…leave me alone. I know I crossed the line, and I will brace myself for anything. He can fire me, and you are the last person I'd appreciate to have around when he does that."

"I will see you after he fires you." She laughed, stopping to watch her walk back of her office, whilst shaking her head.

She had barely sat down, when Bobby entered her office, and he looked at her narrowly.

"What was that about?" He asked squarely.

"Nothing." She replied, "and please spare me the lecture and just say what you have to say."

"Don't boss me around. I'm not here in the capacity of MD or your lover and please make no mistake about it." She listened dumbfounded, for a moment.

It was her birthday and she had earlier been reading her birthday cards from anyone that thought she mattered. She had received a few presents and yet Bobby had not so much as send her a card, except to embarrass her the way he did and cause her to make a complete fool of herself. She felt humiliated and she had no idea how she would get over her worst display of public emotions.

"Are you trying to have me fire you?" He continued.

"Why don't you spare me the lecture and just go ahead and do it?" She challenged him back.

"I could have. It was the first thought that crossed my mind, but then, I thought twice. You need a decent job to support my son."

"Go father yourself a child with the whore you were with." She stated categorically grabbing her bag and storming out of her office, unable to control her anger.

He sighed, before sitting in her office chair for a while, hoping it would help him understand her. He was only trying to be friendly with the woman he had brought to the office, but Kodelly's reaction had ruined all that. He needed to appease her, if that was the only way left for him to get to know his teenage son.

Kodelly drove to father Timdel's office. He talked to her in a sober manner. He asked her questions, wanting to know more about her. She responded to some, to some others she frankly told him that she did not want to lie. He was getting to understand her better, although she had not once attended mass, but it was his vocation to be of service to others, regardless of their ethnic origin, colour or status. She left his office and drove to the mall.

It was almost dark when she got home. There were a few lights here and there in her big house. She opened the door, imagining just how lonely she would be despite it being her birthday. She had screwed up her opportunity of being taken out for dinner by her earlier outburst at the office, even though she was not the one who had caused the whole situation to occur, but Bobby. If only he had not brought that woman to the office, then she would not have known about what he's up to in his free time or when she is not there. Why beat herself on the chest, she said opening the door and entering into the dark hall.

"Surprise!!!" Came a loud shout, startling her for a moment.

"Happy birthday, Kodelly!!"

"Oh..., you shouldn't have." She said, tears flooding her eyes, seeing some of her friends and workmates standing there, with Olly in front of the small crowd.

"Happy birthday, mom." He said, hugging her and leading her into a neatly, decorated lounge.

"Thank you, darling. Thank you everyone. I am really flattered." She said in an emotional voice and wiping the tears from her eyes.

"We thought a dinner party is just what you needed." Spoke Rena, who was beaming with excitement.

"A toss to the birthday lady."

"I need to go freshen up." She said to Rena.

"You are excused. Just make it hasty." She replied holding a glass of wine.

She disappeared upstairs, thrilled that her friends and family had counted her worthy of this occasion. She could hardly wait to get downstairs to the lounge. It was only until then that she realised just how hungry she was. She had been upset for most of the day and had not taken time to have a decent meal. She hurried back downstairs and was met with Bobby.

"Hello. I brought you some flowers."

"Thanks. Were you invited?"

"Yes." He replied giving her a bouquet of flowers.

"I will just put them in the vessel, though you really shouldn't have."

"I wanted to see my son." He continued in a lower tone.

"Don't say that again." She hissed.

"Okay, okay ..." He replied, raising his arms in resignation and following her to the dinner table.

They all had dinner through lively conversations.

"We would like for you to now cut the cake, mom."

"Yeah, and make a wish." Spoke Rena excitedly.

"Okay, okay..." She replied, watching as they brought the cake from the kitchen. Wondering what her wish would be? She was quite undecided about a number of things. There was nothing immediate that she could wish for, she realised. She seemed unsure about so many things. She blew the candles and made a silent wish, and then she went and stood on the balcony after having cut the cake.

"I will be leaving now." Spoke Bobby, who was soon followed by Olly with his guest.

"And what time is she going home?"

"I will take her home, mom, the fun is just starting."

"No, sweetheart it's a little late now, please. I will ask Rena to drop her off."

"Mom, I'm not a kid."

"I know that you are not, but that don't make you fool proof for mistakes."

"Whatever." He replied, walking away with his high school friend.

"That's my boy." Spoke Bobby excitedly again. "I can see that his already dating."

"Whatever…, I think it is time for you to leave as well. I need some time alone."

"Happy birthday Kodelly and good night."

"Good night." She replied, receiving a peck from him on her cheeks.

_____

CHAPTER SIXTEEN

*B*eing the head of a department for such a big corporation involved a lot of work. Month-ends were exceptionally busy because reports would need to be submitted. Kodelly knocked off from work, taking a bunch of files home with her. She would have to work from her study, as she normally did in order to meet her deadlines. She got home and had an early dinner before she set off to work. She piled her files but then realised that she had forgotten one very critical file at the office. She got up and drove back to the office building. It was a bit late, and everyone had knocked off, but fortunately for her, she had the keys to the block she wanted to access.

She went up the elevator and got off at her landing. She began to walk the distance of the corridor to her office door, when suddenly the lights went off for a second. She continued to walk seeing nothing unusual with a florescent tube that was probably about to go off. She reached the office door and unlocked it and switched on the light, despite the light that was coming through the ajar door. She walked to the cabinets and was just about to unlock it when the lights went off again. She turned abruptly and walked in the direction of her office table, just then a man appeared in the doorway. It was fairly dark, and she could not make out whom it was. He stepped in and closed the door behind him. Her adrenaline began to race. She could hardly see a thing as a part of her told her to scream, but even if she did, they were probably the only two in the building.

"Hand me the keys." He hissed. "The key?" He repeated, walking towards her table.

She felt a quiver go down her spine, wanting to scream and yet wondering if the securities that were seated at the entrance of the building could hear her.

"The Key." He repeated, walking to the side of the table where she was.

She began to move away. He jumped over the table and hit her in the face, before she let out a scream. She managed to run, despite the punch that she had received in the face and got to the other side of the table, picking the paper basket and throwing it at him. She let out another scream, while she frantically got to the door and ran out of the office, whilst he trashed her office table. She began to run down the corridor in panic, the lights went on again for a moment, but then they was off again. She heard his heavy footsteps running after her.

"Bitch." He called out to her, as he ran after her.

She continued to run the length of the corridor, in spite of the fact that she knew that she could not run any faster. She wondered if she could have to wait for the elevator but then that would make the situation even worse.

She got to the elevator and as she had feared it was not on that floor. She pressed the bottom, but she heard him drawing closer. She began to run towards the fire escape, as she could not wait for the elevator. The lights came on and off again. She got to the stairs, totally out of breath. She began to descend the stairs. She was not going to make it to the ground floor, she thought in panic, not with the stairs as he was quickly catching up with her. She heard his heavy breath again, above her own. She got back to the corridor and began to run to the elevator wondering what he wanted from her. She got to the elevator and began to fiddle with the buttons. There must be someone else in the building, she realised as the elevator had moved again.

"Bitch." He shouted again.

She began to run away from the elevator, certain that he would catch up with her any moment now. She looked over her shoulder and realised that there were now at least two or three people chasing after her. If only she could get to the stairs on the other side of the building.

She heard a loud thump, as the man that had been chasing her, fell face down.

"Help!!" She cried again, nearly reaching the other flight of stairs.

The second man had stopped also; she could not tell if he was the one who had caused the first man, who hit her whilst in her office to fall. She stopped to catch her breath when the lights came on again. She was panting uncontrollably, before she looked up again.

"Kodelly." She heard a familiar voice. "What on earth are you doing here?" Are you alright?"

"Bobby." She cried out, her mouth totally dry and her legs wobbly from exhaustion, watching as the security men got to the man who was now on the floor.

"Bobby." She repeated, with him rushing to her. He held her in his arms.

"My goodness what were you doing here so late in the night?"

"I came to collect a file." She spoke back, panting whilst leaning against the wall. "Who is he?"

"I'm not sure. Security had reported a fault with the lights, so I came to check on that." He explained. "Did he ask for anything?" He asked after a pause, with a look of concern in his eyes.

"Yeah. Some keys or something."

"Come let me take you home." He continued, aiding her to the elevator.

*　　*　　*

It was a bright morning and her son Olly walked into her bedroom with a breakfast tray. Kodelly had not been to the office for the last two days upon both Bobby and Olly's insistence. She had sustained a dark eye, as well as a sprained ankle. She needed some time to recover and thus would be away from her busy work schedule.

Olly had been frantic when she got home after the incident, with dishevelled hair, a dark patch on her eye from the blow, as well as a limping leg.

"What happened to her?" He'd asked Bobby with scepticism.

"Thanks to him, I'd be worse than this." Replied Kodelly.

"Do you need a doctor?" He continued, holding her on her other side.

"She saw the doctor already." He informed Olly.

"I just need to exercise more often; I feel them muscles ache." She replied, sitting on the couch before Bobby filled him in on what had happened.

Bobby was already standing in the room and was wondering if her condition was perhaps accelerating the pace at which their relationship was growing.

"Here you are mom, just the way you like it. Warm milk, tea, toast, eggs and cheese with a slice of tomato."

"Thank you, sweetheart."

"Will you be requiring anything else?"

"Go to varsity, I don't want you arriving late because you had to take care of 'poor old mama'."

"Okay." He said, kissing her lightly on the forehead.

"Don't you think that I am now fit to go back to work? I mean I can always wear make-up on this patch?"

"Mmmh, I suggest that you give it another day or two." He replied.

"Oh, have a nice day." She called out to him as he went out.

"Thank you and same to you."

"His a very charming lad." Spoke Bobby after he had closed the door behind him. "Shall I pour you tea? I see that there are two cups, so maybe I can have some as well?"

She nodded.

"He is a very charming lad and good at whatever he does." He repeated taking a sip from his cup of tea.

"What do you mean?"

"You should have seen him playing tennis on Saturday. He is very brilliant."

"Wait, wait, on Saturday? You went off to watch my son play tennis on Saturday?"

"Yes." He replied innocently. Surely that was not unusual.

Kodelly was astonished, as she had totally forgotten about the tournament. She had promised that she would go and watch him play, but instead she had been confined in the house with a sprained ankle and a black eye. That bastard could not have chosen a more inapt time to attack her than now, or else she could not be lying in bed listening to Bobby tell her of how brilliant her son is.

"You went to the tournament with him?"

"Yes. I let him drive my car. And everyone was asking if he is my son at the club, after the match. They said we look alike."

"Enough, Bobby Mitch." She injected with her hand raised at him. "Enough. You...I have heard enough...How could you?"

"I did not agree. I did not say yes." He tried to defend himself.

"You bastard, you are taking advantage of my situation."

"I am not." He yelled back, "Olly needs me and I'm going to be there for him." He pointed out.

"I bet you will be. Where were you all those years, you think he didn't need you then?"

"Oh, come off it. He is my son and I want to be there for him."

"No, you come off it and leave us alone." She yelled back sitting up right. "How could you. You think you can fix all the damage you have caused. Just walk right back into our lives?"

"You, damn right I will leave you alone. Does everything have to be about the past? What about Olly? It's all about you, isn't it? You're a very self-conceited, woman." He said walking to the door and out into the corridor.

He sat on the steps contemplating on what to do. Wondering if he would be haunted for life, over a decision he had made all those years back. He had initially thought about her, after he had left Cambel City, but then, he just would not go back. He had thought about her time and again and that was as far as the feelings went. The day he had set eyes on her again was like opening the wall that blocks the dam. His emotions had erupted. She had a right to be angry, but she was not going to shut him out forever.

He stood up and walked back to her bedroom. He gently opened the door and saw her sitting in front of the mirror. Her eyes were focused on her reflection. She did not turn to face him but continued to brush her hair.

"Kodelly, I'm sorry. I know it is hard for me to change the past, but I love Olly and I just want him to be a part of my life." He explained emotionally in a low tone.

"Shouldn't you be at work now?" She paused for a moment and turned to face him. "I'm sorry too, for yelling at you. I guess it was uncalled for."

"I couldn't, I...I placed an order for his dream car. I'd like you to present it to him."

"Wow, wow, I can't afford his dream car. He will know that I didn't buy it for him." She paused for a moment. "Bobby Mitch, you will not stop at anything. Now you want to buy my son's affection?"

"I should have discussed it before hand, with you I mean, but I knew that you would object." He paused for a moment. "Dressing up, are you going somewhere?"

"No, I just wanted to see my eye. So, tell me, has anything been done with the man? Do you know what he wanted from my office?"

He shrugged with his hands in his pockets.

"No." He lied. "Besides, we had to drop the charges against him."

"You what?" She asked with a frown on her face. "That man nearly killed me." She objected. "He could have killed me."

"You have to see things from the whole perspective, Kodelly. News like that filtering to the public can scare people away. Besides, it is just not worth it. We nail him for a couple of months, next he will come out with a vengeance." He explained tactfully.

"I see, so you just let him go?" She reaffirmed, nodding her head.

"We have intensified security, that incident will not recur." He reassured her, walking to her and kneeling in front of her, before kissing the back of her hand. He then kissed her on her lips, her arms wrapped around his neck kissing him back. Their lips parted, fumbling with their clothes, stripping each other naked and making love in a familiar way.

*   *   *

It was a warm, sunny afternoon and father Timdel had invited Kodelly to walk with him in the local park. It was a beautiful park that was frequented by many people. They could hear the children's laughter in the distance as they walked slowly. She had become used to the old, spiritual, parish priest and normally enjoyed listening to him talk as he drew the line between right and wrong.

"Why do human beings strive so much?" She asked after a pause.

He shrugged, listening to the children's happy voices, and then, they stopped next to the pond in the park to admire the fish.

"Look how in harmony the fish are." He answered as though he had just been asked the question. "People strive because of greed, hatred and jealousy. They don't want to share resources like the fish in the pond. They strive because of greed. They do not have the natural love, for neighbour." He emphasised.

She smiled looking at his ageing status, clad in his cassock, and some huge beads around the waistline of the garment. They stood for a while by the pond, before deciding to leave. She walked him to his car, declining to be driven to her house as it was not too far from the park. She could do with a little bit of exercise, she thought as she walked home.

"Madam…Madam a phone call for you." Announced the butler as soon as she had stepped into the house.

"Thank you." She replied, going to answer the call.

"Hello." She answered.

"Hello beautiful." The voice on the other end responded, "If only I could see the panties, you are putting on today or aren't you wearing any?" He continued, before Kodelly cut the line on him. She had received weird, obscene calls in the last few days and had no idea who could be behind them. She began to go up the stairs with only one desire, to wash the perspiration from her body after walking in the sun.

She opened her bedroom door only to find Bobby lying on her bed, with his tie loosened and a bottle of champagne on the side table, with two glasses, one of which was already in use.

"Where were you? I missed you." He spoke upon seeing her.

She stepped in and closed the door behind her, trying to make out what was going on. She was still thinking about the prank caller, even though she had instructed the butler not to put any calls to her from anyone that refused to disclose their identity.

"Come love. I just couldn't get you out of my mind." He motioned. "I just had to see you."

She obliged and sat next to him, sipping from the glass he had just poured for her momentarily, before taking a swig from the glass and then she asked for a refill.

"How was your day?" He continued to ask.

"As usual, pretty much the same." She replied, not wanting to mention the prank caller to him.

He kissed her lightly and then he pulled her to him. She kissed him back whilst they caressed. She unbuttoned his shirt and threw it onto the floor. Then she stepped out of her shoes, kissing him urgently and running her fingers through his hair. He took off her blouse and skirt and then she watched him undress. She smiled getting up from the bed and grabbing her robe, which she put about her.

"You can go and tell her where I left off, I'm sure that she will be glad to finish off." She said sarcastically, picking up her skirt and blouse, before going into the bathroom.

"What do you mean?" He asked after her stupidly.

"Jill." She said knowingly. "Of course, she will be willing to finish off. Now get out of my house."

He sighed, putting his clothes on. He got the bottle of champagne and took a swig from it whilst walking out of her bedroom.

She sighed, wondering if Bobby truly was having an affair with the other woman as Rena had insisted. She soaked herself in the tub and thought about the prank caller, with his perverted way of talking. His voice was harsh and deep. He spoke about sex and made it seem like a wild, barbaric act. Some very dirty act. He explained it in an aggressive manner, each time he had an opportunity to speak. She dried herself up, wondering if there was need for her to be alarmed. He was probably just someone trying to play a big joke on her, she concluded before going to bed early.

*   *   *

She walked into the office premises in her usual cheerful mood. She had not seen Bobby in the last few days, making her wonder if there was anything wrong in her wanting to know the truth about his activities. She had a right to know anything that he was doing, least she could be caught off guard the way she had been all those years back. It was a harsh lesson, one that she would live to remember, no matter how hard she tried to move on. She walked into her secretary's office and found Bobby waiting for her there, with a red rose in his hand. He gave it to her and pecked her on the lips in the presence of the secretary. She felt flattered, considering that she had already received a call from the prank caller before leaving her house. He had hissed about how disgusting he found women to be.

She had barely walked into the office, before her direct line began to ring. She picked up the call, her usual professionalism in her tone of voice and for a moment the line was quiet.

"Hello?" She asked, a bit alarmed.

"Hello, bitch." He replied.

"What do you want?" She asked the prank caller, having recognised his voice.

"What do I want?" He asked back in a hiss, before laughing.

"What do you want?' She asked frantically.

Bobby stood in the doorway and listened to her, watching her as she spoke, wondering what or whom she was talking with.

"You are phoney." She continued in a hurried voice, "You don't exist. It is just my imagination working on me." She said, before slamming the receiver down.

"Those are not telephone manners." Cut in Bobby jerking her back to reality.

"Bobby…" She said fearfully, bringing her hands up to cover her mouth, momentarily. "I mean, that was nothing."

"Kodelly you are so worked up right now. What is going on?"

She sighed for a moment, contemplating on whether to tell him everything or not. She walked to the other side of the table and sat down heavily in her chair.

"What is going on? Who was on the line?"

"I don't know." She began, deciding that she needed to talk to someone. "It is just some man who has been calling me for the last couple of days and he seems to be watching my movements."

"What man?" He asked with his eyebrows raised, before they were interrupted with the ringing of the phone again.

She looked at the phone not wanting to answer it.

"Come on, answer it. Put it on the speaker."

"Okay." She said nervously.

"Hello." She said trying to sound firm.

"Well, well, well, so you told on me to your rich boyfriend. You cunning bitch, you told on me? So, what's he gonna' do, hey, spank me?"

"It's him." She said, cutting the line. "It's him. It's wired and he heard us. This room is wired." She said, running out of her office and past her secretary.

Bobby stood for a moment, before walking to her office table to see if he could see any unusual devices. He knelt down, being unsuccessful for a moment, before finally getting hold of a device.

"My word, Kodelly." He said to himself, pulling it off and rushing to her secretary's office.

"Kodelly, you were right. Your office is wired." He said and then stopped for a moment, looking at the secretary who looked back at him. She seemed puzzled, wondering why her boss had run out of her office and past her without saying a word.

"Where is she?"

"She hurried out. She didn't say a word." She answered, feeling a bit perplexed.

"Thank you." He replied, slipping his hand into his pocket to put the device away.

He hurried down the corridor towards the elevator.

"Come on. Come on." He spoke to himself impatiently, as he waited for the elevator.

She must have decided to go home, he thought to himself. The elevator doors opened and there were two elderly women inside.

"We are going up, sir." Said one of the two.

He stepped in though, ignoring the remark, wishing he could get them out; instead, he nodded politely to them.

"Hello to you too." Spoke the other.

"We are going to see the MD of this corporation." Informed the other.

"What about?" He asked irritably.

"What about?" Laughed the other. "It ain't any of your business, if you ask me."

"I see." He replied, watching as the elevator door opened to let them out.

"Oh, just so you know, I'm Mr. Bobby Mitch." He said politely, knowing that they were going to his office.

"Bye, Mr. Mitch. You've got quite a nice butt." Laughed the other.

"I am the MD." He said again, holding the elevator doors open, with the button for a moment.

"Oh, don't we all wish." Replied the other. "Close the lift, be on your way…son."

"Okay." He said, closing the door and heading for the parking floor with the elevator.

Kodelly must have driven off by now, he thought in frustration. He hurriedly opened the door to his car. He started the engine and began to speed off. He got into the driveway, and parked in front of him, was a huge delivery truck. He sounded the horn, to alert the security personnel, who were conducting their routine check.

One of the security men hurried to his car and saluted at him.

"Good morning, sir."

"I want to drive out now…" He demanded.

"Well sir, we are…" He tried to explain.

"Never mind the routine, just get that truck out of my driveway NOW."

"Okay sir." He replied excitedly, signalling to the driver of the truck to move his vehicle onto the premises.

Bobby sat tapping his fingers, watching until the truck was out of the driveway and then he sped off into the main road. He cursed every stop that he had to make, before getting onto the highway and then he accelerated further. He looked in the back mirror and chasing after him was a police car. He decided to stop when he heard the siren.

"License please?" Spoke the police officer as soon as he had reached the car window.

He pulled out his license and gave it to him, cursing every moment of it to himself.

"I'm sorry, sir. My wife is just about to have a baby."

"Your wife, hey?" He replied, peeping in the back window.

"She's at home."

"Ooh, but you really want to be there and see this new one, don't you?"

"Yes, officer."

"You know the traffic rules?"

"Yes, officer."

"Okay." He said taking his details. "Drive slowly." He cautioned.

"Thank you, officer." He said politely again.

He pulled off, trying to keep his word. He drove within the stipulated speed for a while; he could not imagine another delay. Kodelly needed him and this time he was going to be there for her. He wondered who the prank caller was. Could it be a man from her past, or someone with a crush on her? He pulled the car to a halt in her driveway, and quickly got out of the car. He hurried to the front door and rang the doorbell. Within seconds, the butler appeared in the doorway.

"Good morning, sir. How may I help you?"

"Good morning. May I come in?"

"No." He replied, despite having seen Bobby on several occasions before. "Madam gave strict instructions not to let anyone in."

"Tell her that it's me and please hurry up."

"Yes, sir." He said, closing the door in his face before going to consult with the madam. He reappeared minutes later and allowed him into the house.

"Where is she?" He asked hurriedly.

"Upstairs." He replied, watching him run up the stairs.

He hurried to her bedroom and there she was, sitting on the bed staring at the dressing mirror.

"He was here." She said emotionlessly as soon as he entered.

He raised his eyes and followed her gaze and smeared on the dressing mirror with lipstick were some writings.

Bitch for wealthy boy.'

He sat next to her and embraced her, not knowing what would be appropriate for him to say. The phone began to ring before he could think of anything to say. She looked at him and he gestured to her to answer.

"Hello?" She answered.

"Tell your man a quarter of a million for your boy. He should pay by tomorrow. We have your boy."

"Oh my God..." She exclaimed. "They have my son. They have kidnapped my son." She screamed, holding the line in her hand and beginning to sob.

Bobby quickly got the receiver from her hand.

"Hello." He answered authoritatively. "Hello." He repeated, the line was quiet and then the caller, just hang up.

"It's going to be okay." He assured. "How much does he want?"

"A quarter of a million. I don't want my son to be hurt. I don't want for that to happen."

"He won't be." He reassured, wondering who could be behind this. "I have to make a few phone calls and make sure that we have cash available, immediately." He said, beginning to phone his bank.

They spent the rest of the day indoors. The caller had called them minutes after the first call, cautioning them not to have any ideas or to do anything that would jeopardize the whole situation. He insisted that he would let them know where to meet him, in exchange for the boy.

Kodelly refused to eat for the entire day. She jumped at every phone call, but the caller did not call as he had earlier informed them. Bobby had rushed to the bank to collect the money. A part of him kept asking him, why he was doing it? It was his child for damn sake. If anything, this would be his second chance at being there for them. He could not imagine any other man standing up for his own son. He then returned to be at the side of his mother, watching her stressed face. Later in the night, she had resorted to drinking a cup of tea to keep her awake, insisting that she would not sleep at all. She had however, fallen asleep in the early morning hours, despite having insisted that she was not going to sleep at all. He had stayed awake with her, listening to her tell him for the first time, stories of their son's childhood and for the first time he seemed to realise just how much he had missed by not having been there at all. He loved the stories she told him, some hilarious, some difficult, and some playful and yet for Kodelly that was a prayer, a plea, a petition to have him back.

"I didn't want a girl, because girls are often taken advantage of. I didn't think a boy would be fun either, because boys normally have to go and sit in the pub even if they don't have any business there, just to prove that the 'fit' in with the rest of their peers and to avoid being called 'a home boy', but God gave me a son and I want him back, here, safe."

"It's going to be okay." Bobby reassured, half believing in the words he had just uttered.

*   *   *

She was awakened by the sunrays streaming through the curtains. They had both eventually fallen asleep on top of the bed covers from exhaustion. She sat up for a moment, and then quickly jerked into motion. She hurried to the bathroom and took a quick shower, and then she went downstairs, wondering whether the phone had rung when she was fast asleep, and as such did not hear it. She felt very exhausted, but could not go back to bed, in case she missed the very important phone call. She was very tense whilst sitting next to the phone; her imagination seemed to have taken the best of her. An hour later, Bobby walked down the stairs; he had freshened up, even though there were traces of exhaustion on his face.

"Any news?" He asked with concern.

"No. Nothing yet." She replied, beginning to pace up and down.

"What if we call the police. We can't just sit and wait."

"What if that puts Olly in harm's way?" He asked back. "A cup of tea?"

"Strong coffee if you will." She replied, before he disappeared into the kitchen.

The phone began to ring, as soon as Bobby entered the kitchen. He hurried back, watching Kodelly pick up the handset.

"Hello." She answered. There was a pause on the other side, before the caller spoke.

"Can I speak to your man?"

"Yes." She replied, hurriedly giving the receiver to Bobby, as he approached her.

"Hello."

"Bobby." Sounded the man from the other end of the line.

"Yes?"

"Do you have a quarter of a million with you?"

"Yes."

"Now, I wouldn't do anything stupid if I were you. You need that bitch to continue sleeping with you, so do what is right. Pay up. I always looked forward to this moment. It is now payback time. I am the one who should be the MD of the big corporation. I am the one who should have had enough money to start and run my own successful business…but no, you played me out of the deal…"

"When are you bringing the boy back?" He interrupted rudely.

"Your son you mean? I am the one that was supposed to get the money from the exhibition, but you played me. I am coming there now. Don't do anything stupid."

"What is he saying?" Kodelly asked fearfully.

He ignored her question, while the caller dropped the line.

"Is everything okay? Is my son okay?"

"Yes. Yes. I think he is coming to collect the money now."

The phone rang again, and he picked it up hurriedly.

"Bobby." Spoke the caller again cheerfully.

"Yes?"

"Now, listen very carefully. He walks in on his own, you hand me the cash and that is it. No hostages okay, unless you don't want that pretty bitch to look you in the eyes again. You understand?"

"Yes." He replied hearing him drop the line again.

"I think he will be here any moment from now." He informed her again, watching her wipe the tears from her eyes. She would never speak to him again if she knew that it was actually about him and not her, as they had earlier believed. It was not a man from her past but rather a man from his past trying to settle an old score, after so many years. It was unbelievable. If only they did not kidnap Olly, then he could have taught those bastards that he was just as crude as he was when he was much younger.

A few minutes later the doorbell rang, and Olly walked through the door, coming through with him was another man, to whom both Kodelly and Bobby paid attention. Much as Kodelly felt like screaming and running to hug her son, she had been cautioned to remain calm and not to do anything that could aggravate the situation.

"Hello, mum and uncle Bobby." He greeted, walking past them in the hallway.

"Hello." Replied Kodelly.

"The bag?" Asked the stranger that had walked in after Olly.

"Here." He replied, handing him the bag.

"Good work, Mr. Bobby, it better be good stuff."

"It is the amount you requested." He replied.

"Okay." He said, smiling to himself and walking out of the house. He quickly hurried to the parked car and drove off.

"Is everything okay?" Asked Olly, with a look of concern in his eyes.

"My God honey, are you okay?" Kodelly asked with concern, rushing to embrace him.

"Yes I am. Why do you ask?" He asked quizzically, seeing the look of concern on her face.

"Thank goodness it is over and done with. I promise you that that won't happen again." Cut in Bobby.

"What on earth is going on here?" He asked again.

"Come on darling, did they hurt you?"

"Who? Nobody hurt me." He protested having pulled away from his mother.

"So, they just kidnapped you?"

"Kidnapped? Who told you that? I went to Cambel city yesterday. I left a note for you as usual on your dressing table."

"You what! Wait a minute, so all this time your mom and I were stressing out you were out having a good time?"

"Stressing over what, uncle Bobby?" He asked back innocently.

"Don't leave notes next time." He scolded. "Tell your mother where you are going to. Just tell her." He yelled.

"Oh, my goodness." Spoke Kodelly bursting into tears of relieve, "Oh, my goodness. I am so happy to see you." She said, embracing him again.

Bobby looked on for a moment before excusing himself from their company. He needed to go home and rest before going back to work. The prank caller had really taken the best of him, and he had managed to clean him out by a long, short. He wondered if he had been too irrational in dealing with the situation. He certainly had not been assertive, or he could not have been duped of his hard-earned income. He certainly might have paid even more if the man had requested for more, making him wonder if his guilt of the past had made him pay out, without even thinking twice. The lad was his son and there was no doubting it. He had promised that he would be there for him regardless of the situation. He thought about Olly and the relief that he felt when he saw him walk through the door, even though he had been in no real danger. He wondered how their relationship would be if he knew that Bobby Mitch was his natural father and not just a fond friend of his mother.

He yearned to be acknowledged as a dad, if not by his first son but at least, if he could have another child, yes, one whom he would be there for from the beginning and watch him grow. He would guide his every step, he sighed, wondering if he was daring the wind.

* _____ *

BOOK THREE

CHAPTER SEVENTEEN

Kodelly sat in Rena's sitting room, with a rose flower in her hands. She looked at it intently for a moment, admiring its beauty and then slowly she began to pluck its petals and throwing them on the table.

"He loves me, he loves me not, he loves me, he loves me not." She repeated softly.

Rena walked into the sitting room with a glass of Vodka, drinking of its contents. She had spent the evening with Kodelly at a party and then they had returned to her flat in the early hours, after Rena insisted that she drive with her to her flat. Kodelly had been very distracted, allowing herself to drink into a stupor.

She had finally believed Rena's allegations about Bobby. She had accompanied him to an elegant restaurant a day before, and halfway through their meal, a woman had walked to their table, whom she later learnt to be Jill. She greeted Bobby, before pulling a seat not minding Kodelly, who became infuriated. Bobby did not seem to mind the intrusion, and the woman began to make a conversation with him in a husky voice, before Kodelly stood up from her seat with her plate half complete, emptying its contents on her. Before either of them could do anything, she grabbed her bag and stormed out of the restaurant. She left Bobby to deal with the ruckus she had just caused, as the staff approached him to question him on what was going on? They had probably concluded her to be the jealous wife.

She drove back to the office, not minding how Bobby felt about the whole thing. He tried to call her after a few hours, but she had declined all his calls. She found his behaviour to be rather horrendous, besides she was still too embarrassed and annoyed to talk with him.

"That is very childish of you." Addressed Rena.

She shook her head, still feeling drowsy from all the alcohol that she had taken the previous night.

"I did not realise that I was in love with him again." She spoke motionlessly.

"Again?" Rena asked with a puzzled look on her face. "What do you mean again?"

"Oh, I mean, well… I mean… I didn't realise that I was deeply in love with him. I mean after we slit up, after I shouted at that woman, he came with to work." She lied, not wanting to disclose the past.

"Well, I had no idea that the two of you had actually split up." Replied Rena, with her eyebrows raised.

"For a short while." She said brushing it off, with the waving of her hand. "I must go now."

She excused herself, afraid that she might just divulge the past. She was afraid that she would disclose her past secrets, especially not to the big-mouthed Rena, otherwise everyone would know about it.

"Don't you want to have some breakfast?"

"No. No, thanks. I will go and eat at home." She said, getting up from the couch and walking out of Rena's apartment.

She still felt angry at Bobby; she felt betrayed and worst of all she hated her own guts for spilling food on that woman. She felt that she had overacted. No. She would not call it overacting, she just wasn't going to allow him to walk all over her like he had done when she was still young and naïve, she told herself feeling renewed vigour.

She drove back to her house. She expected it to be quiet, especially since Olly had travelled to Summerset to see his grandparents. It would be even quieter, since she was not working, and Bobby would certainly not call on her. She wondered what she would do to keep herself sane. She got inside the house and was only two steps up the staircase when she heard a voice behind her.

"Hi, Kodelly." She stopped in her tracks, wondering if her mind was deceiving her. She turned slowly to face the person.

"Hi." She said again.

"Laura. What are you doing here?" She asked in surprise.

"I hope that you don't mind me coming over here without calling." She replied.

"No, I don't." She replied, "It's good to see you." Looking at her pale figure and troubled face.

"I hope you don't mind me putting up with you for a couple of days." She spoke again.

"No. No. You don't need to be apologetic. You know that you are always welcome." She paused for a moment. "So, how are the children and your husband?"

"Fine. I well, I…"

"Listen, I will get the butler to get you a room ready. Let me just go upstairs and take a bath and catch some sleep. I'm really exhausted."

"Was out having fun?" She heard her ask.

"No. Not really, just a party."

"Oh, I see." She replied, watching her give instructions to the butler, who had appeared in the hallway and then she turned to face Laura again.

"If you need anything, please don't hold yourself back." She said, before excusing herself from her company.

She could not imagine what Laura was doing in Goldring city, but again she had enough worries of her own to start speculating about her cousin. She would get to the bottom of it after resting.

Within a moment Laura was standing in the middle of one of the bedrooms that were rarely used in Kodelly's two-story house. It was well furnished, and the linen had just been changed, making the room smell fresh. Having tucked her bags away, she sat on the bed. She had been in Goldring city for the past month and a half. She had been staying at the hotel and determined to find a job. She would wake up each day with renewed vigour, but her efforts had proved futile. She would go to bed in the evening, telling herself not to give up, until this morning when she'd had to pay for the hotel accommodation again and realised that she had no more money left to spend. She only had enough money to pay her transport fare to Kodelly's lovely mansion. She still recalled her vivid arguments with Dinkley Mills. She even accused him of being behind Kodelly's sound, financial standing and that he bought the house for her.

She shuddered at the memory of her walking out on her husband. She had woken up in the morning, after having had a row with him the previous night, which had caused Dinkley to go out drinking. He came back late and sat in front of the television set, unaware of the fact that his wife had packed her bags. She walked down the short flight of stairs to the lounge, where he was. She had a suitcase in her hand and a cheque leaf in another. She had filled it in and just needed him to sign it.

He sat on the sofa with a bottle of beer in front of him, with an odour of liquor surrounding him.

"Sign here." She demanded, putting the cheque in front of him.

"Where are you going?" He tried to ask.

"Don't," She said raising her hand in the air, "There is nothing left for us to discuss. Just do me that favour. Please..." She replied emotionally.

He got the cheque, too tired to continue arguing with her, especially after their previous night's ordeal. He signed the cheque and handed it to her. She got the cheque, picked up her bags and walked out on him. They'd had several arguments in the recent past and somehow their arguments never ended without her mentioning Kodelly's name. She felt that her cousin still overshadowed her, despite the great distance between them. She sighed, walking to the window to see what was going on outside.

Kodelly lay in her bed, wondering how long her cousin would stay with them and if she would meet Bobby, before going back to Summerset. She envisaged her to be on some business trip or something and would soon go back to her husband's loving arms. She had no idea that her timid cousin had actually walked out on her husband and their two beautiful daughters.

*   *   *

Kodelly had not seen Bobby outside working hours, since the scene at the glamorous restaurant. She had decided to take a stance, although she did not know exactly what it was. She missed Bobby, but she was not yet ready to play second best, nor was she ready to be entangled in a relationship with so many players in it. Being away from him made her realise just how much fond of him she had become, again. She realised that she missed him and yet she hated herself for harbouring such emotions. She had gotten used to living with Laura again, who had bluntly explained that she was on separation from her husband.

"Whaat?" Kodelly asked in shock, spitting the coffee from her mouth. "What did you say?"

"Dinkley and I are on separation." She repeated flatly.

"Does mother know about it? It will break her heart and the children?"

"Don't tell me that I did the wrong thing." She charged. "What we decided, was the best thing for both of us."

"Okay." She replied raising her hand in resignation, wondering how Lidy would take the news.

She figured that Lidy should have gotten over the notion that Laura came between Dinkley and her. She could not imagine what her life would have been if she had married Dinkley Mills.

A part of her told her to phone Dinkley and find out what exactly was going on, and yet a part of her told her that she would convince her cousin to go back. Laura had so far emphasised one thing, and that was to get a job and move on with her life. She sighed, thinking about Olly, who was quite good friends with Bobby, even though his relationship with his mother had become strained. She heard a car pull through the driveway and she went to the window to peep. It was Bobby's car; she saw Olly disembark through the driver's seat and Bobby came out too.

They stood and talked for a while, then the back door opened as Bobby got into the driver's seat, a woman came out from the backseat and spoke to Olly for a moment, before getting into the passenger's seat. It was the woman she had met at the restaurant, she realised in frustration and anger before watching the car drive off. How could Bobby do this to her? How could he have the audacity to bring her onto her premises? She could not help but to blame herself, wondering if perhaps she had not been receptive enough or maybe she should have put up a fight, but then again, she felt she was too old for that.

She picked up the receiver and began to phone father Timdel; he seemed to be in a position to ease her disappointments, she had realised with time. He made her believe that she was a worthy being who deserved better than to be disparaged.

She ended her conversation with him and yet the heartache still seemed eminent. How could he actually have the guts to bring his girlfriends onto her premises, she still pondered? She wondered how she would feel if perhaps he married that woman. She could not imagine the humiliation that she would have to live with. Rena had encouraged her to continue dating Bobby despite their differences, telling her that she could have stood for such treatment as long as she got her fair share of him, anyhow. She would marry him if anything, just for the money, not his good looks or his charisma and most importantly not for love.

She sighed again, only too glad that she would be able to see father Timdel the next morning, as they had earlier agreed.

*   *   *

It was on a Saturday morning and Kodelly woke up early. She took a shower, wondering how she would spend her day. She had only one appointment scheduled for the day. The memory of Bobby with that woman gave her a pang of jealousy emotions. She could not imagine that he was delighting her in the same way that he enchanted her with his charm and she, was definitely smiling back into his eyes, those gorgeous eyes of his. She dressed up casually and went downstairs into the kitchen. She had a glass of juice and some cereal and then she walked out of the house and drove to the local church, to which she was now familiar. She parked the car securely, and then walked to his office; she would then go and check at the chapel if he was not in his office.

She knocked on the heavy, mahogany door and the woman who was tidying his office allowed her in.

"Good morning." She greeted. "Is father Timdel available?"

"Good morning." Replied the other middle-aged woman. "Yes, he is. He will be back within a minute or two. He went to answer the phone in the other office. Please take a seat."

She obliged. "Thank you."

For a moment she wondered if she was feeling nervous. There was no need for her to be nervous, she consoled herself, or perhaps it was her guilt that was bothering her. She only seemed to want to see him when she was not handling herself emotionally. She had managed to attend one of his Sunday morning services, but had after that been unable to commit, even though she had found his sermon interesting.

She looked around in the antique furnished office, with the bookshelf covered mostly with religious books and a few files on the other side of the office shelf. It was a dimly lit room, she noticed, watching as the old priest walked through the door.

"Miss Mollar, good to see you. So how is the morning?" He greeted, remembering his appointment with her only then.

"Fine. It is good to see you too."

He turned and looked at the woman that was tiding up.

"Do excuse us for some time, please, my angel."

"Yes, Fr. Timdel." She replied, walking out of the office.

"Yes. What can I do for you or is this just a courtesy call?" He paused for a moment, "And I must say it was a generous donation you gave to the church this month again. Your generosity goes a long way in aiding us to reach out to the community."

"Oh, thank you and yes, it is just a courtesy call. I mean, no..." She replied, feeling unsure again.

She wanted to talk to somebody. Yes, somebody who could help her understand her feelings, her disappointments or maybe she should let her big secret loose about Olly's paternity. Somebody who could help her untangle herself from the mess she had gotten into.

"Did you say your prayers this morning?"

"No." She replied, frankly.

"Why not? Surely you have a God you must worship?"

"I forgot or maybe my life, well…"

"You mustn't forget. It is very important…" He cut in, in his firm accent.

"Father?" Called out the woman who had earlier been tidying the office from the doorway, "a telephone call for you. They say it is important." She explained her intrusion.

"Okay." He replied to her and then he faced Kodelly again, apologetically. "Excuse me."

She sighed, as soon as he was out of sight and pulled one of the books from the shelf, beginning to browse through its pages. The elderly priest walked through the door again.

"Oh, the line got cut before I got there. I must be getting too old to walk fast. Was it the father of your child you wanted to talk to me about, Mr. Bobby Mitch?" He referred to plainly whilst looking her in the eyes.

Her eyes dilated; her mouth opened in aghast. How did he know about her past with Bobby Mitch? She had mentioned him only as her friend and senior at work and not as her lover from Cambel city. Was it that obvious that the two of them had shared a past together once before? She was too stunned to speak, but instead stared at him before the door opened again.

"Phone Father. It is the same person. He says you never took his call." She insisted, not wanting to be taken as an unnecessary intruder.

"Just tell them I'm on my way." He called out. "Excuse me." He spoke softly to Kodelly.

Kodelly nodded as he excused himself from her company. She sat still for a moment, hearing their footsteps become faint. Instinctively, she got up from the chair, feeling the adrenaline run fast, feeling the heat engulf her. How did he know, she questioned, walking out of his office? She hurried to her car; she got inside and fumbled with the keys for a moment, before starting the engine. She could not think of anything, except how stupid she must appear to the old priest who had seen past her and into her past. She joined the main road without seeing the oncoming vehicle. It was too late to react when she noticed the vehicle; she let out a loud scream, hitting her head on the horn before everything went dark.

*   *   *

Laura woke up late. She still had not found a job, hence to her Saturday was not exactly any different from her weekly schedule. She went into the kitchen after dressing up. She realised that Kodelly had already had her breakfast, by noticing the dishes that had been left unwashed. She was feeling good about herself for a change, since coming to Goldring city. She had asked Kodelly for some money, and now all she needed was to change her image. She wanted to reduce on her weight by eating toast and juice like Kodelly often did. She had already planned a trip to the mall, to get some new clothes, something that would affiliate her to Kodelly's class. She had in mind some elegant outfits. She walked out of the house, after having had her breakfast and asking the butler for the car keys for the extra vehicle.

"May I have the car keys?" She'd requested.

"Madam never instructed me to give them to you." He replied firmly.

"Don't patronise me." She charged at him. "I'm as good as her sister if that should mean anything to you."

"Yes madam." He replied as a matter of courtesy with a smile on his face.

"The keys?"

"I will fetch them for you." He replied disappointedly.

She drove through the driveway with her head above her shoulders. She was filled with a new sense of determination; to make a new image for herself.

*　　　*　　　*

Bobby woke up to a bright, sunny, Sunday morning with a smile of content on his face. He shifted his gaze to his wife who lay beside him. He gently stroked her hair, not wanting to wake up, his lovely, newlywed, wife. He felt like a teenager in love all over again, as he admired his bride and enjoyed the feeling and pleasure of being married.

He slipped out of bed and contemplated on making them breakfast. He quickly washed his face in the adjacent bathroom and went into the kitchen. He opened the cupboards and began to think of what he would prepare for them. He felt very proud of himself. He could not imagine anything that would surpass the joy that he felt now, despite that their marriage had been so quiet for a tycoon like himself. He would have loved a big wedding party, but that could always be done later. They had gotten married in haste, more on the spur of the moment, but he had enjoyed every minute detail of it.

She opened her eyes, her head still banging and for a moment she wondered where she was. Then, slowly she got out of bed, pulling on Bobby's gown, which was an oversize to her. She had no changing clothes other than the casual outfit she wore the previous day. She looked at her hand to admire her expensive diamond wedding ring, which had been slipped on her finger the previous day. They had stood in front of the priest as she and Bobby exchanged their wedding vows, to make a lifetime commitment.

She walked to the dressing table. She sat in front of the dressing mirror and recalled the previous evening's events. They had kissed and caressed, eventually making love again and again and for the first time she had no guilty feelings or fear of being left or abandoned. It felt very right now that she wore his ring, now that they were man and wife. She shuddered, remembering the screaming of the tyres, with her eventually letting go of the steering wheel, before hearing a loud bang. She was fortunate to come out of the wrecked car with a few bruises and mostly just shock of how soon and fast the whole incident had happened. The church personnel had pulled her out of the vehicle. Father Timdel and the other people who had heard the crush had run to the scene, helping both victims. He had then phoned Kodelly's workplace and managed to get hold of someone, who had phoned Bobby and informed him of the ordeal. Kodelly eventually came around but was still in so much pain. She could not help but to wonder what could have happened, should the accident have come to the worst. Who could have stood up for her son other than her parents? She knew without a doubt that Bobby could have made a good parent had the worst transpired. She had cried uncontrollably in Bobby's arms after he'd arrived, although, they had not been together since the scene she had caused at the restaurant. Yet his heart had been longing for her. He asked her hand in marriage, to which she agreed. They had agreed that there was no better time than the present. Olly and Rena were then invited to witness them exchange their vows.

Her face lit up as soon as Bobby walked through the door. He was carrying a tray in his hands.

"How is my beautiful wife feeling this morning?" He greeted her.

"Slightly better, well almost, anyway." Watching him as he set the tray on the side table.

"Well, it might suffice for you to know that your husband is also feeling fine too." He said, kneeling in front of her and kissing the back of her hand and then her lips, with her kissing him back, even though her mind was not up to it.

She had not so much as gotten used to the title yet. She actually would have to learn to be a wife, she told herself, wishing that she could turn him down. But then again, the thought of letting him down on their first morning together as husband and wife might just spark ill feelings between them. Instead, she yielded to his desires, recalling only the vows she had made the previous day that earned her the title of being called *missus* Mitch, among other privileges.

* _____ *

CHAPTER EIGHTEEN

Bobby and Kodelly had just returned from their honeymoon. They had enjoyed a time of seclusion on the Island. Kodelly felt more vibrant now, than ever before. She had almost given up that the two of them would ever be together and happy again, after she saw Bobby with the other woman. She no longer had to play second best, she was his official wife, and nothing would change that now, even though it had taken her a bit of time to get used to living in Bobby's mansion.

Her first few days had been accustomed with her giving excuses to allow her to go back to her house. She seemed unsure of her impulsive decision to marry him. She had gone back to her house two days later after insisting that she needed to sort things out in her bedroom, when night had fallen, she went and stood on the balcony, admiring the bright moon. She stood in the quietness of the night, admiring the stars in the sky and meditating on her new life.

Olly walked onto the balcony and stood behind her. She was so engrossed in her thoughts that she did not realise that he was there. He spoke, startling her from her meditation.

"I thought that you would be happy." He stated. "But I can see that you are not."

"I am." She lied, hiding her confusion, and hugging herself from the cool breeze. "I wish that everyone else couldn't remind me of how fortunate I am."

"Then, what are you doing here?"

"I was just having a feel of the evening breeze."

"No, I mean away from your new home, with uncle Bobby?"

"I don't know, are you sure you don't want to come and live with me, I mean us?"

"No, I will be fine, besides the two of you need some time alone." He replied. "You just got married and you deserve to be happy, mom."

"Thank you, darling. Please call us anytime. You will always be my baby. You must know that. You'll always come first."

"Thanks mom. I have to go and finish off my assignments now." He said excusing himself from her.

She stood on the balcony a while longer, before finally driving back to her new home, where she would be embraced in the loving, welcoming arms of her husband.

Their wedding party was grand; Lidy had been at the forefront with the preparations. She had insisted on being involved with the guest list and choosing Kodelly's dress. She insisted on choosing the snacks and the venue, as well as the menu and the design for the invitation cards.

"Well, a wedding comes only once in a lifetime." She said excitedly, wanting to be involved in everything, "Or, so it is supposed to be." She added with a chuckle.

Kodelly still recalled how hysterical she was, after decoding what her daughter was actually telling her.

"Hello, is that mom?"

"Yes, my love it is. How is Olly?" She had responded from the other end of the phone.

"He is fine. How are you and dad?"

"We are fine, just missing you and that handsome son of yours."

"You spoil him so much, mom. I just wanted to tell you that I got married yesterday."

"Married! What! Were you engaged? Was there a wedding?"

"No. No, we just exchanged vows and I was not engaged."

"What are you saying, could you please start from the beginning?"

"I am, Mrs. Bobby Mitch. We will throw a party in two weeks' time. Please come as soon as you can."

"Oh my God, Kodelly, my Kodelly is finally tying the knot." Came the excited voice. "I am so proud of you. Wait till your father learns of it." She paused for a moment. "Congratulation's sweetheart, Bobby Mitch you said?"

"Yes, I have known him for some time now. I must go now, give my love to dad."

"Oh, this is too good. I thank God it is true. The whole of Summerset shall be proud of you. God has heard my prayers for you. I shall get you the best dress. You shall be the most beautiful woman that walks down the aisle. Oh, I am so proud…"

"Mom," She cut in. "I shall see you soon."

They had ended the conversation, with Kodelly ultimately realising that she had made a mature decision, one that had made her parents proud and one that would take away the stigma to being unattached. She thought about Lidy and how she adored her husband, wondering if she would feel the same about Bobby. Lidy had married when she was still young and bore her husband their daughter and had been faithful to her husband from then on. Their love was the fuel that kept the fire burning, the water that turned the turbine. Their trust and respect for one another was the honouring bond and security that they needed to be in love and live happily, thereafter. Trust, love and respect, such simple words and yet they can make or break a relationship, she realised.

Lidy arrived much earlier than her husband, who still had to attend to a few things before setting off for Goldring city. He was, however, very aware that his wife well represented both their interests in any matter. She was to stay at Kodelly's house with Olly and Laura. Her visit; however, caused Laura much discomfort. She had questioned her on her separation from Dinkley, which she had come to learn of through Kodelly. Laura had maintained her passive stance, insisting that their decision was the best ever. She was sick and tired of Dinkley Mills control, telling her whom she must associate with, what to wear, what cup to drink her tea from. No, she had told herself, she had taken more than she could actually handle from him. It was time for her to move on and make a mark in her life.

On the night before the wedding party, Kodelly sat chatting with Lidy and going through some of Bobby's childhood pictures. Lidy felt that Bobby Mitch, whom she had met in person, actually bore some resemblance with Olly, though she could not quite put her finger to it and yet she was sure of that from the first day that she had met with him. But she convinced herself that she did not travel this far to speculate, but rather to be present for an event she had dreamed about from the time her baby was born and that was to host the finest wedding party ever.

Lidy and Kodelly's father had gone back to summerset after helping the newlyweds choose and book their honeymoon resort.

It was a fabulous wedding day, one that stood too clear in Kodelly's memory. Her father, Mr. Mollar, had walked his daughter down the aisle in full view of all their guests; giving her hand in marriage to the man she already called her husband. The reception was then later held at one of the five-star hotels and another party was held later in the evening.

They danced into the early hours of the next day. Rena had been one of the bridesmaids. She danced the night away with excitement. She beamed with excitement through the whole ceremony, drinking to her satisfaction. She enjoyed the party with admiration, as the woman she considered to be her best friend, celebrated her marriage. She wondered if she would spend as much time with her as they had done in the past. She considered her to be very fortunate, stealing Bobby's heart and wrapping it around hers. But maybe they deserved each other, she had reasoned. Maybe they were meant for each other she had thought rationally, watching them kiss in front of everyone.

Olly was happy for his mother, watching her and the man she was in love with celebrate their nuptials. They had surprised him with a brand-new car on the eve of their wedding party. He watched with content, while his mother and Bobby danced. Then he looked at Laura, seeing her visible efforts to change her image. He sighed, wondering if that was what being grown up was all about.

*   *   *

Laura woke up early as she had normally done in the past two weeks. She was content of her notion of how she expected to look. She took a long bath and then dressed up and descended the stairs. She went to the kitchen and much as she craved for sweet things and a beefy breakfast, she instead settled for a bowl of cereal and a glass of orange juice.

She drove into town moments later, even though she was not exactly sure of the place where the offices were but had a vague idea of the location of the building. She parked her car securely and then went up the escalator, onto the landing; she paused for a moment before stepping into the elevator. She could not remember the directions clearly but was hoping that she was heading in the right direction. She stepped out of the elevator onto the floor where she thought it might be. She stood for a moment and tried to use her intuition, not wanting to ask around for directions.

She wore a neat suit with dark glasses covering her eyes, with a bag strapped over her shoulders and mature ladies' shoes. Her hair was neatly tied back. She found herself in an open reception area.

"Hello." She greeted the lady behind the desk with a smile. "I am looking for the MD?"

"Good morning ma'am. Do you have an appointment?"

"No." She replied, watching the lady raise her eyebrows, "but I am family." She immediately added. "He'd asked me to come through, but I didn't bother to make an appointment."

"Okay, just sign here for me." She instructed her. "Then you can go through to his secretary's office. She will take it from there."

"Okay." She replied filling in her details before proceeding.

"Good morning, madam." She was greeted by the lady in the office she had just entered.

"Good morning, I'm here to see Mr. Welnar Zalpah." She replied, admiring the elegant office.

"Do I have you on my appointment list?"

"No, well… no. Just mention my name he knows am coming through."

She scrutinised her briefly, before buzzing her boss.

"Sir, you have a Ms. Laura Mills here to see you."

"Laura." He interjected knowingly. "Send her in."

"Okay, sir."

"You can go in." She informed her.

"Thank you." Replied Laura, feeling a bit nervous.

She had met Mr. Welnar Zalpah at Kodelly's house once. They'd had a brief conversation, through which Laura had learned of his company and was invited to call on him anytime she was in town.

This was anytime, she thought, walking into his big office after knocking formally. She had been contemplating on calling on him for the past few days, especially since her job responses had so far not been fulfilling.

"Hello." He said in a gullible voice.

"Good morning." She replied, sounding a bit too formal for her liking.

"Take a seat."

She obliged.

"Well, Laura, what can I do for you?" He asked in a friendly tone.

"I need a job." She stated, surprised at her boldness.

"A job?" He repeated, twitching his thumbs, in front of him, with his arms resting on the table.

"Yes."

"What type of a job?"

She quickly narrated her work experience while he looked at her without paying much attention to what she was saying.

"May I see your résumé?"

She handed it to him.

"Looks good." He said after browsing through it, for some minutes. "How is the new bride doing?"

"She is fine." She replied not wanting to be rude, wondering if he was going to give her the job or not.

He handed back the résumé.

"I am afraid I do not have anything to fit your field at the moment. I'm sorry, Laura."

"Well, I guess this is it." She said, getting up from the chair. "Thanks for your time anyway."

He watched her pick her handbag and place the strap on her right shoulder before she began to walk the distance to the door through which she had just entered, hearing the noise from the television set that was on, in the other side of his huge office. He shifted his gaze to the TV, and she was just about to turn the knob when he spoke again.

"Can you do deliveries?"

"What?" She replied, turning to face him again.

"Deliveries." He repeated, lighting a cigar. "I will pay you good money for it, real good money."

She had stopped in her tracks, paused for a moment, wanting to assimilate what he was talking about.

"What kind of deliveries?"

"Do you want to start today? I have something that needs to be delivered. Come." He motioned to her.

She held her bag close to her and walked to his table, her eyes curiously looking at him.

"This." He said giving her an envelope, "Deliver it at this address and to the specific name." Giving her another paper on which he had scribbled an address. "I will pay you for your transport; in fact, I will buy you a car if you do well. Just be careful and please remember, it is between you and I." He paused for a moment while she read the address silently. "You wanted a job and I have given you one. Now are you going to stand here the whole day or do some driving around?"

"I will do it." She replied, partly aware of the contents of the envelope.

But she had to do it, she told herself. She was not ready to go on driving Kodelly's car and asking her for money. She needed the job; it certainly would not be too strenuous.

"That's my girl." She heard him say. "That's my girl."

She walked out of the office building to where she had parked her car earlier. She memorised the address she had just been given for her first delivery. She started the car's engine and told herself repeatedly that she was going to do it, with a part of her feeling good about herself.

She went back after the first delivery and he immediately knew that she was easy to trust and that they were now, in it together. He then made her do more and more deliveries, guaranteeing her with a pay cheque each time. Within a couple of weeks, he was able to fulfil his promise to her, by buying her a car. Nothing seemed to bother her anymore. She enjoyed the freedom that came with the money he was paying her. Shopping sprees became a part of her lifestyle, while she continued to be on Welnar Zalpah payroll.

_____

CHAPTER NINETEEN

Kodelly travelled to Summerset with their month-old baby girl. Lidy had insisted that she visits with them and take the much-needed rest, from the busy city and her demanding chores as a wife and mother of a teenager. Little Bimora was a very beautiful and delightful baby who had drawn Bobby's attention and captured his heart, and for the first time he knew exactly what it took to be a father. He now realised what an amazing thing he had missed out on the first time and was learning what an awesome task being a parent entailed. He could still remember how selective and moody his wife had been during her pregnancy. He remembered her impulsive cravings and yet he loved her even more. He enjoyed going with her for the childbirth classes, although he dreaded the idea of being by her side when the actual time arrived. He was excited and was proud to talk to anyone about the soon to be born baby.

He took her to the shops to buy all the things they thought would help them to be better parents. He loved his older son Olly, even though neither of them had revealed the truth to him yet. He felt more secure with him, now that he was married to his mother, but he still had to obey her wish by not revealing the truth about their relationship.

Olly too had been eccentric, holding his baby sister in his arms for the first time and looking at her small, beautiful face.

"She's adorable mom. She is so adorable." He'd said time and again.

He had been so taken by her that he moved in with them for a full month until the day before they left for Summerset. He had always thought that the newlyweds, needed time alone and had decided to live at Kodelly's house all along.

Kodelly was overwhelmed, she was happy to be finally getting her figure back after what seemed like countless months of expansion. She felt overshadowed and listened to Bobby make endless plans for their new baby. The arrival of the new baby simply meant, sleepless nights or at least less hours of sleep, feeding the baby and a countless list of chores and she could not delegate all of them. She needed to bond with her baby, and she was not about to start feeling bored yet, especially since Bobby had insisted that she takes twelve months leave. She had objected, but he seemed adamant with his decision, making her accept her persistent mother's invitation to visit with her for a month or two.

Lidy and her husband had been enthusiastic about their visit. Kodelly was happy to be in Summerset after a long time. She seemed to get more rest, as most of the people around her helped her with little Bimora. She definitely also had a break from the much-polluted air of the industrialised city. She missed Bobby though, and she often wished that she could feel his muscular arms in the night. She missed him hushing love words to her in the secretness of the night. She missed talking with him, even though he telephoned her every day, enquiring about how she and the baby were. He often enticed her to cut her stay short, telling her that he just could not live without her. They had not been apart since they got married and she too was finding it hard to be away from him, but she had the guarantee of their wedding ring that no matter how far or where she was, her heart would always belong to him.

*   *   *

Bobby sat in the lounge after having a wonderful, homemade, Sunday meal. He still had a month to be alone in the mansion before his wife and daughter returned from Summerset. He had a glass of beer before him and was listening to some classic music. The house was exceptionally quiet since no one worked there on Sundays.

The doorbell rang; he got up from the couch and walked to the door, wishing that his butler had not been off duty and then he would have to do what he knows best. He opened the main door and standing in front of him was a well-groomed lady, with dark glasses covering her eyes. She wore a long thick fur coat, which seemed to cover her entire length, with cream sandals on her feet, holding a small bag in her hands.

"Señor' Bobby Mitch?" She spoke, after having stared at him for a moment through her dark glasses.

"Yes." He replied sounding surprised.

"May I come in?" She said, walking past him and taking the gloves off her hands simultaneously, stopping in the hallway to watch him close the door.

"What can I do for you?" He enquired, seeming even more astounded as he led her into the lounge.

"Oh, do for me?" She asked back with a soft laugh. "It is what we can… maybe do for each other. I thought you might be lonely, so I came to keep you busy. I thought we might get acquainted."

"No. Well, I don't know what you mean by acquainted. I am quite a busy man and I chose to be at home not because I am lonely but…"

"Shh, say no more." She cut in softly. "Let our bodies do the talking." Taking her fur coat off to expose her bare body only clad in her underwear.

He looked at her admiringly for a moment, watching her advance towards him. She then threw her arms, gently around his neck, after allowing the coat to drop to the floor.

"Let's have some fun." She whispered.

"No." He replied forcefully. "No. Please, just get dressed and go." He ordered, having pulled away from her.

"Why sugar pie? Nobody has to know. Must I get you in the mood? Should I do some dancing for you, or must I be totally nude?"

"Not here. Not in my house. Please go. I do not appreciate what you are doing?"

"Why?" She asked walking towards him again.

"Because I am married." He replied, surprised at himself. He picked up the coat and threw it at her.

"Afraid of your wife?" She teased.

"I love her, okay… So please just go."

She smiled and then she put the coat back on. She then put on her dark glasses and walked to the door, she stopped before turning to face him.

"You can always give me a call; in case you change your mind." Blowing him a kiss shamelessly. "Bye, Bobby Mitch." She added from the doorway.

He sighed, watching the door close behind her. He was totally flabbergasted by her. He could not believe that she could try and seduce her own cousin's husband. He wondered how long she had been thinking of him in such a way. What was she trying to do? Did she honestly think that he would get down with her? She was attractive, and all the current information on her was that she was on separation, but he never thought that she could actually throw herself at him. He walked to the kitchen and got himself another beer, wishing only to harbour thoughts of his wife.

She walked out of Kodelly's house after failing to seduce her husband. She walked to her car and drove to Mr. Welnar Zalpah's office. She went up the escalator and then up through the stairs like she had done on several occasions, only this time she was not there to collect a delivery but to make a social call. She had been to his office before on Sundays, to collect some deliveries and was almost certain and without a doubt that she would find him there. She let herself through the secretary's office, before opening the door to his office. He sat on the sofa in his office; he was in his late forties but took considerable good care of his image. He shifted his attention from the TV set to the door, watching her approach him.

"I don't remember calling for you." He began.

"Hello, Mr. Zalpah." She replied, ignoring his comment. "Tell me, don't you ever spend time at home?"

"I have a nagging wife and so if I have to think constructively, I need to be somewhere quiet." He admired her coat for a moment. "I didn't call for you, did I?"

"No. No. I just thought we could maybe spend some time together."

"As in?" He asked bluntly.

"Do you have any alcohol here? I can't help myself; I need something to drink."

"Check in my secretary's office."

She knelt in front of him instead and held his face in her palms, caressing his lips with her tongue. His arms went around her body. Their lips parted, feeling the warmth of each other's tongues. Slowly she dropped her fur coat, exposing her bare body. He kissed the length of her stomach whilst undressing. He took her fur coat off completely and undressed her and made love to her savagely on the couch.

* * *

Bobby had just finished taking a bath; his wife and baby would be coming back in a week's time. He had agreed to meet with Olly at the Tennis club; he stepped from the bathroom into the dressing room when he heard some noise in the bedroom. Still wrapped in a towel, he opened the door to their bedroom and there she was, lying on top of their bed cover.

"Come." She said enticingly.

"No. Not you again. What do you want?"

"I want you." She said, getting up from the bed and walking towards him. "And this time you aren't escaping me."

"Nice body." She continued. "Shall I oil you, mmmh?"

"No." He replied. He felt a tingle with her finger movement on his chest.

"Yes." She whispered, "You need me, and I need you." She continued unwrapping the towel from his waist, kneeling, stroking his thighs gently and kissing them, raising herself up before he pushed her away from him. He hurried to the dressing room and shut the door tightly, breathing heavily. No. No. He repeatedly told himself. No Bobby you must not. He quickly pulled some clothes on before opening the door again; to his surprise she was not there and yet her clothes were still on the floor.

"Laura." He called out, leaving the bedroom. He walked towards the staircase and heard someone talking. He could not tell if she was talking on the telephone or if she was with someone. He raced down the stairs and saw her dressed in his towel, closing the door and turning to go back upstairs.

"Where to?" She charmed again. "We aren't anywhere close to finished yet."

He walked past her ignoring her comment; all he wanted was to see whom she had been talking with. He opened the door and saw Rena walking to her parked car. He called her name, causing her to stop in her tracks; she turned to face him and watched him trot to her.

"What do you want?" He asked.

"I came to check if my faithful friend was back, but oops, I had no idea…" She replied.

"It's not what it looks like, damn you."

"Damn me? I didn't say anything, and I didn't come to check on you so don't damn me." She stressed with her finger raised. She paused for a moment and clicked her fingers in the air. "You don't need someone to remind you that you are married, do you Mr. Mitch?

"Bitch, don't you go telling people lies about me. I did not invite her over here. Do you understand?"

"Oh, so you just found it convenient to…"

"I did not." He yelled at her. "I am warning you, if ever I hear a word about what you saw, you will be grossly sorry you ever knew my name."

"So, you are asking me to keep my mouth shut, not to tell my own best friend about what I saw?"

"You heard my warning." He charged turning to walk away, as he was afraid that he might just strike her in the face if he continued to stand there.

He walked back to the house and heard Rena's car drive off. He went upstairs to his bedroom where he found Laura standing in front of the dressing mirror, with a glass of wine.

"Nice wine. Care to join me?" She said, with her eyebrows raised.

"You bitch." He charged, grabbing the towel from her, and throwing her clothes at her. "How did you enter my house?"

"I used Olly's keys."

"Can I have them?" He demanded.

"Why?"

"I am not playing games. Can I have the keys?" He spoke again in enraged.

"They are in my bag."

"Now dress up and go. Don't come throwing yourself at me again. You understand?"

She looked at him while handing him the keys. He got the wine glass from her and the bottle of wine.

"Out." He yelled, seeing her still standing there without bothering to start putting on her clothes.

"Out. I don't fucken' care if you dress up in the car or not just get out."

She obliged, hurrying out of the room and down the flight of stairs. She slipped on her clothes at the foot of the stairs and let herself out.

Rena drove back to her apartment, wondering why Bobby would choose to cheat on Kodelly, with her own cousin. She certainly was not going to be the one to tell her of her husband's infidelity. She had her own life to lead and certainly getting mixed up with that would for sure complicate matters, besides she still needed her job, so if ever she let loose the secret it would cost her, her job. Stupid Bobby Mitch, she thought, still feeling the pain on her arm from his handgrip, while he tried to stress his point to her.

Poor Kodelly, her own dear cousin must have been hitting on her husband for the past two months that she and the baby had been away and definitely nothing ever stays a secret; she smiled to herself with content.

*   *   *

Kodelly walked the length of the corridor to her office; she still had the extra weight hanging about her and was just glad that her long leave was finally over. She was aware of the many heads that she was making turn from the office windows she was walking past. She was glad to be back to her busy office, even though she would require a lot of adjusting after having been away for such a long time.

She had returned from Summerset after two months as they had agreed with Bobby. She was hoping that he would have changed his mind about her staying home with the baby for a year, but he had not. She spent the months sitting at home with the baby and entertaining the guests in the garden, over a cup of tea with some cookies, or cake or scones.

Sometimes, she could have wine with cheese later in the afternoon and just wait for her husband to come back from work. What a life, she mused. Bobby would then come back from work and compliment his adorable daughter, sometimes even without taking much regard of his wife. Olly too, was very drawn to Bimora and he hardly stayed away from them. He visited them as often as his busy schedule could permit.

He enjoyed being a part of her life and taking his baby sister for walks. She seemed to be the centre of attention to everyone, making Kodelly feel a little bit jealous. She was only too glad when her leave finally came to an end, as she was tired of the routine.

She knew she had to get rid of some of the weight that she had put on during her pregnancy and during her long leave. She wondered if she was looking presentable enough to fit in the corporate world again.

She had spent a lot of time trying to decide what clothes to wear in the morning. She wished that she would not worry about petty things, especially what people would think of her. She wished that she could be like Lidy, who was content with staying at home and just making herself useful around her husband and home. But again, Lidy was more particular about how she dressed, the way she talked and whom she associated with.

She entered her newly furnished office, smelling the fresh paint on the walls, which had been repainted in anticipation of her return. She walked to her office table. She put her bag on the table, before walking to the window. It was good to be back; at least she would have to use her brain again. She looked forward to meeting with business executives and running her department again. She had lots of work to catch up on though, she reminded herself with a sigh.

The door opened and Rena walked through the door. Her face lit up in a smile and for a moment she wondered why Rena had never visited her since she came back from Summerset with the baby. She had called her occasionally to find out how she was, but had turned down every invitation to visit her, and come up with excuses each time. Kodelly had come to the conclusion that perhaps she felt uncomfortable to spend as much time with her, now that she was a married woman, unlike in the past.

"Rena how have you been?" She greeted her delightedly.

"Fine. Look at you. Look at all that weight." She replied whilst hugging her.

"Don't remind me. I am trying to get myself back in shape."

"And the little girl?" She asked after letting go of the embrace.

"Oh, she is fine. She celebrated her birthday two weeks ago, I thought you would come?"

"I was going to, but something else came up." She lied.

"Thanks for the present. We received it though."

"How is Laura?" Asked Rena again, "I wanted to tell you…" She began to say uncomfortably.

"Rena." Spoke Bobby from behind her. "Shouldn't you be in Production, aren't you busy?" He walked in time to hear her mention Laura's name.

"I am."

"Then what are you doing here, if you are busy? I don't pay you to make idle gossip." He charged firmly.

"Excuse me." She said, leaving the couple alone.

"And what was that all about?" Enquired Kodelly.

"Nothing. I just wanted to spend some time alone with you, my darling wife." He walked to her and kissed her on the lips.

"Not now." She said, pushing him away.

"Why?"

"Because I thought we had enough of that at home, already." She replied crossing her arms in front of her.

"I can never get enough of you, I'm sure that you know that by now."

"I do, but if you don't mind…" She said, stepping away as he tried to kiss her again.

"Oh, I get it. You had enough of me. You don't want to be around me; besides you were so bored to be at home with Bimora. Is that what we mean to you?"

"Stop it. You know that I love you. But I have to be active. I have to do things that require me to think."

"We are so easy to satisfy that you don't need to think anymore?"

"I did not say that. Now either you walk out of this office or …"

"Or what?"

She raised her hand in resignation.

"Fine." He said kissing her on the forehead before walking out of her office.

She sat down in her office chair and picked up the phone to call her maid. She needed to find out how Bimora was doing, even though she felt bad about how she had just treated her husband. She knew Bobby too well and she had a feeling he had something to do with why Rena never visited her. She could not bear to live without her close friends; neither could she live away from Bobby. She did not want him around her all the time, although she loved him. She thought he was just a little, too pushy at times, but again that was all part of the entire marriage package; to have, to love and to honour, she could not deny him his right to be intimate with her. Couldn't he just accept that she had missed being at work though, and not weigh it on a scale of what roused her interest the most? She enjoyed being married to him. She appreciated the respect and stability that came with it. Yes stability, she thought again, thinking about Rena who was still single and attending every party that was rocking the city and she could not blame her entirely.

Maybe Rena just could not trust anyone anymore, or perhaps she had not yet found the kind of person that she wanted to spend forever with. She sighed, thinking about Laura and the changes she had made in her personality and image. She had assumed an expensive lifestyle, which she claimed was augmented by Dinkley Mills, making her wonder if that perhaps, was a step towards their reconciliation. She never for a second doubted her cousin's faithfulness to her husband. She could not have suspected that Laura could have an affair with anyone.

She sighed before getting back into the working mood and forgetting about all the hustles and bustles that surrounded everyday life.

————————————

CHAPTER TWENTY

Rena entered Kodelly's office after she'd been summoned and closed the door behind her. She rarely found time to visit her during working hours; neither did they ever manage to have lunch together, since Kodelly often had to drive back to her home to see Bimora. Rena was content with the arrangement as it meant them seeing less of each other and ultimately, reducing her guilt and chances of opening up on the 'big secret', involving Laura and Bobby.

She had told herself never to gossip about it and each time she came close to opening up, she would remember Bobby's stern warning to her. She wondered why Kodelly wanted to see her. Maybe she had heard of her husband's infidelity and wanted to verify if Rena had heard anything to the same effect?

"Rena." She began, as soon as she'd entered her office. "I hope you will not find an excuse to go away just now?"

"It's Bobby I'm afraid of actually." She confided, talking almost in a whisper. "He doesn't seem to like me hanging around you."

"I will handle Bobby." She interjected. "Is he the reason why you have distanced yourself from me?"

"No. No." She lied, hating herself for being there. "What did you want to ask me?"

"Ask...Oh...It's about Laura..." Kodelly continued, raising her hand in the air for a moment.

"Laura...What about her?" She asked back urgently, causing Kodelly to raise her eyebrows in surprise.

"Is there some conflict between the two of you? Why did you react sharply when I mentioned her name?" She asked again with concern.

"I did not." She defended.

"Oh, come on, is it the expensive car she now drives or the expensive clothes?"

"No. No, you know that she is just not a pleasant person and if you called me to gossip about her, I'm not interested..."

"Tell me about it. You, not being interested in gossip?"

"Yes." She replied firmly, biting her lower lip, least she talks about the big secret.

"Never mind." She said dismissing her suspicion. "But I'd like you to do me a favour." Watching Rena listen to her intently, her arms folded in front of her.

"I want you to go to the coast for me."

"What for?" She asked curiously.

"Dinkley Mills is currently living there. I will give you his details and his photo. He hangs around at one of the pubs. I'd like you to pretend…"

"No. No. No, I ain't doing any of that nonsense." She protested. "If they can't be together… too bad, but we won't help them fix their broken relationship. The love between them is dead, honey, forget it."

"Please, I'm begging you. It hurts me to see Laura here, away from the ranch, Dinkley too. She doesn't belong here. Mum now has to help out taking care of her two, teenage girls."

"What do you want me to do?"

"No sleeping." She giggled. "I just want you to give him a hard time, swindle him or something. Anything to make him come back to his senses, please?"

"Really, I don't know if I should do this. I don't really like Laura."

"You won't like Dinkley too. He is more of the old-fashioned type."

"I see."

"Does it mean you will do it?" She asked with renewed enthusiasm.

Rena nodded.

"I will book you into a nice hotel and if you could please be on tomorrow's flight."

"And work…leave?

"Leave that to me. Bobby is my husband, remember?" She said winking at her as she spoke.

"And please remember also that I am only doing this for you and not for Laura."

"Okay, stop nagging and put up your best act."

"Okay. Does Bobby know about this?"

"No, I'm just worried about Laura. I think that she is probably lonely and of course Dinkley Mills is making a perfect jerk of himself down at the coast; spending the family fortune he has worked so hard for on beer and women, I suppose." She paused for a moment rubbing her fingers on her forehead.

"Thank you, Rena, and please keep me informed."
"I will." She replied, before leaving her office.

*   *   *

It was a hot Saturday afternoon; Bobby entered one of the rough middle-class pubs, which was normally not his pass time. He had decided to have a beer or two with the down to earth folks. He was tired of the high-class pubs with all the sophistication, class and affluent people. He felt bothered by Laura, and yet he did not know how to draw the line. How could he turn down such persistent seduction from a woman? For how long could he deny her, he wondered whilst ordering a cold beer. He was also bothered by the fact that he had not informed his wife about her behaviour, but then again, she would never find out about the time that Rena found her at his home, their home. Maybe he should let her know, but again that would spoil the relationship between the two cousins, he thought, taking a swing from his glass of beer.

The pub was quite full and hot. He listened to the mostly rough men discuss their private lives, talking about women and their fantasies carelessly, with t-shits sticking onto their sweaty backs. He ordered his second beer, taking a swing at it and allowing his worriers to drown in the glass of beer. He felt relaxed, as he watched the women dressed in their cheap jeans and shirts, seemed to be having a great time. He wished for a moment that he could frequent such places and not the high-class pubs, where it was all about who was CEO of what corporation and who had the bulls or the cash-cow or the dog? Who was driving what car and definitely the woman present in one's company normally mattered and naturally, they could be very expensive to satisfy. He felt relieved that he was now married and so many steps away from having to please such women.

"Hello Bobby…" He heard a voice speak from behind him, above the noise. "Here's a man who gave up his freedom to a day's joy and recognition. Your wedding only lasted a few hours, but you my darling, are now miserable for life."

He turned, still sitting on the stool by the bar.

"Come." She invited, before he could say a word to her.

He followed her through the jammed tables and seats to the exit door, amid sweaty odours. She certainly did not fit into the crowd. She appeared too decent for the place, unlike most of the women there, who were busy taking swigs from the glasses not minding who saw them. She was dressed in an expensive blue dress, with slits on both sides and expensive silver shoes.

They stepped outside of the pub and the sunlight greeted their eyes. He then stopped in his tracks and turned her to face him.

"What do you want?" He charged.

"I have a surprise in store for you." She replied, motioning him to follow her again. He obliged, crossing the road and walking a short distance before they entered into the hotel foyer. It was not such an expensive hotel, he noticed upon entering the premises.

"They serve beer, even here." She spoke again, emphasising the fact that he did not belong in the pub from which they had just come. He followed her up the stairs to the rooms. She produced a key and unlocked the door to one of the rooms and he entered after her. He felt enraged by her but kept himself calm.

"Is this the surprise?" He asked in a level voice.

"No, it is only about to begin." She replied seductively, unbuttoning his shirt hurriedly, wanting to kiss his chest. She unzipped her dress while standing in front of him.

"Let's make love." She whispered. "Make love to me…"

He pushed her away from him and then grabbed her on her arms, shaking her fiercely and then slapping her on both sides of her face.

"Laura, make this the last time, you hear? You understand?" He charged with rage, watching as she squirmed and covered both sides of her face with her hands.

"No." She screamed. "You are hurting me."

"You disgust me." He said, letting go of her and walking away from her while buttoning his shirt, before storming out of the room. He hurried out of the building and crossed the road to where he had parked his car, contemplating on how to tell Kodelly.

He needed to get home and take a bath. He felt filthy from the conversations he had been listening to, as well as from Laura's touch. He needed to be home with his wife and their baby. Yes, their baby he told himself whilst driving back home. He got home to the loving arms of his wife. He made love with her, blocking away any obstacles that could have been in the way. He loved Kodelly, he repeatedly told himself while holding her close to himself. She was the one he had chosen to spend forever with. Yes, she and their children were what mattered the most to him. They were his family, his life, he reassured himself again and again.

*   *   *

Kodelly stood looking through the bedroom window in the darkness of the night. The lights had been turned off and Bobby was asleep, she on the other hand could not sleep. She had not heard from Rena since she flew out a week ago, making her wonder if everything was okay? She wondered how she was going to know Dinkley Mills, since she had left the photo on Kodelly's office table? She had never met him in person. so how was she going to carry out their plan, she wondered? A part of her insisted on travelling to the coast to see how things were and yet a part of her kept asking her what excuse she would give her husband. She wished that she had been more open with him about it in the first place, and then he could have known and understood her concerns for her cousin.

She had thought about it the whole day and yet she could not find an excuse that was believable. She could not let Bobby know about the expedition with Rena. He could talk them out of it. But she had to do it for Laura's sake. She needed to get her back with Dinkley Mills.

Bobby turned, trying to feel his wife's presence in the bed before he opened his eyes.

"I could swear it feels like winter if you are not lying next to me." He said in a sleepy voice. "Sweetheart, what are you doing up so late?"

"I just couldn't sleep." She replied, coming out from the curtains, and walking towards the bed.

"Wanna talk about it?"

"Yes." She heard herself say. "I wanna go to the coast tomorrow."

"What?" He exclaimed, becoming fully awake. "What?"

"I want to go to the coast for a day or two, please?"

"Why, what's there?" He asked again, sitting up and leaning against the pillows after turning the lamp on.

"I... well want to go and buy something."

"Something like what? Shouldn't we go together? Bimora would love that."

"No. No. I need to go alone. I already made ..."

"Okay, okay you don't want to be seen around with me?"

"No. No. I just need to travel. Must I explain everything? In fact, there is nothing to explain. I just want to be down at the coast, please?"

"Well, if you insist. I'm sure you have a good reason for your decision."

"Thanks." She said before hugging and kissing him. "Thanks, honey." She felt relief from part of the stress and confusion.

At least she could travel the next day, she told herself and then she would find out why Rena had not called her yet and if she was still going to do as they had planned.

*   *   *

She arrived late in the afternoon. She could feel the heat as she walked to the cab. She hired a cab and informed the driver of her destination, after sitting in the back seat. She pulled the newspaper and began to read through it until they arrived at the hotel where Rena was booked. It was not the same hotel that Bobby had booked her in the time which seemed so long ago; in fact, it was quite a distance from the coast even though one could hear the raging waters. She got out of the cab and paid her fare as the porter hurried to welcome her. He carried her bag whilst she stood for a moment staring at the hotel.

Kodelly wore dark glasses to protect her eyes from the sun, with a fine dress, with sandals on her feet. It was quite a long flight, and she felt a bit tired, if not too tense she realised. She walked into the foyer and to the reception desk of the huge, beautiful hotel. The porter stood behind her, waiting for her to get service.

"Welcome Madam, what can I do for you?"

"I'd like to find out if Rena Goof is still booked here?" She began.

"In a second." He replied, typing something on the computer.

"Yes, she is." He said after a pause.

"Is she in her room, perhaps?"

"No. She went out. Would you like to leave a message for her?"

"No. I'd like to check in. I booked a double room yesterday?"

"And your name is?" He asked, taking the details, and handing her the room keys thereafter.

She went up to her room, with the porter still carrying her bag.

"Thanks." She said, giving him a tip after reaching her room.

She shut the door and took off her clothes, thereafter, she took a long refreshing shower.

She dressed up quickly, too eager to see Rena. In a moment she left her hotel room for Rena's. She got to her room, knocking on the door for a while, and then after realising that she was not yet back, she went back to her room and ordered a meal.

She fell asleep after the meal and woke up only an hour later. She washed her face again and walked to the window. She drew the curtains and looked down onto the pavement and right in front of her eyes, she saw her coming out from a car that had just pulled in the driveway. A gentleman came from the driver's seat, kissing her on the lips, they stood for a moment, and she realised that it was Dinkley Mills. Great she told herself, Rena was working exactly according to their plan. But why hadn't she called her to let her know how far she had gone with their plan, she wondered watching as Dinkley got back into the car before driving off. Rena walked into the hotel building and Kodelly pulled away from the window.

She felt excited, wanting to run to her hotel room, but she restrained herself. She would give her some time to rest a bit before calling on her; after all she was working according to their plan. She envisaged that they would definitely go to the beach the following day.

About half an hour later, Kodelly stood knocking on Rena's hotel door. The door opened a few seconds later and Rena's mouth opened in surprise.

"Kodelly!" She exclaimed. "What are you doing here?"

"May I come in?" She asked calmly, ignoring her friend's surprise.

"Yes. Yes." She replied, still unable to hide her surprise.

"So, you managed to meet Dinkley Mills? How have you been?"

"Fine. Fine." She replied carefree. "I just love the beach."

"So, how are things going on between you and Dinkley?" She asked quizzically. Kodelly looked refreshed from her shower, and she had no make-up on.

"How did you know that it was him? I noticed that you'd left his picture, that's more so the reason why I came." Kodelly continued.

"Well... I didn't know that it was Dinkley." She replied, catching her unawares.

"What do you mean? Why didn't you call me? So how far are you with our plan?"

"I went to the pub for the first two days, I was trying to get hold of you, but it was always after hours, and you were not in the office." She paused for a moment.

"And...?" Kodelly cut in.

"And some man approached me, he was nice to me, he treated me like a lady. We had a drink or two. We arranged to meet the next day. I didn't know that it was him... He gave me a different name..."

"Well and then...?"

"We went to the beach. We had fun... Kodelly, I didn't mean to, but we fell in love. I am in love with him."

"You are kidding me, right?" She said, looking her in the eyes and smiling at her and yet she did not smile back but instead, she kept a serious face.

"No. No, Kodelly that is exactly what happened." She said, raising her arm and with the movement of her hand she lite a cigarette that she took from the counter.

"Rena, you can't be in love with him." She charged, sensing the magnitude to what she had just said and following her in her steps.

"I found out his real name afterwards." She replied, stopping to face her.

"After what?" She paused, waiting for an answer that never came forth, "After sleeping with him?" She finished off and raising her hand to her forehead.

"How could you do this to me? My own friend sleeping with my cousin's husband?"

Rena felt like this could be an opportunity to stand level and tell her about her own husband's infidelity with her cousin. Maybe that would ease the disappointment and make her understand that some things just happen.

"I'm sorry," She said instead. "but we're both in love with each other." Adding as a matter of fact.

Kodelly stood in shock for a moment, unsure of what to say or do. She looked at Rena who could only confess of her newfound love. She could never have anticipated that Rena could fall for Dinkley Mills. But who was she to decide who must fall in love with who and whom not to fall in love with?

"I'm sorry." She heard her say again. "But that's just how things are between us. He loves me. I know he does."

"I have to go." She said firmly, unable to hide her disappointment and outrage at herself for being so naïve. "I will fly back to Goldring city tomorrow. I will pay your hotel bill up to today. You still have your return air ticket, should you decide to come back to your senses." She added coldly.

"Can't you be happy for me?" She charged. "All my life I have been looking for someone. Someone to treat me with respect, not someone to call me… a bitch. I have finally found him. He brings out the best in me…" She said to Kodelly, who had turned to leave her hotel room, causing her to stop in her tracks. She turned to face her again.

"He is already taken Rena. Dinkley Mills is very married, and I will not discuss any options. Bye." She said softly, but firmly before walking out of her hotel room.

* * *

She flew back to Goldring city. She could not help but to blame herself for making Rena fall in love with Dinkley Mills. If only she had not come up with her so-called brilliant plan, to get Laura and Dinkley back together. If only they had not separated in the first place! Dinkley Mills had some of the attributes that Rena always wanted in a man, she realised, he had the looks, a bit of class and money. Which is everything she had been looking for in a man. She pushed away the gloomy feeling and opted to think about her husband. He would probably be just knocking off from work she realised, by the time she gets home. She needed him to whisper loving words to her and make her feel good about herself again. She had totally been let down by Rena and just needed to be with someone she could always love and trust. Yes, her husband.

She arrived at the airport and was driven home in a cab. She got out of the car, watching it drive off before she saw the butler hurry to her.

"Good afternoon, madam." He greeted as he picked up her bag.

"Good afternoon." She replied.

"Master Bobby said to tell you to go to the house as soon as you get back." He informed, walking to the house with her.

"What?" She asked startled, stopping in her tracks for a moment. "Anything wrong?"

"No."

"Is Olly fine?"

"Yes, master Olly is fine, but they said you must go there as soon as you arrive. He said they phoned the hotel and you had already booked out, so they thought you might be flying back." He explained, standing in the hallway with her.

"Thank you." She replied, turning to go to her car and wondering why they wanted her at the house.

She drove through the busy roads with caution, despite her fatigue and stress and finally found herself at the house. She got out of the car and hurried into the house.

Bobby met her in the hallway. He had heard her car from upstairs.

"Thank goodness you are here." He stated, hugging her.

"What's wrong?" She asked again, feeling alarmed.

"It's Laura. She is quite not well. We called the doctor for her. Let's go upstairs, I'm sure he has finished with the examinations."

"I see." She replied, feeling less anxious and following him up the stairs.

"Mom," Greeted Olly. "how was your flight?"

"Not so tiring I must say, though I got a bit of a scare when the butler summoned me here." She paused for a moment when the door to Laura's bedroom opened.

"How's she Doctor?" She asked, as soon as the doctor was out in the corridor with them.

"She needs some rest. But the indications so far seem to show that Laura is on some sort of mmmh, an addictive drug." He paused at Kodelly interjection.

"What! I must see her…"

"This is not time to play jungle my lover. You will go in there only when you are calm. I will send the rest of the test results tomorrow."

"Thank you, Doctor." Spoke Bobby.

"It's a pleasure to be of service to you."

"I will walk you to the door." Offered Bobby.

"Thank you." He replied, going down the stairs with Kodelly and Bobby.

"I suggest that you all give her time to rest before disturbing her. I just gave her some medication. You can go home and relax a bit. I'm sure you must be tired after your flight?" Advised the doctor obstinately.

"Is that okay honey?" Cut in Bobby. "Olly is staying over at our place, he came yesterday. Did you enjoy the coastal air?"

"It was hot." She replied not wanting to divulge any more details, especially since she had not even been to the beach.

*   *   *

Laura woke up in the middle of the night, still feeling drowsy from the medication she had been given by the doctor. She got out of bed and changed from her pyjamas, into some other warm outfit. She walked to the door, opening it gently; not wanting to wake the maid who had been instructed to occupy the room next to her in case she needed anything in the night. She walked down the corridor, hearing only her breath. She entered the room that used to be occupied by Kodelly and went to the wardrobe. She opened the wardrobe and found what she was looking for without much effort. She then tiptoed down the stairs still feeling drowsy. She got out of the house and got into her car, before driving herself into town.

She stopped in front of the familiar building, feeling weak but determined to go all the way. She sat for a moment in the car to regain her strength. Then she got out of the car and went up the escalator, and then she got into the elevator, up to the floor where, Welnar Zalpah's office was. She could see that the light was still on in his office. He probably had not been home since he came to the office earlier in the morning. She opened the door and saw him coming towards the door, just about to leave.

"Laura, what are you doing here so late?" He began.

"Shut up and just do as I say." She said in a shaky voice.

"What the hell is wrong with you?" He asked again firmly, "I employed you to deliver stuff, but it looks to me that you have been using it."

"Do as I say." She said through clenched teeth, feeling the perspiration all over her body. "You and I," She continued to speak beginning to cry. "are going to the Islands for a holiday. Okay?"

"You must be out of your mind. I have got a wife."

"I said, do as I say." Pulling a gun from her pocket and pointing it at him.

"You will phone them after we have reached the Islands. After all, you have a nagging wife." She reminded.

"Laura, you must reconsider what you are doing." He tried to reason with her.

She laughed, wiping away the tears with one hand.

"I love you." She said with a chuckle through her very dry lips. "Don't we love each other? Don't we?"

"Yes...yes, we do." He said with his arms raised, obeying her every command, after noticing her drastic mood swings, too afraid of what she might do to him.

She was very high on drugs it seemed, and anything could happen to her at any moment. She was irrational but she was also armed and knew every bit of detail about Welnar Zalpha that could cause a stir in society if he was linked to drug dealing.

"Yes, this is what this is about...love. Yes, love." She added with another feeble laugh. "Love of money and love of lust...I love you..." blowing him a kiss as he walked next to her, her lean body covered in a coat. She then smiled at him as they exited the building.

*　　*　　*

The maid phoned Bobby's house early in the morning and informed them that madam Laura was not in her room. She seems to have left the house at some time in the night because her car was also not in the garage, she explained painstakingly. They, in turn had phoned the doctor who had confirmed that she was on a drug. Bobby and Kodelly had then been forced to inform Dinkley Mills, cutting short his rendezvous with Rena. They had no idea where she could have gone, especially since they were not aware of her association with Welnar Zalpah.

Dinkley Mills had promised to immediately fly to Goldring city and had managed to get there on the same day in the afternoon. Kodelly appeared worried throughout the whole day, wondering what could have happened to Laura? She had been consoled that her dear cousin had just ran away, since she had taken off with her car, although no one had seen the car anywhere so far.

How could they have not known earlier that she was on drugs, she wondered, wanting to take responsibility for her cousins' actions?

The butler introduced the presence of Dinkley Mills, who had just arrived, to Kodelly and Bobby who were sitting in the lounge.

"Dinkley, how good of you to come." She said, getting up from her chair and shaking hands with him, with him kissing the back of her hand.

"How have you been, Kodelly?"

"Fine." She replied lightly. "Please, meet my husband, Bobby Mitch."

"Dinkley, it is nice to finally meet you." He spoke shaking his hand, at that moment the butler walked through again to introduce another guest, Doctor Marcus.

"Good afternoon lady and gentlemen." He greeted them all, having been in no haste to bring the test results after learning that Laura had already ran away.

"Doctor Marcus." Kodelly spoke urgently, eager to know the details of the test results.

"Are they what you suspected yesterday?" Enquired Bobby.

"Yes, unfortunately she is on drugs." He replied, turning to look at Dinkley before disclosing all the details, in line with the doctor/patient confidentiality ethics. "Who is he?"

"Her husband. Laura's husband." Filled in Kodelly eagerly.

"Congratulations." He said, turning to face Dinkley again, "despite the addiction, your wife is going to have a baby... soon."

"What!" They all exclaimed in shock, with Dinkley taking a step forward and grabbing the doctor by the collar.

"It is not my baby." He said between clenched teeth.

Bobby stepped in quickly to separate the two.

"Dinkley, no. Let's all be rational." Bobby advised him.

"Rational. My goodness what has become of her?" He said moving away from the doctor.

"I'm sorry Doctor." Bobby apologised on Dinkley's behalf. "But are you sure that she is going to have a baby?"

"Yes. I thought you all knew about it." He said, straightening up his shirt. "She only has a few months left to go. That, I could tell even without doing the test, but I did a test just to be sure." Supporting his theory with the test results, which were on paper before handing them to Bobby, as an awkward silence filled the room.

"I have to go now. I have other duties to carry out. For the sake of the baby she is carrying, I hope that she beats the drug addiction."

"My apologies." He repeated once again to the Doctor, while Dinkley paced in the background.

"It's okay." He replied, looking with loath at Dinkley for a moment.

"I will send the cheque tomorrow." Spoke Bobby again.

"Thank you." He said, showing himself to the door, wondering whom the father of Laura's baby was if her husband claimed not to be.

He got into his car and drove away, leaving everyone in the house wondering what to do next or if it was well worth their while to worry about Laura with her drug addiction and her purported pregnancy, especially since she was an adult?

* ——————————— *

BOOK FOUR

CHAPTER TWENTY-ONE

They had not heard from Laura since the night that she had ran away from the house. Lidy and her husband had been very disappointed when they heard the news about her disappearance and the fact that she was on drugs and was expecting a baby. She had always been a nervous wreck, but no one could have suspected that she would resort to taking drugs. She must have gone into depression, since she had been suppressing the fact that she was not hurt by her separation from Dinkley, they all speculated. But one might have thought that the expensive cars and shopping sprees could compensate, perhaps in kind for the loneliness. Everyone speculated without conclusion or having a clue on whom the man behind the pregnancy could be?

Rena had learnt about Laura's disappearance with a paroxysm of joy. She had continued her relationship with Dinkley Mills, who had promised her hand in marriage as soon as they could find Laura and get her to sign the divorce papers. Then, Rena Goof would become the new Mrs. Dinkley Mills. She too was expecting Dinkley's baby. She had however, no idea or knowledge of Laura's pregnancy, which Kodelly had made sure to withhold from her. She had betrayed her trust and friendship, making her feel forever guilty for having initiated the whole plan, instead she had fallen hopelessly in love with Dinkley, who had brought out the woman in her with his gentleman's charm.

Bimora was quite a big girl and was still adored by the two men in her family, who made her believe that she was a princess who deserved to be treated as such. Olly had been forced to move in with his parents, especially after they had realised that Laura had ran off with Kodelly's gun. The affection between Kodelly and Bobby had also grown stronger. She could almost hopelessly wonder what her life would be without him. He seemed like the only person she could trust, especially after being betrayed by her best friend, who was now living her fantasy life with Dinkley Mills. She had insisted that she had not gone between the two of them. They had already been on separation for over a year when she got involved with him. She found him to be sweet and charming, making her wonder, how he had ever lived his life with the quiet and secretive Laura for so many years.

Dinkley Mills had not been initially aware that his new girlfriend and Kodelly were close friends, even though he seemed to have learnt later on that they knew each other by working for the same corporation; from which Rena had subsequently resigned. He had no idea that it was Kodelly's cunning way of thinking that had permitted him to meet with such a beautiful, highly sexy, looking woman with big breasts.

He had phoned Kodelly once, after flying back to the coast. He had requested them to keep him informed should any news on Laura reach them, following her disappearance. Kodelly was however, a bit surprised to receive a call from him since she had not heard anything about Laura as yet.

"Hello." She'd answered.

"Hello, is that Kodelly?" Came a male voice on the other side of the line.

"Yes. Who is this?"

"Dinkley."

"Dinkley…, how are you?"

"I'm fine." He replied, pausing for a moment.

"Is it news about Laura…?"

"No. No…I just wanted to talk to you. To hear your sweet voice; Kodelly you are still so beautiful. You have defied age with your beauty. My sweet…"

"Dinkley …" She interjected. "We have not heard from Laura, okay. I will call you, should we hear anything. Bye."

"Wait…Wait." Hearing the phone go quiet on the other side.

He tried to call her again, but she had declined his calls. She was happily married to Bobby, and nothing was going to change that. She blamed Dinkley for Laura's situation, if only he had loved her as he should have and helped her overcome her insecurities, then none of this could have happened. She could not have disappeared with a pregnancy of a man whom no one knew of, neither could he and Rena, her ex-best friend have been sharing a bed in intimacy. It was just too much for Kodelly to comprehend.

*   *   *

Kodelly's mother and father had been visiting with them; they had arrived the previous day, after Bobby persuaded her to invite them. He felt that it was now time for everyone to know the truth that he actually was Olly's real father, and not anything else that they had all along been made to believe.

She stood in front of the full, length-dressing mirror and admired her image for a moment. Then she looked at her fingers, rubbing her wedding ring. She felt uneasy about the whole thing. She was happily married, yes happily married and so it must be the best thing to do. Yes, after all these years, it was not going to be a secret anymore. Everyone would know. Indeed, they would all know, she told herself. The bedroom door opened, and Bobby walked in. He was dressed in one of his tuxedos, expensive shoes, and wore a rich perfume. He came and stood behind her, sliding his arms around her waist.

"You look beautiful. If you could only stop worrying." He began, trying to encourage her, "Everything will be fine. I am Olly's father. Everyone deserves to know. Olly has a right to know."

"I know, but I am not just sure how he will handle it?" She replied.

Thinking for a moment about the years she had spent alone without Bobby by her side, wondering if they could all just overlook that and carry on, as though, he had been there all their lives.

"I don't know too. But whatever happens, happens. You and I will still be together, whether they accept the news or not. I am here for you, now and forever."

She nodded.

"I love you Kodelly." He continued, "Now, I want to see a smile on your face and in your eyes. Come on…" He enticed playfully. "Dinner is almost served; we don't want to keep anyone waiting."

"Okay." She said before kissing him passionately.

They had decided to break the news at dinner; it would be the most appropriate time, most convenient and the most decent way.

"Dinner is ready." Announced the butler after the couple had gone downstairs.

He watched the wealthy family walk into the dining room, grandparents, child, son-in-law, and grandchildren. They all took their seats at the table, chatting causally for a moment.

"Must I bring the first course now?" Enquired the butler after a moment.

"Yes." Replied Bobby, waiting for him to disappear before clearing his throat and attracting everyone's attention.

He felt hungry above everything else and was looking forward to eating the food that smelled lusciously, through the kitchen doors.

"We have some very important news to share with you all." He said, looking from one person to the next in the order in which they were seated at the table.

Before he could go any further, the dining room door opened and Laura walked through with her six months old baby in her arms, drawing everyone's attention. She looked a bit unkempt, even though she wore clean clothes. Her hair was roughly combed, and some bags were visible beneath her eyes. She looked as if she had gone for some days without getting proper sleep. She looked back at them for a moment and then to her warmly wrapped baby before she broke the silence that had followed her entrance.

"Bobby, your baby." She announced, extending her arms with the baby towards him, causing an immediate mayhem to arise.

*　　　*　　　*

Kodelly sat in her bedroom back at her own house; she still remembered what a catastrophe the evening had ended up in. She recalled Lidy's face darken with rage, after Laura had made the announcement. Bobby charged against her allegations, even though no one really believed him. They all thought it somehow made sense that the child Laura was holding was his. Somehow, in the midst of all the confusion Bobby had stood his ground and made the announcement he had been waiting for, for so long. Olly Mitch it should have been all those years and not Olly Mollar as he was called, causing even more confusion at the dinner table, at which everyone had lost their appetite. Olly had asked Kodelly if it was true, she looked dumfounded for a moment, not knowing what to say. Then Olly had stormed out on his parents, insisting that he needed to go to Summerset with his grandparents for a while. He walked away from his parents as though they were two monsters that he could not even bear to face.

They had followed him to his room, begging him to understand how difficult it had been for them to keep the truth from him and yet he did not even care to listen. As far as he was concerned, they were two of the most selfish people he had ever known. Why even bother to let him know that he was that child they probably had never wanted in the first place? Despite their money and wealth, he could not understand or stand to face them, and he thought that perhaps they would change their minds about his paternity later on down the line. As a result, he had made up his mind to travel to summerset with his grandparents, who had also decided to cut their stay short.

Kodelly, who was still in shock at what had transpired, decided to call Rena in the middle of the night and informed her of Laura's reappearance and her allegations against Bobby. Rena had then sat up, fully awake and narrated her encounter with Bobby the time when she had been away.

"Why didn't you tell me?" She'd asked sobbingly.

"Because Bobby told me not to." She replied stupidly.

"But...I was your friend?" She cried.

"You still are my friend." She tried to comfort. "We still are friends." She added, only too glad to receive a call from Kodelly after such a long time. "I will come over tomorrow if you need me?"

"No. No. I will be fine. I will deal with it, somehow." She'd replied, cutting the line and dismissing all her doubts about Bobby's innocence.

He was not innocent; he could be the father of Laura's illegitimate child, or else he could not have threatened Rena from telling her what she had seen. The bastard, she thought with rage. She stormed back into their bedroom and announced to Bobby, who lay wide awake that she was divorcing him for what he had done to her. She could not stand the fact that everyone else knew about his sleeping around with Laura, except her of course. He had tried to deny it again, but when he heard her mention Rena's name, he knew that it would take more than just convincing her to prove that Laura was lying.

How could something so perfect go so wrong, how could she have not known that her husband was having an affair with her own cousin? If, maybe, it had been some other woman, she could have forgiven him, but not with her feeble, cousin Laura, she thought again. Looking at the wedding ring that she had removed from her fingers and was now on top of the table.

She had filed for divorce through her lawyer. She believed that what Bobby had done to her was unforgivable. What made it worse was that he did not even have the decency to take her somewhere else but defiled their wedding bed. Laura had no boyfriend, making all the pieces to the puzzle fit in. It just had to be Bobby's child, that Laura had borne.

Lidy and her husband had returned to Summerset with Olly, insisting to take Bimora too, until the two could sort out their problems, but Bobby had refused to hear of it. He was fond of his daughter, and it seemed like she was the only one who had remained loyal when everyone else had deserted him.

Laura was considered unfit to be around the baby and much as Lidy was hurt with what she had done to her daughter, stealing her man again, she decided to go to Summerset with the baby, until Laura was fully rehabilitated. Laura, whom she hated to talk to because of her uncouth behaviour, had agreed to go for rehabilitation.

The baby, thought Kodelly with renewed pain, wondering if that would be the constant reminder of her husband's infidelity? Bobby had refused to do what everyone had insisted, going for a DNA test. Insisting that his word was enough to be trusted, not even if it was the only way to salvage his marriage. Kodelly sighed, wondering if she would ever get used to sleeping in the bed alone, without Bobby by her side. She wondered how long it would take to get over the loneliness, but her biggest pain was her son's constant refusal to speak to her.

*　　*　　*

Bobby adjusted his collar; it was the third time he was going on a dinner date with his mother-in-law in the last three months. Lidy had over the last three months kept close contact with Bobby Mitch, even though she found her son-in-law's behaviour disgusting. She was not ready to lose contact with Bimora. The poor child needed her more than anything. She wished that she could get her from him and raise her into a perfect lady. She was outraged to find out that Bobby Mitch was the one who had walked off her pregnant daughter and that she could take him back after so many years was unbelievable. It was shameful for her daughter to take him back; it made her stoop very low. He just hurt her again, she realised, by sleeping with her own cousin. She had not been so much in touch with Kodelly, whom she blamed for her husband's behaviour. She had allowed Laura to come too close to her family and permitted her in the process to destroy her marriage.

"First she steals Dinkley Mills from you. No. No, that was not enough, now this? You shouldn't have trusted her again. Are you happy now?"

"Mom, I had no idea that Laura could do this to me."

"No idea? I did say to you the first time 'look at what Laura has done' but you said you were not in love with Dinkley, but what about this… reducing your husband to a jerk?"

"Mom I only wanted to find out how you are." She tried to explain, upon realising that her mother was still very bitter about everything,

"I will call you some other time." She said, ending her conversation with her.

Bobby sighed, wishing things could go back to what they used to be before Laura came and ruined everything with her lie. He hated to be in the house without Kodelly, whom he now only saw at work. He still was not ready to do the DNA test. He would expect his wife to know better than to believe every story she heard. He had never slept with Laura, why could they not just believe his word like they had believed Laura's word. She did not go for a test to prove that what she was saying was true, she just said it, and everyone believed her.

He thought his relationship with Lidy had actually grown stronger, than when he was happily married to Kodelly, because, now she was able to talk to him more frequently and directly and she seemed to like him more. She had initially insisted that she would stay in a hotel each time she visited, but Bobby had eventually managed to persuade her to stay at his house. She was after all, there to be with Bimora and so she could spend more quality time if they were in the big spacious house. He even gave her one of his cars to drive each time she was around town.

They were taking Bimora for dinner this evening to a very expensive hotel. Kodelly had been aware of it, even though she had not been invited. They drove to the hotel and sat at the table, which had been reserved for them. Kodelly drove to the same hotel with one thought in mind, to see how the two had managed to consummate their relationship. She wanted to know why Bobby was not in Lidy's bad books. Lidy had objected to Kodelly's request for a divorce and she thought it unspeakable that her daughter had kept such important information about Olly's father for so long, away from her and the rest of the family. She should have at least trusted her mother, even though trusting her mother would have meant revealing the secret to Bill and of course the rest of the world. She had refused to intervene for now, and have Olly speak to her again. It was too soon for the lad, whom she believed needed more time to deal with it.

It was a hotel to satisfy Lidy's taste and definitely to make the spoilt Bimora even think of herself as a little princess. Kodelly had no intention of joining them or even so much as to let them see her there.

She went and sat at a table in the corner allowing the menu and the potted plant, which was nearby to conceal her presence. She ordered a drink, watching them as they talked and laughed. She wished that she could go and join them, but then she had not been invited and could not have known of it, had she not had a chat earlier with her daughter on the phone, earlier.

She finished her drink and paid her bill, declining to have dinner when asked by the waitress, but she decided to leave instead. She got up hurriedly and walked quickly out of the dinning sector and was almost out of sight when she bumped into a man.

"Gee, I am so sorry." She apologised, realising that his drink had spilt on both of them.

"Pardon me." He also said, thinking it was his mistake and not hers.

"I am sorry; I should have been looking to where I was going. I can pay for your dry cleaning."

"No, that won't be necessary." He replied. "I'm sure it is not that bad." He paused for a moment, "Leaving already? Would you like to join me for a drink instead?"

"No. I have to go. I'm in a bit of a hurry."

"Okay." Said the well dressed, middle aged man.

"Were you expecting a date?" He asked again.

"No, I was not." She replied firmly again.

"It was nice to meet you. Rather bump into you Ms…?"

"Kodelly Mitch, no Mollar," She replied shaking her head. She extended her hand to shake hands with his already extended hand.

"I am Pedree Laskador."

Pedree Laskador, she thought for a moment, that could not be him. That could not be the man she had seen at the exhibitions. She looked at him, stunned for a moment before he spoke again.

"I would have loved to have dinner with you." He spoke again, realising that she had heard of his name from somewhere, "But since you are in a hurry, please give me a call, we can talk later." Giving her his business card.

"Can I have your number?" He asked again.

"My word, I don't believe that it is you." She said, fishing in her handbag for a business card. "I have actually been to your exhibitions before, in Cambel city."

"How is the older Laskador?" She heard herself enquire.

"He is fine. So, you are an art enthusiast? Anyway, who isn't? There is…, art in almost everything around us. Even human beings are such arts, and my eyes tell me that you are a masterpiece."

She smiled, blushing a bit.

"Do excuse me, I'm not always such a forward speaker, but like I said I'd appreciate if there could be a next time, if you are keen on it?"

"We will see how it goes. Give me a call and then maybe there will be a next time. Gotta' go." She said slipping from his company.

He watched her disappear and then he looked at the business card she had just given him, before he went and sat down to have dinner, amused with himself.

———————

CHAPTER TWENTY-TWO

It was raining heavily and Kodelly was straining her eyes to read the road posts. She stopped the engine by the roadside to retrieve the map once again, trying to figure out where she was. She still had to drive for at least another ten minutes or so, she realised before putting the map back and starting the engine again.

She finally reached the place where she was going, pulling the car to a halt. She sat in the parking, in the open area waiting for the rains to stop. She noticed after a moment or two, a woman hurrying to her car with an umbrella. She seemed to be one of the workers there.

The woman tapped on the car window.

"Hello, I brought you an umbrella." She tried to say showing her an umbrella.

Kodelly opened the door and came to stand in the already opened umbrella. The woman led her into the house, which was being used as office premises. Kodelly closed the umbrella once they were in the building and gave it to the woman who had fetched her from the car.

"Can I help you?" Asked the woman in the reception area.

"Yes. Yes, I am here to see, Laura Mills."

"Oh! Laura, she is so fond of this place, and she is doing quite fine now, I must say." Interjected another woman who was standing next to the reception area. She wore a clean uniform and was well-spoken with a firm figure.

"Come, I will take you to see her." She invited.

Kodelly obliged and followed her lead.

"Are you family?" She asked again.

"Yes. I am her cousin."

"Okay, just wait over here." She said, stopping at the entrance to one of the rooms. "I will be with you in a moment."

Kodelly entered the almost empty room with just a cushioned chair on one side of the wall. She decided to remain standing. She had not seen Laura since the time that she had decided to start her rehabilitation, after ruining an evening that was supposed to unite Kodelly's family. She shuddered at the memory and then, she saw her walk through the door with the elderly woman who had led Kodelly to the room standing behind her.

Laura wore a plain, long dress, with her hair roughly combed, with a good pair of shoes on her feet. She stared at Kodelly emotionlessly.

"I will leave the two of you, for some privacy." She said, closing the door behind her as soon as she had spoken.

"How are you, Laura?" Kodelly began, after the door was closed.

"What do you want?" She asked emotionlessly.

"I wanted to see you. I wanted to know how you are doing?" She spoke, extending her hand to touch her arm gently.

Laura pulled away.

"I am doing fine as you have seen. Now can I go?" She replied, turning her back to her.

She pulled a cigarette from her pocket and lit it through a shaky movement.

"I thought you are not supposed to take any...any...?"

"Drugs?" Laura filled in for her almost yelling as she talked. "Drugs? Well, I'm not. But you know what, I will for as long as I want." She paused for a moment. "Do you want one?"

"No."

"Oh... you just think you are everything. You think you are so perfect..." She said, raising her hand in the air and puffing the smoke from her mouth, "But..." She continued through a laugh, "you are not. You are absolutely nothing..." She charged.

"Why don't you quit what you are doing to yourself and try..." Before she could finish her sentence, Laura charged at her with all her might, causing Kodelly who was caught off guard to stagger until she hit herself against the wall.

Kodelly quickly pushed her away, but she grabbed her again and swung her around pushing her until she fell onto the floor. Laura quickly got on top of her, screaming in the process.

"I hate you. Stay... the hell... away from me, okay. Staaa....y away." Shaking her repeatedly. "Stay away from me, Miss perfect. Stay away from me."

The door opened and two women stepped in, grabbing Laura by both arms, and pulling her up. The elderly woman who seemed to be in charge of the institution stood in the doorway, watching Kodelly get up with Laura still yelling.

"Let go of me. Let go of me."

They dragged her out of the room, past the elderly woman whilst Kodelly got up from the floor and began to straighten herself up.

"What happened?" Asked the elderly woman, awkwardly.

Kodelly looked at her without answering her back, whilst panting.

"She gets a little bit like that sometimes. Aggressive I mean." She continued.

"I see." She replied, her heart still beating fast.

"She is going to be fine. Those are just withdrawal symptoms." The elderly woman spoke again with a wink.

"I see." She replied again with little interest.

"Well, I have to go now." She said, excusing herself from her company and going out from the direction she had just come through a few minutes earlier.

The elderly woman followed behind her. She hurried through the reception area without saying a word and out through the rain to her car. She kicked into her car in disappointment and frustration. She opened the door and let herself in and then she drove back to her house.

It was hot and sunny, unlike the rainy part from which she had just been. She got out of the car in her damp clothes. She got into her house still feeling a bit gloomy. She wished that she could help Laura, but she did not know how. She was glad she had taken a day off from work. She took her clothes off, to take a bath. She took a bath and walked into her bedroom with just a bathrobe about her. There was a gentle knock on the door, before it opened. Pedree Laskador walked into the room with a bunch of flowers in his hands.

"Hello." He greeted, as he walked towards her, "You look lovely." He said, kissing her on the lips.

"Hello." She replied, trying to shake off the gloomy encounter with her cousin.

"I just wanted to see you. I phoned your office, and I was told that you were not in."

"I see." She replied.

He put the flowers on her bed and pulled her gently closer to him and for the first time he kissed her passionately. She kissed him back urgently, throwing her arms about him before the door opened softly, then closed again quickly. She freed herself quickly from him, pulling the bathrobe tightly about her.

"We can't do this." She said urgently, while he looked back at her startled, for a moment.

"Excuse me." She said whilst hurrying to the door.

She knew there could only be one person that could open her bedroom door without knocking. She hurried down the stairs after him and he stopped at the foot of the stairs to confront her.

"I thought you needed a day off," He began. "but I had no idea that you just wanted to have sex."

"It's not what you think." She tried to explain.

"Not what I saw. I bet you couldn't wait to have those divorce papers completed so you could go about doing whatever you wanted, could you?" He paused for a moment, then continued. "I never had sex with Laura, why didn't you believe me?"

She looked at him momentarily.

"I see. You still believe that I slept with your pathetic cousin. She lied to you. But I guess now you do not owe me any explanations. Ex-Mrs. Bobby Mitch." He ended before storming out of her house.

She stood dumbfounded for a moment, whilst holding onto the rail and then, she turned and began to climb the stairs. She knew that he still loved her, even though he did not object to their divorce. The only thing that could have proved that he had nothing to do with Laura could have been the DNA test, but he had objected to that. She remembered how he came to her house every night after she had left his house for the first two weeks. They would make love as if she had not even filed for divorce, then he would leave in the middle of the night and go back to his house. It had been hard for him to let go, but slowly his visits had reduced. She recalled how she often cried after he had left her house, feeling the loneliness all over again.

She could smell his perfume on her beddings and question herself, why? Why something so perfect had to go wrong. But she was determined to stand her ground. If he was not ready to do the test for her, then maybe he just did not care. Maybe Laura was telling the truth; maybe Rena was right about what she claimed to have seen. She reached the top of the stairs and was met with Pedree Laskador.

"I just came to give you this." He said, handing her a piece of paper with his new address on it. "I am no longer staying at the hotel."

"I see. Thanks, anyway. I will see you some other time." She advised, before kissing him back lightly on the lips and then watching him leave her house.

*   *   *

Bobby entered the pub that he had been frequenting in the previous months after Kodelly had left him. It was a glamorous pub and disco. It was usually here where he would start his evening, before going to her house. He would make love to her as if everything was still okay between them, until he felt he just couldn't do it anymore. He had to let go once again. She had hurt him by not trusting him or standing by him.

She should have known better than to believe her cousins allegations and yet he had no way of proving it except to take the DNA test. Maybe if she had decided to trust him, he could have done it for her, but she had decided to act like everyone else. He had certainly disgusted Bill, Kodelly's father, especially after he learned that he was the one who had ruined his daughter's life; by leaving her all those years back. Bill Mollar could not understand how she could have trusted him again and for him it was almost obvious that Laura had told the truth. He had taken advantage of her state of loneliness and vulnerability like he had done of Kodelly, the time when she was still young and naïve.

Bobby sat at his usual seat at the bar, ordering one beer after another. Young girls usually approached him, whom he normally turned away and preferred to enjoy the company of his beer. Then he would drive back to his big house and would normally find his daughter sleeping, except for the maid who normally would appear in the passage and ask if he needed anything, to which he would decline. He wondered if she thought that for one crazy moment, he would go to bed with her.

The music was playing loud, and he had just ordered his second beer. He noticed a group of young girls sitting opposite to the counter, they appeared to be talking about him and giggling. He ignored them for a moment, before one of them walked to him. She sat on the stool next to him. She gave him a smile before speaking.

"Hello, my name is Ariel Nopo." She introduced herself.

"Hello and I have no time for you." He replied.

She immediately laughed.

"We normally see you around, so I thought you probably would do with some company." She continued.

He looked at her exaggerated mark-up as she spoke.

"Do you want a drink?" He heard himself ask.

"Yes."

"Wine?"

"Yes. Thank you."

"Okay get your wine and leave me alone." He said, placing the order with the bar man. "Go back to your friends."

"Okay." She replied, having slipped her hand into his jacket pocket, which hang loosely on the back of his stool.

He stayed on for a while before leaving this time he did not drive back to his house but went to Kodelly's house, even though he wondered if he would find her again with the man, he had seen her with the other afternoon. He allowed himself in with the key he always carried and went up to her bedroom. He opened the door and realised that she was asleep and to his satisfaction, she was by herself. He slipped between her covers and began to kiss her and caress her. Then gently he made love with her.

Kodelly woke up the next day wondering if she had just been dreaming about him. She dressed up, after showering and wondered if Bobby had actually come to her house since he had already left when she woke up. It could only be Bobby; he was the only one who had the keys to her house. What was she thinking, she wondered hurrying down the stairs to the car? She drove to work, reminiscing about the previous night. She got to her office and sat at her table for an hour, and yet she could not concentrate on her work. She could not bear the suspense, so she got out of her office and decide to go and see him, and maybe find out if he really was with her the previous night.

She got to his secretary's office and sitting in her office was a teenage girl in a crimson dress, with leather boots and moderate makeup, browsing through a company brochure.

"Is Bobby in?" She heard herself ask.

"Yes, good morning Mrs. Mitch." Came the polite reply from his secretary.

"Good morning." She answered back, before opening the door to his office.

"I'm sorry I had to leave very early in the morning." He began, as soon as she had walked in.

She was not dreaming, after all she realised with a smile. He actually had been there with her. She had thought he would never desire to be with her again after walking in on her and Pedree Laskador, not that they were doing anything sinister, except kissing. She felt a sting of delight at the memory, though wanting to conceal the fact that she had come to question him about last night. She wished that she could appear upset about it, but she could not.

"What did you want to see me for?" He asked, realising that her mind had strayed.

"Oh! Nothing. I just wanted to find out how Bimora is?" She lied.

"She is fine. I drove her to school this morning." He replied swinging in the swivel chair. "Missing us. We can go off if you want?" He teased.

"No. No. I have a report to finish off. I might see you later."

"Okay." He replied, turning to continue with his work.

She walked out of his office and through the secretary's office. She glanced at the young woman still sitting there and assumed her to be visiting the secretary. She was engulfed with content, knowing that Bobby still desired her.

"May I see him?" She asked excitedly, as soon as Kodelly had disappeared into the corridor.

"Well…" Began the secretary wanting to block her again. "His quite busy."

"Please." She begged and then paused. "Please, may I see him?"

"Okay, go through. He knows that you are here, waiting to see him anyway." She replied resignedly.

"Thanks." She said excitedly, getting up from the chair and walking to his office, her sexual appeal about her.

He immediately recognised her.

"You forgot your business card." She began teasingly, putting it on his executive table. She had taken it from his jacket pocket the previous night at the pub.

"Thanks for bring it back. You had no shame taking it. So, what can I do for you?"

"I thought we could spend some time together and have fun." She replied seductively.

"No." He replied firmly.

"Why?"

"Shouldn't you be in school or something and what do you do, anyway, always hanging out at the club?"

"I... I am not busy at night. I have a rich dad who is always so busy trying to make an extra dollar and," She said walking across the office playing with her bag. "a mom, who is always thinking of putting an extra diamond in her ring, so that leaves me with plenty of time to myself."

"I see." He said, watching her now walk towards him. She touched his lips with her young fingers before kissing him on the lips.

"I will see you later at the club." He said quickly, afraid that the teenage girl could sweep him off his feet right in his office. He noticed her tender young, lean figure and realised that she was actually beautiful, especially since she wore less make-up.

"As you say Mr. Mitch." She replied, swinging her hips before walking out of his office with a feeling of accomplishment and achievement about her.

She walked through his secretary's office, making it obvious that she wanted him more than anything. She started to count the hours to when she could see his lovely face again, later in the evening.

*   *   *

Bobby walked into the pub a little later than usual and sat at his usual place, before ordering his beer, even though he knew that he did not just want a beer, but he also wanted to see Ariel. It was only a few minutes after he had been there, before she came and stood by his side.

"Do you want a beer?" He asked her.

"No, I just want us to be alone together." She replied seductively with her short skirt exposing her strong lean legs, even though they were partly covered in leather boots, and she wore a short white shirt, only big enough to cover her breasts.

He finished his beer in one swig.

"Let's go." He invited her, getting off the stool.

She followed him to his expensive car. He opened the door for her and then without conversing much they drove to his house. He led the way into the house and up the stairs, he saw Bimora's nanny, this time she did not ask him if he needed anything but retreated into her room as soon as she saw the woman he was with. He entered his bedroom.

"Do you need anything, a meal, drinks?"

"Ice-cream if you've got some, Mr. Mitch." She said, looking around the room.

"I will be back in a moment." He said, leaving the room to go downstairs.

He returned minutes later with the ice-cream and a beer for himself. He found her sitting on top of his bed covers with her boots lying on the floor next to the bed. He handed her the ice-cream, but she put it on the side table and reached for him instead. She began to kiss him and undress him as she did so, getting the ice-cream and pouring it on his bare torso, taunting him whilst she licked it off him. He could not take it any longer, he stripped her clothes off and made love with her before falling asleep. She smiled to herself, tucking close to him before she too, finally fell asleep.

Bobby woke up the following morning, trying to recollect the previous night's events. He slipped out of bed after recalling that it was the teenage girl that he had spent the night with. He went to the bathroom to take a show, washing her off him, and then before he could even finish his shower, she walked into the shower with him, allowing the water to ran down her body. She began to kiss him and before he knew it, he was all over her, making love to her again.

———————

CHAPTER TWENTY-THREE

Olly had moved back to Goldring city, much to Kodelly's relief; even though he had refused to move in with either of his parents but had instead decided to get his own apartment. He had missed being around Bimora more than anything and that was the main reason why he had decided to move back to Goldring city.

He parked his car in the driveway and then he walked into his father's big mansion. He was sure that he would find him at home since he had actually invited him over. He entered the room where his father was playing snooker with his daughter.

"Dad, how are you?" He greeted, rubbing him on the arm and then hugging Bimora who had ran to him.

"I'm fine." He replied calmly. "So, how is school?" Watching him stand away from his little sister.

"School is okay."

"Get some good grades. Make your mom and I proud." He encouraged.

"Is that what you called me for?" He asked him sarcastically, suddenly changing his temperament.

"No, I thought we might go together for lunch, as a family." He replied innocently, with a shrug.

"Family?" He asked back with a grin.

"Yes, a family." He replied back firmly. "I hope you still aren't giving your mother a hard time by not talking to her and refusing to see her?"

"And why should that matter to you, anyway?"

"You don't know why?" He spoke back. "Don't go acting like you don't know how much she loves you."

"Oh, yeah?"

"Don't 'oh yeah me', I'm not your peer. We made a mistake, and we are sorry. We should have told you in the beginning, but we felt that the time wasn't right."

"What wasn't right? It was better for me to call you 'uncle Bobby' and end up looking like…, like… a fool?"

"It was not about you. It was about us doing the right thing."

"Oh well, the right thing turned out to be wrong. So, don't go telling me how I should feel about it or not. Just leave me alone. If that is what you called me for, I'm out of here."

"Okay, I will talk about something else. Let's go for lunch, please, as a family…" He said, leading them out through the door and into the hallway. They walked out to the car with either of them going to the front doors, before little Bimora spoke.

"And who gets to open the door for me? Am I not supposed to be a lady?"

"You are young lady." Replied Bobby, opening the door for her after apologising and acknowledging her presence.

*　　*　　*

Bobby returned home from work. He opened the door to his bedroom and was met with the expectant eyes of Ariel; she was sitting on the bed with a bowl of popcorns. Her attention would usually be torn between looking at the door to see who had come through and looking at the program on the television set. Then she would switch her attention entirely to Bobby, asking him how his day had been and if he had missed her as much as she did miss him? He no longer went to the pub as frequently as he had done in the past, even though he usually came home late. If he was home early, he would spend time with Bimora until she went to bed and then he would turn his attention to Ariel, who had decided to spend more time in Bobby's mansion than at her rich parents' house. She did not quite like Bimora, whom she considered to be a little, spoiled brat. She always tried to have her father's undivided attention and there was no compromise with that. She was the only one who knew about her dad's affair with the teenage girl, thus far.

"Bobby, how are you, my love?" She said, putting the bowl of popcorns away. She had switched to calling him by the first name other than addressing him as Mr. Mitch, which had been ridiculously too formal.

"I'm fine." He replied, watching her leap from the bed and fling her arms about him.

She began to kiss him and fumble with his clothes. He wished that they could just talk like he normally did with Kodelly and not just jump into bed. He longed to have an intelligent conversation other than to listen to the teenage girl talk about what she wanted to buy, what party they should go to and so on. He had spoiled her on a few occasions with gifts and had bought her an entirely new wardrobe, to fit with how he expected her to dress when she was with him and not the entirely party clothes she seemed to have. She made every effort to please him and did not seem to have an opposing opinion to his. She had recently turned eighteen, although she acted more mature than her age with regards Bobby. He was however, hoping that the new image he was trying to create for her, with the clothes he had bought, would make her seem older than her age. The last thing he wanted was anyone to realise just how young she was. She was actually younger than his son, Olly, who was in varsity. He dreaded to think that his daughter could ever do such things that Ariel was capable of.

Sometimes when he was alone in his office, he seemed to realise that he hated himself for sleeping with her, but he often consoled himself with the fact that she was the one that desired him and wanted him. She was the one that wanted to be with him. She was the one that had approached him. He often wondered what parents she had that did not seem bothered to find out where their daughter was, even though she claimed that she called them daily to let them know where she was. He wondered how Kodelly would react if she found out about his affair with her, notwithstanding they were now divorced.

"I missed you." He heard her say, "Would you like to go for a swim with me and maybe we can… get naughty in the pool?" She suggested. "No, I would like to wake my daughter up and spend some time with her." He said, breaking free from her.

"Oh, the little princess..."

"Yap, my adorable angel." He said, looking at her and yearning for her body, but he decided to walk away from her this evening.

He just could not stand to sleep with her every time he saw her. He had to be strong, he told himself as he walked away and went to the bar downstairs. He poured himself a scotch, before falling asleep on the couch.

*   *   *

Kodelly finished dressing up, she got the address that Pedree Laskador had left with her the previous time and slipped it in her bag. She had not seen much of him lately; nonetheless, he had called her frequently. She drove through the streets and found herself parking in front of the building where he was residing. She got out of her car and entered the expensive apartment building, guiding her way to his apartment. She stood in front of the door, knocking gently, and then she heard movements within the apartment before the door opened.

"Kodelly, good evening." He greeted cheerfully.

"Good evening." She replied, stepping into the hallway after he had invited her in.

"Oh, my apartment is such a mess." He began.

He was clad in a pair of jeans trousers, a t-shirt and wore a pair of expensive sandals on his feet.

"I thought you would never come to see me again. I'm sorry about last time, I just couldn't resist kissing you."

"I allowed you to." She replied flatly.

"We can sit in the lounge or in the bedroom, which is actually more spacious." He explained leading her to the lounge, "I do my work from here." He explained, gesturing at the canvas, the tins of paint and the incomplete drawings and paintings, which had taken up most of the space on the floor.

"I see." She replied.

"My work is not yet complete, so I'm sure that you will find it very boring."

"And your father, where is he?" She asked on impulse, with her eyebrows raised.

"You know my father?" He asked back.

"Yes." She replied confidently. "You did most of your exhibitions with him back then in Cambel city."

"Oh!" He replied with a laugh, "That is not my father, he is my granddad." He corrected.

"Oh, I see." She replied stupidly, recalling how well Bobby thought he knew the two artists in those days.

"His busy at the moment." He continued to explain, "We thought we could work separately for a while, come up with new fads and concepts and then meet at the next exhibition."

"So, would you like to have a drink, or are we going to stand here for the rest of the evening and look at the incomplete work?"

"I will have a drink and the chairs?"

"Down the corridor, you will find my bedroom. I have pushed the lounge chairs there. Let me get us the drinks first."

Pedree Laskador re-joined her moments later with two glasses of orange juice.

"And your father, is he also an artist?"

"No. Grandpa wanted him to be. He tried, but the only painting he ever did was that of my mother. He met this gorgeous woman, who swept him off his feet. He couldn't stand to travel around the world without seeing her face. They got married and had me and the rest of my brothers and sisters and I practically grew up with paint and brush, thanks to my grandfather."

"You are very talented." She complimented.

"Well, thanks, like my grandfather says, 'your support is our inspiration'."

"So, how have you been?"

"I have been fine."

"How did your divorce go?"

"Well, painful I suppose. I sometimes wondered if it was the right thing for both of us… but thank goodness it was over and done with." She paused for a moment. "Let's not dwell on that. Anyway, I'm actually leaving. I just wanted to know your hiding place."

"Well, I actually had dinner in mind."

"Dinner! I am not dressed for dinner."

"Then stay with me. Spend the night with me."

"Well, I am not sure of my feeling for you…"

"Shhh, let the river ran its course to the ocean. Don't build walls to stop the water and call it a dam. I am attracted to you Kodelly, very attracted. I haven't felt this way in a long time." He said taking her hand in his, and slowly rubbing it.

She was attracted to him too, she thought, but maybe she was attracted to his fame and personality, but was that not love? She would not mind being seen in public with him. He was noble and a professional artist. A man that even Bobby would be astounded to realise that she was associating with, especially with the kind of respect that he had for their paintings.

"*This is priceless.*" She had often heard him refer to their work.

"I will stay." She heard herself say, looking deep into his eyes as they held hands, while soft music played in the background.

*　*　*

"And what brings you to my part of the world?" She asked Rena who had just been directed to the study by the butler.

She appeared to have lost a few kilos', even though she still looked attractive. Her breasts stood firm in front of her. The coastal air had done a marvellous job on her skin, despite that she had moved back to Goldring city.

She had been back in Goldring city for the past eight months, awaiting her all-important call, which just did not seem to have come through. Dinkley Mills had left for Summerset with the promise of divorcing his wife, once she reappeared. He had not called Rena or informed her of what had transpired on his arrival back at the ranch. His parents had partly blamed him for what had happened to Laura. If only he had tried to be more understanding and supportive, then she could not have felt so marginalised and resorted to leaving him. He had a baby with Rena, with whom he only communicated by posting a cheque, which normally arrived towards the end of the month. He had not discussed the wedding arrangements any further, even though that seemed to have been the centre of their relationship at the coast. She wished that she could go to Summerset and confront him. But the bastard had just been too unemotional, lately. He had informed her of his decision to go back and work in the family business, at the ranch, and that was the reason why she had come back to Goldring city. He had then informed her that he would marry her as soon as Laura got better, and she would live on the ranch with him. He had initially called her on a frequent basis, but the calls had reduced with time to just a written cheque at the end of the month.

"I thought that we were now past that, Kodelly?" She complained.

"Past what?" She asked back with a grin, "After you betrayed my trust and went on to sleep with my cousin's husband?"

"Well, your cousin is no angel. Isn't she the reason why you are divorced?"

"Oh, don't remind me." She said, covering her face with her palms for a moment. "What do you want?"

"Where did those flowers come from?" She asked, gesturing at the fresh bunch of flowers on Kodelly's table.

"That is none of your business, or are you perhaps trying to start up a gossip column in one of the local newspapers?"

"Oh, come on. It's all over town that you are dating some high-class celebrity. The deeper the pocket the stronger the love bond should be, mmmh?"

"Oh." She said with a laugh.

"Bobby...," She said with the count of her finger, "and now this rich celebrity, you are very fortunate." She paused for a moment. "How is Laura doing?" She asked again.

"Why do you want to know how Laura is doing, so you can set your wedding date?"

"No, I'm just curious to know. Frankly, we haven't talked about that lately. I can't continue depending on the cheques he sends for the child. Is there a possibility that I can get my old job back?"

"Speak to Bobby, I'm sure that he will be able to squeeze you in. I do not know the 'happenings' in that department."

"Oh, I get it." She said, nodding her head.

"Rena, I have a lot of work to catch up on. So, if you will excuse me now..."

"Okay." She replied disappointedly.

"So, how is your relationship with Pedree Laskador?"

"Perfect, if you really want to know. His got class. Is there anything else you want to know?"

"Is it true that his father is a womaniser?"

"Firstly, that ain't his father but his granddad and secondly from the bottom of my heart take this piece of advice." She paused for a moment, looking at her as she looked back at her eagerly. "Go work for the gossip column, you seem to know all the dirty stories about everyone."

"Come on, I'm only trying to break the ice. So how are things between you and Olly?"

"Oh, he's still not talking with me, but he simply adores his dad. Okay, how does that make me feel? Like only half of my world is in existence. I don't know why he is fuming with me, but I hope he gets around it soon. I can't bear the thought of us not talking."

"I'm sorry to hear that." She said, wanting to win her friendship again.

If only she knew what button to press next? But talking about Olly was a good start; she seemed to have eased a bit.

"I won't keep you long. I have to go now." She said, feeling a bit empty and wondering if she would be able to get her old job back.

"And how is your baby doing?" She heard her ask. "and the girls."

"Fine, fine, they are all fine…I just need a job." She added desperately. "I have to go now."

Kodelly waved at her as she turned to walk out.

She walked out of Kodelly's house, certain that she had no choice but to face Bobby and ask him for a second chance, even though she doubted if he would even give her audience. He probably also resented her for having ran off with Laura's husband. But hell, it felt right at the time. She had no idea that he was just using her, maybe to get back at his wife who had deserted him. She went home to try and figure out how best to approach Bobby Mitch.

*   *   *

Lidy had arrived at Kodelly's house two days ago. She had listened to her daughter give her sentiments about her desire to have Olly back in her life, to be friends with him and to be, just his mother again. She had made it clear that Lidy was the only one who would get through to him on her behalf. She knew he had great respect for his grandparents, and he would obey them if they spoke with him about how important his relationship with his mother were to her. She claimed that their strained relationship was actually almost drawing her into a depression.

Lidy had phoned Olly and told him about how his mother felt about him and how she still wished to be a part of his life, although he was now a grown up. He agreed to his grandmother's proposal, to host dinner for his family. He invited both his parents and Bimora.

It was a touching reunion, one that could have transpired that evening, if only Laura had not come and spoiled it. It was obvious that Olly had also missed his mother; except that he did not know how to go around the edge he had built about him. He thanked his grandmother for having intervened.

Kodelly was happy and equally grateful that her mother had come through for her. She sat opposite to her ex-husband in their son's cosy apartment. They all chatted softly, avoiding any topics that would seem sensitive. Lidy ended the evening by cautioning them to take care of each other. She seemed to have aged a bit, but her beauty and vibrant energy was still evident and her taste for elegant, glamorous clothes was still the same as her loyalty to her marriage was.

"I will be going upstairs to pack my bags." She announced, as they finished tiding up after dinner.

"Do you have to go back so soon?" Asked Kodelly.

"Well… yes. I have finished my assignment to bring you and the rest of the family 'back together'."

"Yes mom, and you do not know how much I appreciate that. I love you forever."

"It is good to hear that. I love you too, but I must go back tomorrow. I'm sure that your dad is lonely and missing me."

"Alright then." She said resignedly, watching her mother walk out of the kitchen.

She turned on the kettle to make herself a hot cup of tea, and then, she sat on the kitchen chair, putting the cup on the table. She began to think about the dinner function her son had hosted the previous evening. It was her first time to enter his well-furnished apartment. She was proud of herself for raising such a loving and understanding boy. She had noticed his endless concern for his sister, and she knew that Bobby loved him just as much as she did.

The kitchen door opened, disrupting her chain of thoughts. She turned to look at the door and was sure that it could only be her mother who had walked in, but her eyes dilated in shock when she looked up. She quickly swallowed the hot tea, which was in her mouth.

"It is only you and I today, just you and I." Began the person that had just entered the kitchen, with a gun in her hands.

"I will sort you out. I always knew that I would be the winner. Yes, the winner." She continued. "I won't have to walk in your shadow anymore. I won't have to compete with you anymore. I win."

"Laura." She hissed fearfully. "I don't understand you…"

"Oh, you don't?" She said with a laugh. "You don't have to."

"Laura, we can talk things through."

"Don't Laura me." She interjected, "Your mother is not here to sing your praises of how excellent you are and how I am a failure." She said beginning to cry. "Say your prayers before I shoot you."

"Laura, you don't mean to do this."

"I am so tired of tugging behind you. You always have had the best of everything. I just can't take it anymore."

"Wait. Put the gun away."

"You don't want to pray?" She yelled. "You want me to go ahead and shoot you. I have waited for this moment. You will be out of my way once and for all." She said between clenched teeth.

"Don't do it, please." Kodelly said fearfully, recalling how frightened she had been the time her son had pointed a toy gun at her, and yet this time, it was a real gun.

Laura seemed very emotional as she talked. She must have taken quite a dose of whatever that had made her so temperament, she thought, praying within her that this moment just would not be.

"Stand up." She commanded. "I'd like to see you in full. No one will know that I did it. No one will know." She cocked the pistol, watching as Kodelly stood up from the chair and moved towards the wall.

"Noooooo." Kodelly screamed, seeing her mother walk in and push Laura from behind.

The gun went off and the bullet hit into the wall. Laura still had the gun in her hands and was wrestling with Lidy on the floor. However, before Kodelly could manage to get there, Laura overpowered Lidy and stood up from the floor.

"It's you. I should have known that you would be here. I should have known." Pointing the gun at Lidy and ordering her to get up.

Lidy stood up from her fall on the kitchen floor.

"Stand next to your filthy daughter." She hissed. "I have hated you. I have always hated you. I hate the way you mope around uncle Bill. He is such a nice person. He does not deserve you around. I will do him the favour and shoot you too, but first I will start with her." Turning her gun to Kodelly again.

Lidy had heard the commotion from upstairs. She now wished that she had phoned somebody first, before thinking that she could subjugate her niece Laura, who appeared to be perspiring a lot.

"Why are you doing this?" She charged at her, hiding the fear in her voice.

"Because I planned it. She will be out of my way, once and for all."

"And what life will you have after you pull that trigger? A life behind bars?"

"Who asked you to judge me, again? Maybe I should start with you. Yes you." She said, pointing the gun at her again.

"Please don't do it." Begged Kodelly.

"Let her do it." Lidy charged, "She messes up her life and now she wants you to pay for it?" She paused for a moment. "You had a husband, a good husband but you pushed him away…"

"I didn't mess up my life, okay. Things just happened. Just like Dinkley never really loved me…he loved her." She yelled, beginning to cry. "He loved Kodelly, it wasn't me."

"He married you…" Lidy charged on. "You still have a chance, if you hold yourself together." She said more calmly. "Now don't pull that trigger. You have made mistakes and they are all forgivable, but this won't be a mistake. It won't just happen, because you've planned it. You are still a good person Laura…"

"I didn't plan it." She charged, continuing to cry uncontrollably. "Something…told me to. Something just told me, I had to." She continued to cry and dropped the gun onto the floor.

"Wait." Spoke Lidy to Kodelly, watching Laura twitch, covering her face in the process.

She leaned against the wall and began to curl herself, forgetting all about the gun that lay next to her. Then cautiously and with calculated steps, Lidy walked to her, she picked up the gun and moved away.

"Unload this gun and please keep it safe." She ordered Kodelly, and then she walked back to Laura and embraced her.

"Everything is going to be okay. I will go back to Summerset with you. You will see Dinkley and your beautiful daughters. Just stop taking those drugs. See what they are doing to you?" She advised, rocking her gently and allowing her to cry on her bosom. "You are still married to Dinkley Mills. He can still love you…"

"I failed." She repeatedly said through her sobs. "I failed everyone. Why couldn't Dinkley just love me…why could we not just love unconditionally…I have failed…"

"You can start all over again, as if none of this ever happened. We will get you good help in Summerset. Everything will be fine. It will be." She said comfortingly. "Everything will be just fine. We love you Laura…"

———————————

CHAPTER TWENTY-FOUR

Kodelly wrapped up her days work and was just about to leave. She closed her office door and walked through her secretary's office, who had already left. Then she walked down the corridor, feeling exhausted. She heard someone calling her name through the seemingly busy corridor.

"Mrs. Mitch. Mrs. Mitch…" She heard the fat financial manager of medium height call. He took hurried strides and was almost out of breath when he finally caught up with her. He was dressed formal, in a suit, a bag in one hand and the day's newspaper in the other. She had stopped to allow him to catch up with her.

"Sorry to bother you, madam, but do you perhaps have a moment to spare?" He began, standing level with her.

"Well…yes." She replied hesitantly, beginning to walk abreast him, and then entering into the crowded elevator.

"Okay." She heard him say, not wanting to speak in front of the rest of the people in the elevator. They got out of the elevator, separating themselves from the others, but still neither of them spoke but continued to walk towards the parking. When they reached Kodelly's car, he spoke again.

"I wanted to talk to you about Mr. Mitch."

"What about him?" She asked curiously.

"The divorce." He continued, pausing for a moment. "I think it has affected him adversely."

Adverse she thought with a grin. He spoke as if he was presenting the results of the budget, adverse performance, adverse divorce?

"It sounds ridicules I know, but I love the corporation and I have worked with Mr. Mitch for a long time. I have great respect for him. I know that…"

"Could you please get to the point? I am really tired. I need to go home."

"Yes Madam." He continued, "The point is, we need to take drastic measures to stay afloat. We need major contingent measures. I did some forecasts." He said, putting his bag on the bonnet and removing a piece of paper and lying it on the bonnet as though it were a table, then he continued to speak with his attention forecast on it.

He explained his fears and anxieties for the corporation and the need for her to speak to her husband, as he continued to refer to him, even though she kept on correcting him.

"Ex-husband." She would say.

"Yes, your ex-husband." He would correct, before repeating the same mistake.

"Okay, I will try and speak with him. Thank you very much Mr. Glipen." She said to end the conversation.

"My pleasure, Mrs. Mitch. Please speak to him and thanks for your time. At least someone else cares about this corporation; I have been here too long to watch it sink. But please…"

"Yes, I will. Goodnight." She cut him short, before getting into her car.

"Good night." He called back, watching her car drive off with his paper still in one hand and the bag in the other.

He walked heavily to where he had parked his car, half relieved that he had spoken to someone else about his fears and anxieties. He was happy that somebody else seemed to understand his fears. He continued to speculate though, that the divorce must have perhaps affected Mr. Mitch, and that he could be hurting. He wondered how his own life could be without his wife by his side. She was his source of joy and encouragement. She was the one reason why he woke up early each morning to face the challenges of life, as a man ought to, in order to support her and his children. He loved his job, and he got an ego out of announcing that he was the head of the finance department for such a big corporation as Litch, even though things were not looking as promising as they had in the past.

Kodelly drove home discarding the financial manager's fears. She got out of her car and saw Pedree Laskador's car parked in front of the parking. She smiled to herself, walking into the house. She had seen quite a lot of him lately, even though she felt that he spoilt her with too much attention. He was a romantic, shy person and she seemed to have brought out the chef in him. He was widely travelled and seemed to have learnt an assortment of dishes, of which he was always eager to try out and make her taste. She enjoyed some of his dishes but for some, she would laugh and insist on not eating, but watched him munch his own cooking. He normally forgot the real names of some of his recipes, but often gave them his own funny names and he would then confess that he had just made it up. He was funny in a way, she thought, walking into the lounge where she knew she would find him waiting.

"How's work been?" He asked, as soon as she walked through the door.

"Tiring and yours?"

"I had a dull day. No new ideas. I guess I must have been thinking about you a lot."

"I missed you too." She lied. All she wanted to do was to take a bath, eat and go to bed.

"Would you like to go to the opera?" He asked after kissing her lightly.

"Oh, I will sleep through it. I hope you haven't bought any tickets yet?"

"Well, I have, but we can always go another time."

"Okay." She replied cheering up, "I will go with you." Surprised with herself.

She had often heard him tell her just how much he loved going to the opera and so turning him down would be a great disappointment. But why should she care, she thought to herself, wondering if perhaps she was developing feelings for him? For her, the relationship was appropriate, he was a wealthy artist, one that most people would desire to be with. It actually made her proud to be seen in his company, which of course meant that she had not lost touch with being attractive and her femininity. She still was able to attract the most sophisticated man and bring him to his knees, she realised with pleasure, even though she knew that a part of her was still hang-up on Bobby.

He taught her love and all that she knew and of course he taught her how to be ruthless. Going through with the divorce had not been easy for her, but it was done and dusted now, and she had moved on. Yes, moved on with this renowned tycoon she thought with delight. She had nothing to lose by being with him, she told herself seating through the opera by his side.

Watching the opera from the comfortable seats and sipping at her glass of wine. She recalled how Rena had once put the *act* of falling in love.

"Is it not Tom who meets Jill and tells her that he loves her? It is not Jill who approaches Tom, that's the way it has been, and it will always be. Then Jill learns to love Tom based on what he is worth." She had chuckled. "Is it not Kodelly?" She questioned further, trying to defend her hypothesis in an effort to date one of her colleagues.

"I don't know." She'd replied.

"It is the man who should approach the woman, that's how society condones it. Oh, if I had my way." She would say seductively, "I would approach the most charming man and ask him to be mine. But if I did, they would call me a bitch." She said putting her finger on the tip of her nose,

"Of which am not so sure I am. So, I must love 'Tom', because I want to be 'Jill', and he approached me? Hell, no Kodelly you are right. I mustn't date him; besides I earn more than he does." She paused for a moment. "Thanks for being that loyal friend. I have always wanted to have a friend like you."

"What is a woman's' worth? He asked his mother.
Is it in the clothes she wears?
the car she drives, or the beauty that is derived from within her?
When you are down and weary, what is your source of
happiness, relief or joy?
Is it in the smile that she gives… a woman's worth?
The things that she says,
or that jewellery around her neck,
Indeed, what is a woman's worth?
The unselfish love that she gives, carrying you momentarily to
love.
Oh…planet of love, where are you that I may be there?
What is a woman's worth? Is it in that sincere, unconditional?
love that she gives wholeheartedly.
A woman's worth???"

She heard the crowd applaud in part to the opera unfolding, jerking her from her chain of thoughts.

"Are you enjoying the performance?" She heard him ask, whilst applauding with the rest of the audience.

"Yes, I am." She replied with a smile.

"Tell me if you are bored, we can always leave."

"No. No. I think I can live through it." She replied with a soft laugh, whilst the chorused applauding subdued.

They held hands through the rest of the performance. She wondered if perhaps they were building a bond that could stand the test of time and would never be broken, or if perhaps it was just a passing glance. She had mentioned to Lidy of her relationship with Pedree, who had seemed overwhelmed with the fact that perhaps soon, just perhaps soon, she would be able to meet the famous artist, whose work was well respected and whose paintings she had known for a long time.

*   *   *

Rena walked into the company premises, where she had worked until her decision to resign from her position to be with the man, she had believed would love her for the rest of her life. The only man that had treated her like a lady and emphasised her femininity.

She had learnt of Laura's return to Summerset and how much she had improved after being in the rehabilitation centre for only a month. Dinkley Mills had then found his way back to the loving arms of his wife; whose little girl child alleged to be Bobby's now lived with him on the ranch. They had definitely reconciled, and Rena had discerned, deciding to move on with her life. There was no need to hang around anymore. Things would never work out between them, in the way that she thought had they would. His promises had all been a lie to keep her interested, to be there for him when he needed her.

Bastard, she had repeatedly called him, opening the doors to her past hurt. He had reopened the door to deceits that she had put up with in the past before she had decided to be more cautious. It reminded her of the one man she had been so much in love with, Modree, Bobby Mitch's friend. He was wild, unpredictable, and passionate. He was a heavy drinker, but he knew how to treat her. She loved him, and he supported and took care of her. Rena had learnt how to be a heavy drinker and to party from him, and yet he had also taught her to stand on her own two feet, how to always be alert.

"Things ain't wot they appear to be, my love. Sometimes the sun is hot; sometimes it is not so hot… You need a jersey to keep yourself warm. You always try to bring out the best in me, but it is me that is always making a fool outta you. You don't deserve this, my love. You don't deserve this. I love you." He said, holding her hand in his.

"I love you too." She remembered herself answering.

She believed that he cared about her. He had helped her get the job with Bobby Mitch, when she did not even have much going for her. Then, he had promised her that he would start his own company. She had no idea that he was having an affair with a rich woman who lived in the expensive suburbs. But then, there was little she could have done even if she knew about it. He was his own man that did what he wanted when he wanted. He had little regard for commitment and could not believe that one could so much as give up his freedom for the four-letter word, LOVE.

"I'm gonna' open myself a nice club. Yap, we gonna' dance. That is my business, I dream about." He said puffing smoke from his cigarette.

"I am gonna have plenty of money soon."

Then he had walked out on her, making her wonder what she had done wrong? He broke her heart and yet she longed for him for a long time. She had continued to go to the pubs and clubs that they had frequented together, wondering if perhaps she could come across him, but she never did, except to learn of the hard reality of why he had left town. It was from her other friends that she had learnt the harsh reality of his affair with another woman. The rich woman from whom he had time and again gotten money, to buy Rena presents. Then he had convinced her to sell her jewellery shop, which he intended to turn into a nightclub, but all his plans had melted, when her husband found out about him. He changed the ownership of the jewellery shop and stopped her unlimited privileges she'd had to his accounts.

"A man's gotta do what he's gotta do." He often said.

He believed in adventure more than anything else in life. To him life had an adventure to offer at every turn. He was so adventurous that she only got to know him by his first name.

"I would like to see Mr. Mitch?" She spoke to his secretary.

"Rena, how are you? You sure do look radiant." She paused for a moment. "I heard you was getting married. So howz that your, baby?"

"I am fine, and he is not a baby anymore." She replied.

"I hear his father is quite well off, so you must be on top of the world."

"Is Bobby available?" She asked, uninterested in the conversation that the secretary was trying to create.

She then hated to be on the opposite side and be the one being asked about her personal life and speculated if the secretary had heard about her escapades through rumours or gossip, something that Rena was good at.

"Sure." She said buzzing him. "Sir, Miss Goof is here to see you. Can I send her through?"

"Well…Yes." He said with a bit of hesitation, wondering what her visit was all about.

"You can go through. You will fill me in on your wedding plans when you come through." She said winking at her.

"Good morning, Mr. Mitch." She greeted upon entering his office.

"Bobby would do. Bobby is fine with me." He replied, gesturing to her to take a sit and continuing to squeeze the stress ball in his right hand.

"What can I do for you Rena?" He asked, sitting back in his chair, and rubbing his thumbs together, after putting the stress ball aside.

"Well, I'm looking for a job. I was wondering if I could perhaps have my old position back?" She heard herself speak.

"Oh that…. That has been long filled." He replied, pausing for a moment. "How was your, what shall I call it… rendezvous?"

"It was just that." She replied carelessly, "About the job." She continued trying to redirect his attention to why she was sitting there.

"Well, I'm sorry Rena." He replied. "I believe that you have come to the wrong office. I do not process application letters. It's way below me. Considering the number of years, you served in this corporation, I'm sure you would be breasted with such knowledge."

"I need a job." She replied, ignoring his remarks. "Applying through personnel, might take too long."

"But that is the only way it is done. Is there a problem, can't you write a letter? Or are you trying to seduce me and ran off to my wife. Ooops, my ex-wife and tell her lies about me? Is that what you are here for? You would be the last person I do that favour for." He continued with renewed rage. "You can go now. You know where I stand, just follow the normal procedure. Maybe if it was Modree arguing your plight, I would reconsider, but he is no more a part of your life, remember that you never even got this job on merit in the first place? You used your body, but unfortunately I am not Modree, and I am not interested." He enjoyed seeing her twitch in disappointment and humiliation, still sitting in the chair opposite to him.

"I did not come here to be insulted by you." She stated firmly.

"Insulted? Is it not Modree that got you the job? Why, if I may ask there is no application letter in your personnel file?"

"I won't take this." She said bitterly, getting up from her chair and holding her head high.

He also stood up from the chair, leaning forward with his hands on the table.

"You should never have told Kodelly lies about me." He hissed. "Never should have. You were always jealous of her and that was just your way to see us apart. But you should know one thing; I still get down with her whenever I want. Isn't that what makes a marriage? As for you, Dinkley Mills is finished with you. You understand? Finished."

"Nooooo...." She shuddered, turning around, and hurrying out of his office.

"No." she said repeatedly, hearing him laugh before she could reach the door.

She ran through the baffled secretary's office, into the elevator and out of the office building.

She should have known that Bobby Mitch would have a score to settle with her. She hated herself for having given him the opportunity to talk her down in the way he had just done. She hurried to her car and drove off. She got to her apartment filled with rage. Yes rage, for thinking that

Bobby Mitch would give her a job. She needed to get a new job though, but she should not have allowed him to insult her in the way that he just did. She pulled the local paper and decided to start looking from there.

*   *   *

It was a warm, Saturday afternoon when Kodelly drove to Bobby Mitch's house, after having a thorough understanding of the Finance Director, Mr. Frank Glipen perspective. She had taken into consideration his sentiments and they seemed to make a bit of sense to her.

She thought that she could also use the opportunity to spend some time with her daughter, Bimora who had so far adapted to her parents living separately.

"Well, the good thing about a divorce is that you get to visit the other parent when the other parent gets boring. Unlike if they are both living in the same house." They had tried to explain to her.

She seemed to have adapted well with living with her dad, who seemed to do most of the attention giving, love and daily care, unlike Kodelly who only saw her occasionally. She had quite a different relationship with her daughter, unlike the bond she had shared with Olly when he was younger. She had given him too much of her time, which was expected as she'd had to raise him single handedly most of the way.

"Hello." She kissed her daughter on the forehead upon meeting her in the doorway.

"Hello, mom." She replied excitedly, "Dad is on the patio." She informed, holding her mother on her arm and looking as sweet as ever.

"Is he?" She replied, wanting to be interested in her conversation

"Yes. He took me out for breakfast this morning;" She bragged. "and he bought me some nice clothes. I just love my daddy. Grandma brought me this doll the last time she came to see us." Referring to the teddy bear in her hands.

"I see. It is very lovely. So, can we go and see daddy now?"

"Okay." She obliged, running ahead of her mother.

"Hello, Bobby." She greeted, pulling a chair for herself before sitting down.

"Hello. It is good to see you. You never gave me a call to say you would come to fetch Bimora."

"Oh." She said, taking her sunglasses off and waving her hand in the air. "Well, I came to see you too as a matter of fact." Watching her daughter pull a chair for herself.

"Oh, I see."

"So, how are you doing?"

"Fine, though I'm lonely at times. Is that why you came to see me, or you just wanted me to congratulate you for sweeping Pedree Laskador's son off his feet?"

"Is that all that everyone is talking about?" She paused for a moment. "His grandson and my affair with him has got nothing to do with my visit. So, if we can please change the subject."

"Is that why you wanted the divorce so badly?" He spoke between clenched teeth.

"I am not the one that slept with your cousin in our wedding bed and refused to do a DNA test."

"Let's not go there. I think it's time to change the subject." He paused for a moment, before calling the butler in a relaxed tone. "Some drinks please."

"I will have lemonade." Kodelly began.

"I will have a milkshake and Daddy will…" She paused looking at her father.

"A brandy." He filled in.

"Okay, sir." He replied walking away from the family.

He returned moments later serving them their beverages, watching what used to be a happy family now sitting apart. He too could not believe that master Olly was actually his master's son, even though he had noticed that his boss had shown a lot of love towards the young lad. He wondered if his former madam knew about the young teenage girl that normally came around to taunt his master's emotions. He had seen them in compromising situations on several occasions.

"I wanted to talk with you about something." She began in a sombre tone after the butler had left.

"What about?"

"Work. Something to do with work…"

"I'm listening." He said with little interest.

"It is about the future of the corporation." She continued.

"Goodness me, you have been speaking with Glipen?" He interjected, "His fears are unfounded. Yes, it is going to be rough for a couple of months, perhaps a year." He explained. "But for goodness' sake, the economy is in recession. Every business is going through the same thing. Come on Kodelly, I know you to be smarter than that. You are aware that the economy is in depression, right? It is an environmental factor and not a problem with the corporation."

"Well, I did not have the full picture." She said stupidly. "Does he know about what you have just told me?"

"Of course, he does. That's why he is the Head of Finance."

"I'm sorry." She apologised.

"No need to. Now that you have managed to spoil my weekend, what are you going to do to make up for it? Or do you have a date with the younger Laskador?"

"I am not spending the night with you, but I will spend quality time with Bimora and you." She replied. "As long as all the bills are on you."

"Ex-wives! The only thing they ever think of is money. How will I screw that bastard?"

"Exactly the point." She said with a laugh, ceding to spend the rest of the afternoon with her daughter and ex-husband.

_____

CHAPTER TWENTY-FIVE

Kodelly knocked off late from work again, after finishing off some work with Mr. Glipen. He had insisted that she assists him to implement his special, strategic budget. He had his forecasted figures at hand and now, all he needed to do was to edge the corporation against its possible downfall. He had dismissed Mr. Mitch's claim that every business was facing the same crisis.

"Good morning, Mr. Glipen." She confidently entered his office after a well, spent weekend with her daughter and Bobby.

She had spent the entire weekend with them. They had gone out for dinner, returned home late and played some video games until Bimora had fallen asleep and then she too had eventually fallen asleep. She had woken up the next day to his kisses to which she warmed up before he made love with her fondly, after having cuddled next to him through the night. He had carried her up to his bedroom the previous night, after she had fallen asleep. He was happy to see her brilliant face. He was glad to have spent the day and evening having some intelligent conversations, unlike the conversations he normally had with Ariel, who normally just asked for money to buy a new pair of shoes, clothes or whatever was part of the latest vogue. His only consolation was that at least Kodelly was the mother of his two children, even though they were no longer married.

He had been disgruntled when it was eventually time for her to leave. He wished that they could go on living as they had done the previous day and part of the following day. It almost felt like borrowed affection, or stolen passion, with her being there one moment and gone the next day.

"Good morning." Replied Frank Glipen, cheering up and then pausing for a moment, "So how was your weekend?" He'd continued.

"Good and yours?"

"Spent it with the family. We had a picnic." Then he looked at her intently.

"Oh, about what you told me..." She'd began, having sensed his eagerness to get feedback from her.

"Yes?" He acknowledged.

"Well, I spoke to Bobby, and he doesn't think it is an internal concern rather a macro one...temporal." She said uncomfortably.

"Madam, didn't you convince him to put up a fight?"

"Mr. Glipen, I tried, but I seriously don't even know if there is a major…"

"Major," He cut in. "Yes, it is a major concern- 'threat'. Money won't be coming in that easily, if we don't produce. Let's look at the external market. If we can target the export market." He continued, getting serious and shifting his weight in the chair, his hands playing a major role in communicating. "The export markets. But we need more resources and boom that is where the problem starts. We are already being squeezed. Mr. Mitch is the major shareholder, if he doesn't vote for pumping in extra money, this corporation will fall…"

"I see." She replied, getting convinced by him again. "May I have a look at the copy of the report you gave him?"

"Sure ma'am." He said, pulling open the side drawer and handing it to her. "That, Mrs. Mitch covers the plan for two years. I think that it will be most crucial in the next two years. If you go through that, then you will understand what I am talking about. I did my research. I am not talking from without."

"I will get back to you." She'd ceded. "I will." She recalled.

She got into her car contemplating on whether to go home or not? She then decided to drive to Olly's apartment. She wanted to check on how he was doing and if he needed anything. She parked her car and walked through the cold air and into the apartment building. She stood for a moment, before knocking. She heard loud music coming from inside. She knocked for a while before the door finally opened.

A young woman stood in the doorway.

"Yes, can I help you?" She asked rudely, whilst chewing gum.

"May I come in?" Kodelly asked back, wishing that she could walk past her.

"I think you have got the wrong number." She replied, still standing in the doorway.

"Is Olly in?" She asked impatiently.

"Olly? No. He is out."

"May I come in? I'm his mother. I brought him some dinner." She said, gesturing to the takeaway she had bought on her way.

"I'm sorry, please come in." She said, moving out of the way and allowing her in.

"Who are you?" She asked carelessly, scrutinising her son's apartment.

"I'm Nina, his friend…" She replied awkwardly.

"Oh, I see. He has never mentioned you to me." She replied, enjoying the dominion she now had.

"Well …I…Don't know why he hasn't …"

"Listen girl, I mind your staying here with my son. I do give a damn."

"Well, it is only temporary".

"Temporary? Are you helping him with the rent or something?"

"Well, I think you are asking too much."

"Too much! There is no privacy as far as my son is concerned. In short, I do not approve of your stay in this house, and you would do us all a favour if you could perhaps leave, ASAP." She paused for a moment. "Where is Olly, anyway?"

"He went…to the gym." She replied, realising that she had no choice in the matter.

"Any idea what time he might be back?"

"After 10 p.m. He is passing through a friend's place."

"Oh, I see, don't forget to mention that his mummy was here and please next time I come around, don't be here."

"I…I… "

"Just don't be here." She emphasised, opening the door and letting herself out.

She walked to her parked car and realised that the last thing that she wanted was to be by herself. She had a bottle of champagne in the back seat, and she decided just where she was going from there. She drove through the not so busy streets. She parked her car again, got the bottle of champagne and got out of the car. Then she went up the short flight of stairs and knocked on the door once, before it opened.

"Good evening, Kodelly." Spoke Pedree excitedly.

"Good evening." She replied, walking in and giving him the bottle, and then she took her jacket off and put it on the couch.

"I couldn't get hold of you the whole weekend, what happened?"

"I was away. I should have told you." She replied.

"Out on business?"

"No, I went to Summerset."

"Oh, what for?"

"Nothing much. Could I please have a drink?" She replied, not wanting to divulge anymore or rather trying to keep away from lying further.

Men do that all the time, so what was wrong with her doing it? She asked herself. Maybe he did not deserve to be lied to, she tried to reason.

"Please join me for dinner."

"Gosh, am I hungry." She replied, leading the way into the kitchen.

They ate without talking much. Her mind kept straying, asking if he could make her happy; as much as Bobby had done? If he would always be there, which is something they had never discussed. He was not a family man or else he could have been married by now. He followed more in his grandfather's footsteps than his father's, who had married at an early age and had seven other children besides him.

"Would you like some desert?" She heard him ask.

"Yes." She replied, getting up from the chair and going around the kitchen table to where he was standing.

"What?" He asked a bit stunned.

"Let's say, we skip desert and do something else instead." She said seductively, pulling him to herself.

He leaned forward and kissed her on the lips as she threw her arms around his neck yearningly.

*　　*　　*

"Hello dad." Olly greeted his father, who was playing snooker by himself.

"Hello." He answered back, pausing for a while and looking at his grown-up son.

"So, what did you call me for?"

"I just wanted to see you."

"Oh, I see. So where is Bimora?"

"She went out with your mom." He replied, sipping at his beer.

"You want some?" He offered.

"No. I will drink later, with my peers."

"Your mom told me that you had an argument with her?" He continued, gauging his mood.

"It wasn't an argument." He retorted in defence.

"You asked her to stay the hell away from… what's that girl you are seeing? What business must you have with women? Why should you keep her in your apartment?"

"You tell me." He replied back.

"Olly, I'm not playing games. Your mom means well. You can't keep her there; live with her I mean."

"Tell me, as though you are the good guy. You walked out on mom. If it weren't for her would you be talking to me now? What is your track record that you must tell me what to do and what not to do? Dad, Bobby, uncle, whatever…?"

Bobby raised his hand and slapped him in the face.

"No child of mine is gonna' talk to me in that manner." He charged. "I made a mistake; the circumstances were different from yours. Look at you; you've got everything. Great opportunities… I made a mistake."

"Mistake. You call that a mistake…?"

"Olly." He said, suddenly softening up, recalling Kodelly's face a time that seemed so distant now. He could not justify why he had done it, but he now wanted to be with them. They were his family and all that really mattered to him now.

"No. Bobby, I won't do it. I won't have an abortion and hear a debate on the subject and fail to take a stance, because I did it."

"I'm sorry, Olly, but that was the most stupid decision I have ever made in my entire life. But look at you; I don't want you to start making the same mistakes. Do you have any idea how many sleepless nights I had spent after I set eyes on your mother again? Just wondering what her ultimate decision had been. It was stupid of me to have done that, please don't fall into it."

"Well, I love Nina. I do and I know that she loves me too."

"Okay." He said resignedly.

"Would you like to play a game?"

"Yes." He replied, watching his father setup the snooker table again.

"Bobby." She began, walking through the already open door and then stopping in her tracks, after already drawing both men's attention. She was dressed in hot pants and a short t-shirt exposing her belly, with sneakers and she was chewing gum vigorously.

"Ariel, you know dad?" Olly intervened in total dismay.

"Yes." Replied his father trying to stay calm. "Were you guys in high school together?"

"No. No, I know her from the ice-cream shop." He paused for a while. "Speaking of which, you are never found there these days. Don't tell me you are now my little sister's nanny?"

"Not quite." She replied, feeling uncomfortable.

"My girlfriend was actually asking about you the last time from your boss. What did he say...?" He said, clicking his fingers. "Well, I can't exactly remember."

"Well, I didn't mean to interrupt, I'm sorry." She apologised, retreating from the room.

She had not called Bobby to inform him that she would come through. She had wanted to surprise him with her new outfit, which she felt fitted her perfectly.

She had no idea that she would run into another spoilt, loud-mouthed, child of his. She had no idea that Olly was Bobby's son. She hurried through the hallway and past the butler who had just let her in. She wondered what Bobby Mitch would say to her. She had defiled him. She should have called him before coming through. She had actually become fond of him more now, than just the desire to spend his money, she realised, putting her diamond bracelet in her bag. Frustration engulfed her at the realisation that Olly maybe knew that she was not Bimora's maid.

"Does it mean that Bimora now has two nannies, coz I saw the other one when I arrived?" He asked with a quizzical look, and then realising his mistake he continued. "I'm sorry dad. I did not realise that she actually called you Bobby, so she can't be ..."

"It's okay." He replied, submitting to defeat.

"Dad you are not seeing her, are you?"

"That is none of your business." He paused for a moment. "Now, can we continue with the game?"

"Sure, thing sir, sure thing." He replied with a laugh, realising that he now had a basis for arguing with his dad.

Bobby laughed too, filling him in on how she had told him that she comes from a very wealthy family. He was having a causal relationship with her, he explained with little pains.

"I love you dad." Olly finally said, giving him a hug, "You are one hell of a dad, but thanks for the advice anyway." He continued, feeling more comfortable with him.

They finally managed to remove the great hurdle that was between them, yet deep inside he knew that his son had great admiration for his mother. She had always been there for him.

*   *   *

The phone rang just as soon as Kodelly entered her bedroom.

"Hello?" She answered after picking up the handset.

"Miss Goof is on the line for you." She heard the familiar butler's voice.

"Okay."

"Hello. Hello?"

"Kodelly." Spoke Rena's excited voice. "You won't believe this."

"Believe what?" Kodelly asked back, stepping out of her shoes and sitting comfortably on the edge of her bed.

"It's about Laura." She continued, still in an excited tone.

"Whatever it is, I don't wanna hear it." She informed her back, defensively. She knew quite well that Laura was doing better in Summerset. She was back at the ranch with her husband Dinkley Mills, and perhaps, whatever Rena had to say was just something to spite her.

"No. No." She refuted. "It is very important. I work in the payroll department, and I know that I am not supposed to disclose this to anyone, but because you are my friend…" She continued hurriedly.

"What does your job have to do with Laura?"

"Damn it Kodelly, can't you just listen? Your cousin's name is appearing on one of Mr. Welnar Zalpah's confidential payrolls."

"Mr. Welnar Zalpah. What the hell are you talking about?"

"I am employed by his company." She informed her. "In the payroll department."

"What do you mean? Do you mean to tell me that she once worked for him?"

"No. No. She wasn't working here. I checked with Human Resources already, but she still gets a hefty allowance on his confidential payroll. I checked the old reports, and it is much more than what it used to be when she was around town."

"But why would he pay Laura. What connection is there between the two?"

"It beats me too." She replied back.

"Thanks Rena." She said, before putting the phone back on the hook, sitting motionlessly for a while on her bed, unable to think or even know what to do next.

She then hurried out of her bedroom, down the corridor and opened the door to the room that Laura used to occupy, the time when she was staying at her house. She repeatedly told herself that the room had been cleaned over a thousand times and there would be nothing to give her the answers that she was looking for. There would definitely be nothing peculiar. She continued though to open the wardrobe doors, looking hurriedly then closing them quickly. She walked to the drawers, pulling them open one at a time, with still nothing to betray her cousin. Then she went to the dressing table and pulled the drawers out in frustration. She completely pulled the top drawer out. It seemed to have the most papers. She examined the contents that were mostly receipts from expensive boutiques. In frustration she put them all back. She picked up the drawer from the floor and was just about to push it in when she felt something stuck underneath. She upset it quickly, causing all the contents to fall on the floor again. At the bottom was a large envelope, which had been stuck there. She pulled it and opened it. Inside, were a few packets of drugs. She opened one of the sachets and looked closely at the contents and her inexperienced eyes proved that it was a drug. Then, she saw a few notes addressed to Laura from Welnar Zalpah, instructing her to deliver, and among the many papers, she also recognized the direct line to his office.

"Bustard." She muted, picking up the entire envelope and hurrying out of the bedroom.

"Tidy up the room for me." She called out to the maid as she ran past her in the corridor.

She went to her study and picked up the phone, dialling a number that she was so familiar with. Laura picked up the phone from the other end.

"Laura." She began urgently.

"Yes. Who is this?"

"Kodelly." She informed her, trying to keep herself calm.

"Oh."

"Yes." She reaffirmed. "Is it true? I mean I need some honest answers from you?"

"What?"

"That you used to do some delivered for Mr. Welnar Zalpah, and he still supports you and your daughter, his daughter?"

"How did you know? Who told you that?"

"Nothing stays hidden forever. Let's just say I found out from him."

"About the baby?" She asked stupidly.

"About everything." She lied, knowing it was the only way for her to get her to tell the truth.

"He can't. He can't. His wife is not supposed to know about it. It just happened. It wasn't supposed to happen…" She said in a shaky voice.

"So why did you say it was Bobby?"

She was quiet from the other side of the line.

"Did Bobby sleep with you too?"

"No. He didn't." She said firmly.

"Was Welnar, the one that took you for the first rehab?"

"What rehab?" She asked back.

"Remember, I once came to see you on a rainy day?"

"Oh, that was just one of his houses. He was trying to help me. He uses it for business. I was too much of a wimp, to leave the drugs. I couldn't stand being on my own."

"I will talk to you some other time. Thanks Laura." She said, ending her conversation with her.

She put on her shoes and got her car keys, and then she hurried outside. She felt relieved that her cousin's daughter was not actually Bobby's child, as she had claimed, but then again so much had happened since then. She felt relieved that he did not cheat on her with her own cousin, as she had once thought. Yet she wondered why Bobby had refused to do the test, when he never had anything to do with her?

She drove and felt a bit uptight with herself; yet she knew that she just had to confront him. She got into town and out of her car, walking briskly through the cool noon breeze, up the escalators and into the elevator. She could not believe how much gut he really thought he had, but she had to see for herself. She stood in his secretary's office for a moment and without much delay she was shown through to his office.

"Mrs. Kodelly Mitch, what a pleasant surprise." Having turned his attention from the TV set, which was showing on the other side of the office to her.

"You pathetic son of a bitch." She said walking towards him. "You imbecile. Men like you do not even deserve that title at all. The damage you cause is too diverse to ever even be repaired."

"Well, she threw herself at me." He defended, realising that it could be the only reason why she was calling him names.

"Well, I got news for you."

"What?" He asked, sitting uncomfortably.

"I got news that can cause your whole ship to sink all at once. Your business, which of course has been supported by money from an illegal source, your happy marriage can fail, in but a second and of course the whole of society will shun you. And this is not a threat. In addition, you can be locked away for several years."

"What do you want?" He asked, sitting like a man about to hear his verdict.

"You are such an imbecile. Why? Your name will truly become a legend." She paused for a moment, narrowing her eyes before speaking again.

"I won't have you talk to me like that. Get out of my office."

"You got my feeble cousin on drugs; you got her pregnant."

"I never told her to taste of it. It is a rule. She was not supposed to. I gave her a job when she had absolutely nothing."

"You destroyed her life. Gave her a child you don't even want to look at."

"I supported her. I still do support her, but I never supported her drug habit. She is a married woman; it would be best for her to be where she is." He argued back.

"Oh, stop the justification act. I did not come here to hear your side of the story, but this is what I want." She said, sitting on his table and turning her attention to the TV set. She picked up the remote and switched it off.

"When I switch on my TV," She said whilst switching it on, "to see your company campaigning against drugs. I want to see you, as a business pumping in money to help the Rehab centres." She tortured him. "I have got so much information on you, so don't even think of crossing me."

"You blackmailing tart..." He charged back.

"That's not all. I want you to sell your hold in Litch Corporation. I can't imagine you having shares there."

He twitched his thumbs and shifted his weight.

"Is that too much to ask?"

"No." He replied uncomfortably. "No."

She put the remote back on his table.

"Your shares must sell immediately." She said, turning to walk away, half content with herself for having come to confront him.

Even though a part of her wondered why Laura had to accuse Bobby of such a thing, when she knew the truth all along. Maybe, it was the drugs she had been taking, because she had certainly done a lot of things she could not have possibly done in her right senses. She wondered if Laura was no longer in love with Dinkley and yet, she could not imagine that, since it was always Laura who desired him and wanted him to talk with her. Well, she had gotten the man she wanted, so she could not imagine her being out of love with him. She got to her car and drove home, wishing that she could spend the rest of her day alone.

_____

CHAPTER TWENTY-SIX

Bobby sat on the stool by the bar. He sipped at his beer, while the music played loud as usual. He had not set eyes on Ariel, since her encounter with Olly. He had refused to take any calls from her. He felt that he had probably overreacted, but she was not the type of girl he really wanted around him. He had made up his mind on not allowing the teenage girl back into his life. He stopped to watch the people on the dance floor, and then almost at the same time, their eyes locked. She was dancing with a man, a younger man. Bobby quickly looked away, wondering what kind of deceitful stories she had told him. He paid for his beer and set off to leave.

She had not seen him in weeks; she realised still standing on the dance floor. She quickly left her dance partner and followed behind him. He hurried out of the club and was soon on the open parking, walking towards his parked car, whilst feeling the drizzles on his face.

"Bobby." He heard her call out in the quietness of the night. "Bobby, please wait. I wanna talk to you."

He walked on. He stood for a moment only after reaching his car, watching her hurry towards him and then he opened the door to his car and got inside, before deciding to drive off.

She was just a teenage girl, he told himself. He did not owe her anything. She wanted sex and he gave her that including other material stuff. There was no commitment at all from either of them. It was not a question of love. There was no love involved; in fact, love was the last thing on his mind. He was content with what he currently had, stolen passion with the woman he had once called his wife.

He parked his car and hurried into his house; he went upstairs to his bedroom and sat on the bed with his head buried in his hands. He contemplated on what to do, yet, deep inside he prayed that his daughter Bimora would not grow up to be like Ariel and so many other young girls he saw in the pub. He wished he could always be there to protect her, to keep her from any harm. He prayed that she would not be as tough hearted as her mother Kodelly, neither, but as gentle as her grandmother Lidy. Yes, if only she could be as feminine as her grandmother he prayed. Lidy was a high calibre lady and not time, fame or anything could ever derail her from her track. Slowly, his bedroom door opened, and Ariel stood in the doorway. The maid had allowed her into the house. She closed the door behind her, while Bobby raised his head to face her. She took two steps towards him, and then she stood in the middle of the dimly lit room.

"I wanted to talk to you." She began.

She was clad in a short leather skirt and boots, with a white blouse and a small bag in her hands.

"I wanted to…to explain, to…apologise." She continued.

"For what? You lied more to yourself than to me. Is it about your rich dad and your glamorous mother?" He said with a hand gesture.

"Well… sort of." She replied looking away from him for a moment.

"So, how long have you been…doing this?"

"I have to make a living. I have to think about my family and help them ensure even that one meal a day?"

"By doing what? Selling your body?"

"I don't sell my body. I work. I used to work at the ice cream shop, but I work somewhere else now."

"Screwing up my bank balance?"

"No." She replied with a chuckle looking back at him. "It's not about your money, but your charm and personality…"

"Hey." He said cutting in. "I have heard enough. I'm sure you are happy now that we have talked, so you can now leave?"

"What about us?"

"There is no us. There is just you standing there and I sitting here. No 'us'. Understand. Now, please go."

"You can't sleep with me now that you know I'm a nobody?"

"No." He replied firmly. "It is not about that."

"Then what?" She asked walking the rest of the distance to him and dropping her bag onto the floor. She knelt in front of him, "Then why?" She asked, with her arms surrounding him and kissing him fondly. "Why?" She asked, begging again before he began to kiss her back, being ruptured in a moment of passion with neither of them uttering another word.

* * *

The boardroom was well lit, and the table was covered in papers for the late evening meeting. Men walked towards the boardroom dressed in their expensive suits. It was a crisis meeting, one at which they would discuss the future of the corporation, in the face of the prevailing recession.

Kodelly walked into the boardroom too, just as soon as the meeting was about to commence. She had been working late with the Finance Director for the last few weeks. She felt exhausted, but she still had to be present for the meeting. She sat in her chair. They all sat around the boardroom table. The room was quiet before Bobby walked in. He sat down and signalled to the chairman to commence the meeting.

It was no sooner opened than the order lost, with everyone wanting to speak at the same time.

"Order please." The chairman shouted to be heard, but everyone continued talking, wanting to be heard above the noise, papers were thrown in the air.

Bobby got up from the chair and began to walk out. The rest of the people remained, wanting to air their views, aware of the possible threat that the company was facing. She saw Mr. Glipen defend himself through the heated argument with the other managers. While other managers sided with him, others cursed him to the skin.

She too got up from her seat and walked out of the room. She saw the elevator doors open and Bobby walk into the elevator. She felt like calling him for a moment, before changing her mind. She waited for the elevator and went down to the parking. She drove home feeling very exhausted, after having had some dinner in a restaurant. She parked her car and entered her house, and then she went upstairs to her bedroom.

She opened the door and switched on the bedroom light, wondering how the office argument had ended. She had never seen those men act so unruly. She thought about Bobby, who indeed had acted indifferent by simply walking out on them as soon as they had begun their misconduct. She wondered if it really was true that their divorce had affected his performance at work, which she highly doubted.

She put her bag on the floor, before sitting on the stool in front of the dressing table. She stopped to watch her image in the mirror. She got up and walked to the bathroom to wash the mark-up off her face. She opened the bathroom door and let out a loud shout.

"Aaaaah!"

"Shut up, Kodelly. Shut up." He charged, grabbing hold of her wrist, having emerged from the dark bathroom and stepping into the lit bedroom with her as she retreated.

"Oh, my God what do you want?" She managed to say, having seen his face in the light.

"I want you. I have always wanted you." He replied with a grin.

"Let go of me or I will scream." She charged, still moving away from him even though he was still holding her on her wrist.

"Oh, I have waited for this moment for a long, long time. I have always wanted you."

"Dinkley, no. Let go of me." She continued to retreat and to pull away from his grip.

"Why don't you scream?" He charged again, slapping her in the face. "I have watched this damn house for the past three days, and I know there is no one else. There is no one else in the house, but you and I."

"Okay. Then let's talk."

"Talk?" He asked back with a chuckle. "What do you do when I call you to talk? You drop the line."

"Well…just go away."

"I ain't going anywhere. I want you. I want you." He said pushing her onto the bed.

"You are crazy, they're people downstairs. They must have heard the commotion by now." She tried again.

"Is that what you take me for, stupid? It's only you and I."

"You are crazy. Let go of me…" Pushing his weight off her.

"I'm crazy about you. You will love it baby. You will."

"Nooooo." She screamed, wondering how she would ever overpower him.

"It should have been you all the time. It should have been you. But no, first it was Laura waking up by my side and then it was Rena. It should have been you." He said, softly touching her lips.

She bit his fingers, causing him to move a bit and then she got up and headed for the door, but he tripped her and held her roughly from behind, then he flung her onto the bed again.

"I have waited for this for too long. You will love it, honey." He said fumbling with his belt.

"No." She cried, pushing him away, but failing to under his weight.

Then the door opened and Pedree Laskador stood flummoxed for a moment. He had a bottle of champagne and two glasses, which he quickly put on the dressing table. He charged on Dinkley from behind, who immediately swung around and pushed him against the dressing table, causing all the contents to fall onto the floor while Kodelly watched in fear.

He quickly jumped back onto her as she tried to move away from the bed, tearing her dress open with his hand.

"He ain't better than me. He ain't. It's you and me tonight. Nothing is going to come between us tonight."

"No." Kodelly hissed fearfully, "No." She cried.

Then the Champaign bottle landed on his back, he turned in rage for a moment, before falling on his face. Pedree had managed to get up from his fall and hit him from behind. Kodelly dragged herself from the bed and hurried to him, wondering how she could have fought him, if Pedree had not decided to come to her house tonight. She embraced him, feeling very shaky, while he soothed her comfortingly.

"It's going to be okay." He reassured.

"I'm so terrified." She sobbed.

"What do we do about him?" He asked, watching him come around.

"Let him go." She said softly, turning away from Pedree.

"Let him go? Just let him go?" He exclaimed, moving away from her with a frown on his face. "After what he tried to do to you?"

"Yes. I can't deal with this right now." She said, walking away to the bathroom, too embarrassed to say that he was her cousin's husband.

"You heard her. You good for nothing, get out of here."

Dinkley got up from the floor and began to walk away from the room, shaking his head from the fall. Pedree walked him to the door and allowed him out, before securely locking it to ensure their safety. He shook his head, still in disbelief as he heard Kodelly run the bath water. He was too upset to even think of touching her after what he just saw, he decided to spend the night just to make sure that Kodelly would be safe through the night, without having to fight off a ruthless man like the one he just allowed to go.

*　　*　　*

Rena walked into the hallway to Kodelly's house and found her sitting at the foot of the stairs.

"You look very radiant." She complimented.

"I do?" She asked back. "Maybe…I feel good."

"What do you feel good about?" She asked curiously.

"My son decided to move back and live with me."

"Olly, that is great!"

"I guess it is, but…"

"But what?"

"I think I'm a horrible mother."

"Why?" She asked curiously again. "Why, would you think such a horrible thing?"

"Because I paid his girlfriend to leave him. Now he is all sulky, saying she was just trying to use him. But I don't want him to make the same mistakes his dad and I made. I want him to make a decision to marry the woman he will love and try to live happily with ever after."

"If that scenario actually exists." Rena replied with her eyebrows raised.

"Yeah."

"Oh, and guess who came to see me late, last night?"

"Who, the town mayor or something?" She teased.

"No. Dinkley. He said he was on business, so he dropped in to say 'hello'."

"I'm happy for you." She lied.

"Well, I know it is the last thing you want to hear, but I gave him the boot. I'm not the sort to settle for a long-distance relationship. Pity, things didn't work out the way we had planned." She paused for a moment. "I should have listened to you. It was a big mistake, but then, I thought you just didn't want me to be happy."

"So, you are completely over him?"

She nodded.

"Come, give me a hug." She genuinely invited her as she stood up from the steps.

"Shall we have a drink and a toss to old friendship?"

"Sure. I'd love that." She said, following her into the Kitchen.

Yes, to old friendship, she thought, even though she could not tell her about her horrifying encounter with Dinkley the previous night. He was savagely obsessed with her, which was too embarrassing to even imagine. Maybe his absurd behaviour was just an indication that he had made the wrong choice on impulse, so many years back, when he had hastily asked Laura's hand in marriage. But Kodelly could not for a second imagine what her life would have been, had she been married to him. She could not ever imagine wasting her life away on the ranch. She was not meant for such a lifestyle and never would succumb to it, not even for love. She realised with a grin.

His affection towards her would always be a savage affiliation, a journey that never got started. His emotions would go around in circles, until he acknowledges that she never harboured fond feelings for him, she thought, drinking from her glass of wine whilst looking back at Rena.

She never wished for him to be her husband or the father of her children. She grew up in the country, but that was it. She never could have stood by his side on the ranch, Laura did, and he must be grateful for that and for all the love she had given him. She thought with a sigh, after putting the glass away.

*   *   *

Pedree Laskador had not been in touch with Kodelly since the following morning, after the bizarre incident at her house. He could not come to grips with the fact that she just let such a savage man like him walk free from her premises, after causing her so much trauma and physical pain. She had waited for the phone to ring and hoped each time that it would be him on the other side of the line.

"How often does that happen?" He'd asked her.

"What?"

"What I just saw?"

"It was the first time that happened. I just can't explain any further, but there was nothing else for me to do. I need time to think about it and I promise you that I will take all the necessary precautionary measures to ensure that it does not happen again."

"I see." He had said with little interest. He did not speak about it further and left her house the next morning.

She got into her car and drove to his apartment building. She parked the car securely and then entered the secure, elegant complex. She walked through the corridor to his apartment door. Two ladies stood opposite his door chatting softly. There were some children playing around them. She paused for a moment, to gain composure and then she rang the doorbell. She stood for a while, and then rang the bell again.

She tried the door handle and found that it was unlocked. She allowed herself in. She walked to the lounge where he was, a brush in his hand, with an assortment of paints on the stool, standing in front of a canvas he was working on.

"Pedree." She spoke softly, but loud enough to be heard.

He continued to paint, as if there was no one there besides him. It was an abstract painting, she noticed.

"Pedree." She spoke again, drawing his attention for a moment.

He turned to look at her, and then he carried on with his work.

"You lied when you said that you loved me. You lied to me. I never meant a thing to you." She charged softly, before turning and walking out of his apartment.

She opened the door she had just closed a few moments ago, facing the same women who were still chatting with the children still playing by their side. She walked the length of the corridor and was just about to descend the short flight of stairs, when she heard him call her.

"Kodelly." He began, "I never lied to you. I meant every word I said. I love you, Kodelly..." He said running to her, not minding the people that were standing there and watching him. She watched him as he ran towards her, before he embraced her.

"I love you." He said holding her close to him, "I do. I know, I do. I'm sorry, I didn't mean to hurt you." Stopping to face her and then holding her face in his hands and looking intently into her eyes for a moment, before letting go of her.

"How have you been?" He asked as he walked her back to his apartment. He offered her a seat before opening a can of beer for himself.

"Fine," She'd answered after a pause and after sitting comfortably, "except that I have been missing you and I was concerned."

"Concerned…?"

"Yes…" She said, recalling how disgusted he had appeared before leaving her house.

Yet she could not explain about Dinkley Mills. She could not tell him why she just did not want to blow the whole thing out of proportion. It would certainly break Laura's heart, and she did not want her to go back on drugs. No, not ever again. She had to be strong for both of them. Yes, if it was the last thing, she did; but to keep the integrity of her family intact. They'd had enough to deal with, as was already, other than to face another impediment yet again. If Pedree loved her, then he would know better than to force her to discuss things she did not feel like discussing.

"I have been well, except I have too much work to catch up on." He paused for a moment. "We will be exhibiting soon. Grandpa wants us to exhibit at the coast. Preparations are already under way, so I had to work harder."

"Harder?" She repeated, looking at the paintings that had earlier stood incomplete now complete. That probably explained his absence in a way. Just in a way, she realised.

"So, are you ready to talk about the last night I was at you place, now?"

"Well… yes." She said uncomfortably.

"Well?" He prompted again.

"His…an old, family friend. It could have spoilt a lot of other relationships." She heard herself say. "We grew up in the same neighbourhood."

"Oh, is that it. So why didn't you just let me know?"

"Well, I didn't think that that would be reason enough for you to let him go."

"I consider it. I'm sorry for having stayed away."

"I have to go now. I don't want to stand between you and your work." She spoke in a sombre tone.

"Stay the night. I have missed you. I knew that there would be a good explanation for what you did." He persuaded her.

"I love you." She heard herself say. It was different, she was now a mature and confident woman who knew more of what she wanted in life. Pedree Laskador was a good man, she had come to realise.

"I love you too." He replied.

* —————————————— *

CHAPTER TWENTY-SEVEN

Bobby answered the call on his direct line; it was Ariel, he had continued dating her after the night that he had spent with her again. He kept her at bay, even though she wanted to please him. She called him every so often and usually apologised, even though she hadn't done anything to cross his path. He liked to spend time with her, but he had absolutely no love connection with her. He listened to her talk on the phone, emphasising her dependency on him, which was in contrast with what he had shared with Kodelly, who was a strong and independent woman. He felt he would never experience such a relationship with anyone else. Maybe someday, Ariel too, would learn to be independent, but it was not any day soon, neither did he think he would be around her that long. She needed to move on with her life, he realised as they spoke on the phone. It was easy to find a woman of her nature, but seldom would a man find one like Kodelly, who just had rare attributes.

He put the receiver down and again began to think about Bimora. He recalled sitting her down on his laps and taking his wedding pictures and going through them with her.

"Now this is your mother. She is a good woman." He paused, pointing at her in the picture. "And this is grandmother, Lidy. She is a fine woman. I want you to be like her, when you grow up."

"Yes, dad I wanna be like grandmother when I grow up. I wanna be a lady, just like her."

"I love you." He said, wishing that he could go and protect her from love.

Protect her from abusive love. He could not imagine his daughter being vulnerable. He wished he could keep her safe and he promised himself that he would do that. Bad men are everywhere, and he once was that bad guy, but he never could have fallen for Laura's seduction.

There was a soft knock on the door, before his secretary walked in.

"Sir, the draft reports from the F.D." She said, putting them in front of him.

"Yes. Frank Glipen, what does he have to say this time?" He said cheerfully, getting them from the table. "Anything else?"

"No, sir."

"Okay, then I will quickly go through the reports." He said, dismissing her from his office and beginning to flip through the pages.

"Yes. Yes." He muted to himself. "Correct, good."

"Bastard. I don't pay him to …" He said, getting up from his chair and going out of his office, heading to the Finance Director's office.

He saw Mr. Glipen standing in the pool office that was almost empty, as it was nearing lunch hour.

"Frank. Frank…" He called out rudely. "I don't pay you to make such colossal mistakes. Now, withdraw these drafts and change this shareholders' page, immediately."

"Change? There is nothing to change, sir." He replied calmly, pulling his reading glasses from his pocket, and putting them on.

"Kodelly owns twenty-percent shares, after we divorced and nothing more." He corrected, "Your report gives her sixty-percent, which is incorrect." He said showing him the page whilst, tapping it with his finger.

"It is not, Bobby." She said, standing behind him, "I own sixty-percent of Litch Corporation and so I have the most voting powers now."

"What nonsense." He charged again turning to face her. "How did that come about?"

"Sir, we had shareholders like Mr. Welnar Zalpah and his affiliates selling their shares. Your wife bought them."

"Why didn't you tell me that Mr. Zalpah was selling his shares?"

"I did sir. It actually is in one of my earlier reports to you."

"It was just a recession." Kodelly reminded him with a grin, enjoying the look of defeat on his face, especially since she had gotten wind of his affair with the teenage girl.

"I'm sorry, sir." Mr. Glipen apologised.

"No need to be." He said, pulling himself together and waiting for the FD to walk away from them.

"Congratulations, Kodelly." He began to talk sarcastically.

"Thank you." She replied.

"Well, you will soon realise that running Litch Corporation is not as easy as you find taking your pants off for me."

"I will take that as a compliment." She replied, before excusing herself from his company.

*　　*　　*

She sat in the elegant restaurant, to which Bobby Mitch had invited her, to celebrate her high achievement at managing to own more than fifty percent of Litch Corporation; one in which he had laboured so much, for in so many years.

She had been waiting for the last fifteen minutes and was getting a little bit weary. She knew Bobby would try at anything to get his majority shareholding status back. Yes, majority power that he had ruled with since the inception. Kodelly had tested of those powers only after their divorce. But Bobby's slack attitude caused her to acquire the rest, after she had ordered Mr. Zalpah to sell his shares, or rather 'blackmailed' him as he had put it. But then, that had been more like insider trading, she told herself.

She watched Bobby walk in with a man she had only been formally introduced to earlier in the morning, Modree Mitch. She had met him before in only outlandish circumstances. She recalled him from the party incident in Cambel city, so long ago and as the man who had caused her a black eye after he had attempted to break into her office.

He was Bobby Mitch's younger brother. She wondered if he would perhaps handover the directorship to him, to make her stay at the corporation unpleasant.

"We meet again." He said in a firm voice.

She nodded; her gaze fixed on Bobby.

"We aren't staying." Spoke Bobby.

"Why? What? You won't have lunch with me Bobby?" She asked hysterically.

"Ayah, his busy. Big business ma'am." He answered on Bobby's behalf.

"I can't stay. We can't have lunch. But stay, I will foot the bill."

"No. I'm not hungry. What else do I need to know?"

"Nothing," He said pausing for a while. "except that am gonna' be away for some time."

"Away… What do you mean away?" She asked softly.

"He means his got business to attend to." Emphasised Modree.

"Where?"

"Bobby." Interjected Modree. "Hurry up. We've gotta go."

"It's business. I need something more challenging. I will be back soon. Take care of Bimora for me."

"Let's go." Insisted Modree, fearing that he might change his mind.

"Wait." He said, looking into her eyes intently.

"Where are you going?" She spoke softly.

"To gamble." Modree replied.

"Why are you going with Modree? His never been serious about anything…" She charged, "I won't let the father of my children turn himself into a gambler." She said uncontrollably.

"I'm the one that decided to do this." He replied calmly as he could see that she was visibly upset and disappointed. "It is not exactly gambling, but new openings. That is all it is." He said kissing her on the lips. "Take care."

"Okay." She said softly, watching them turn to walk out of the restaurant.

She wondered when she would see him again. She recalled what Rena had once said about Modree.

"Aye, woman, there is plenty of them. Just make sure that the one you love the most is always at the front of the queue. Aye."

She paid her bill for the beverage, having refused Bobby's offer to pay and then she walked out of the elegant restaurant. She walked to the car, a feeling of emptiness about her. She believed he would come back, soon. She hoped so, especially since she knew just how much he loved Bimora. He loved her too much to ever stay away for a long time.

She drove to Pedree Laskador's apartment. She felt the need to talk to someone, someone that would understand her. She could not think of anyone else other than Pedree Laskador. She entered the building and went up the short flight of stairs. She tried the handle and found it unlocked. She stepped in, closing the door before calling out his name, but she was greeted with an echo.

She hurried to the lounge but found it bare. She walked down the short passage to the bedroom, and it too was empty. She walked back to the empty lounge, sure that he must have gone for the exhibition, but he never called to tell her anything or that he was leaving town.

Standing against the wall was one painting. She went to it and turned it around. It was a painting of her, clad in nothing but a pair of jeans trousers, her hair being blown by the wind and her arms encasing her bosom, standing on the beach, the waves of the sea rushing towards her.

She wondered if that was his goodbye note to her. If that was his note to say, he was headed towards the coast. She realised only then that she would miss him. She had taken her relationship with him for granted and had overlooked the fact that his career required of him to travel. He should have called to tell her, she insisted. She could have understood that he had to do his job.

The door opened and she turned to see who had walked in. She heard footsteps in the hallway, and then standing in the doorway to the lounge was Pedree, with his two bags, which he immediately dropped and ran to her.

"I couldn't go without you." He mumbled, embracing her. "I promise, I will never leave you."

"What about the exhibition?" She asked with concern.

"Grandpa will take care of it by himself. I sent the paintings by flight, but I couldn't get on the plane. I couldn't leave you. I won't." He said kissing her hair.

She held onto him, imagining Bimora's gentle footsteps running up the stairs in her house and then she realised that she loved Bimora much more than she had ever cared to show.

THE END

EDITORIAL: WHAT THE BOOK IS ABOUT

The story is about two fine ladies raised in the Victorian era. They are chic and courteous. They move to the city to work. The one soon falls in love with a city bred man and later becomes a single mother, who soon works relentlessly to build the rest of her life. The other marries a man who is on re-bound and her loveless marriage eventually takes its toll leading to a separation and soon after she gets hooked on drugs and deceit for some time, whilst trying to emulate the now successful life of her single cousin.

It is indeed the life story of love, lust, money and betrayal. Does the single mom ever find love at last?

The life story of love and how sincere one's first encounter with it can have a lasting bearing on what one does and on what one, endeavours to do. It speaks of humour, love, prestige and savage, affiliation all on every page of Ferocious love.

FEROCIOUS LOVE.

FEROCIOUS LOVE

ISBN 978-0-620-60554-0

www.ingramcontent.com/pod-product-compliance
Lightning Source LLC
Chambersburg PA
CBHW072349020726
47506CB00004B/1072